V. Mahanenko

CONDEMNED

Lord Valevsky: Last of the Line

A Progression Fantasy Series
Book 7

Magic Dome Books

Condemned Book 7: A Progression Fantasy Series
(Lord Valevsky: Last of the Line)
Copyright © V. Mahanenko 2024
Cover Art © Lunar 2024
Cover Design V. Manyukhin
English translation copyright © Taylor Elise Margvelashvili 2024
Published by Magic Dome Books, 2024
All Rights Reserved
ISBN: 978-80-7693-828-1

This book is entirely a work of fiction.
Any correlation with real people or events
is coincidental.

All Series
by Vasily Mahanenko:

The Way of the Shaman LitRPG Series

Dark Paladin LitRPG Series

Galactogon LitRPG Series

Invasion LitRPG Series

World of the Changed LitRPG Series

The Alchemist LitRPG Series

The Bear Clan LitRPG Series

Starting Point LitRPG Series

The Bard from Barliona LitRPG series
(with Eugenia Dmitrieva)

Condemned
(Lord Valevsky: Last of The Line)
a Progression Fantasy series

Law of the Jungle
A Wuxia Progression Fantasy Adventure Series

Table of Contents:

Chapter 1

"MAXIMILIAN, YOU THERE?"

Naira Jode's soft voice was melodious, guiding me back to the world of the living from the clutches of darkness. I even opened my eyes to get a look at this vision of divine beauty.

Now that I was no longer under the effects of the *First Impressions* perfume, I noticed a few flaws in her complexion. A small scar on the forehead, an uneven contour of the lips, a mole on the cheek. However, this not only did not spoil her appearance, but on the contrary, it turned the artist's depiction into something real, human.

"As if I could be anywhere else," I replied and tried to get up. It didn't work — my body responded, but somewhat begrudgingly, as if not yet fully recovered. Raising my hand with difficulty, I saw a bag of skin-covered bones. The level thirty-one rift had taken its toll. And then some. I opened my map and chuckled in surprise. If the point marking my location was to be believed, I was in the very epicenter of the Light's power.

"Since when was the Citadel open to grey humans?" I asked."Magister Meram warned us that you wouldn't remember your meeting with the padishah," Naira suddenly declared, making me fall silent. "Maximilian, you were killed. By Karina Fardi at a dinner with Bayazid the Third. You really don't remember any of this?"

Naira did not look like a person who was ready to joke about such topics. I tried to get up again and this time I almost managed to sit up, but a sharp pain in my lower back made me groan, collapse back onto the bed and roll over on my side. It felt like my entire lower back had been branded with a hot iron.

"Lie down. Burns from destroyed symbols don't vanish just like that. You will need to visit my cousin. Our clan has a device that allows you to remove deep burns. Including those that remain after the dark fire."

"How's our patient doing?" Kimal Sarento entered the room. "I'd heard you could lose your mind over a girl, of course, but I didn't realize it would be so dreadfully literal. Naira, my love, please leave us. I need to have a talk with one of my careless students, who somehow managed to die in a place where it was simply impossible to do so.

Naira looked at me as if asking permission. I

nodded, and only then did she leave the office.

"Gentlemen, please leave us. You have thirty seconds," he said, addressing the air, and I bared my teeth angrily when the door opened and closed on its own. The invisible men still dogged me, and I no longer had the hoop to identify them.

"Yes, Maximilian, you certainly gave us all a challenge." Kimal Sarento sat down in a chair not far from my bed. Because I was lying on my side, I didn't have to bend over or raise my head to see him.

"Why don't I remember anything?"

"Because for you, everything that has happened since awakening after the thirty-first level rift, including the conclave of the Citadel, our reconciliation, and also the journey to the palace of Padishah Bayazid III, does not exist. When you were dragged out of the infected rift, per his agreement with the Citadel, Magister Meram applied one of his sigils on you. I was unaware of this. I thought that your fate would be decided at the Conclave, but it all ended much earlier. As I managed to discern, our mutual friend, the High Priest of the Zarak Empire, tried. Father Urg described your usefulness in terms of searching for dark ones and converts, so removing the dome at the conclave was a completely conscious step, and not some kind of whim. Brother Lin had long suspected that there was a dark one among the cardinals, but there was no evidence. So that beautiful episode when you heroically defended your right to life, in fact, was an ordinary Citadel farce, crafted to determine which of its highest hierarchs had surrendered to darkness. And besides, you so favorably called the Inquisitor yourself, accepting whatever his price may be. A true servant of the Church of the Light. Although you recall nothing from this meeting. Right?"

I strained my memory, but the very last thing that emerged from the depths was the terrible Master of the infected rift. Everything that happened after that was one continuous curtain of darkness for me.

"Magister Meram placed a fixation cast on you, as he called his creation. The concept is simple as a dimple: if a person dies, but their body remains intact, the cast allows one to restore life from the time the sigil was cast. A very painful procedure — you were lucky you were unconscious. When you were killed, the cast burned off, so you won't be able to lie on your back. Everything below your shoulder blades and all the way to your behind has now turned into one huge burn. By the way, it took twenty human souls to create such a protective sigil, and the Citadel agreed to it. Be grateful! But seriously, everyone got a pretty strong rap on the knuckles. Starting with Magister Meram, who was allowed to see the padishah without being checked, to the padishah, who did not provide adequate protection to his guests.

"What about Fardi?" I tried to say the name calmly, but a note of vitriol still slipped into my voice.

"What about Fardi? Nothing of the sort happened to your Fardi. Brother Lin forbade anyone from touching her. She's still the pride of the Citadel. She is already single-handedly closing level-four rifts. By herself! And all the loot goes directly to the Citadel, bypassing any rift conquerors. A true Sweeper…"

"Kimal!" I raised my voice, which immediately caused a sharp pain in my back.

"There it is folks, human gratitude," the chancellor sighed eloquently. "You raise him, teach him, trust him as you trust yourself, and what do you get in return? He raises his voice at you!"

"What about Fardi?" I repeated my question forcefully.

"Nothing has happened to her. She's sitting somewhere in the Citadel, waiting to meet with you."

"I have no intention of meeting with her."

"And yet, you must. The execution will not take place until you appear."

"Execution?"

"Of course. There is only one end to the path Karina has taken — the stake. The bonfire has already been built, we only awaited your return to consciousness. So today, in about two hours, she will be burned in a solemn ceremony. You can rejoice — your overarching plan for revenge is beginning to come to fruition. One of the Fardis will be wiped from the face of the earth today."

"If you're trying to inspire some sort of warm

feelings for this monster, you're out of luck. True, I don't remember our encounter, but if everything you told me is right, then she's getting off light."

"Maximilian, what's with the attitude?" Kimal Sarento scowled. "The hallmark of a true winner is not achieving your goal, but achieving it while remaining alive and well. Both physically and morally. What is with this desire to inflict more pain on Karina, when her only crime is being the daughter of the man who committed atrocities against your family? Was your family murdered? Yes, that is a fact. But they died quickly and practically without suffering. Karina doesn't have to suffer. So show some respect to someone who has followed her beliefs to the bitter end. Yes, she is your enemy, but that doesn't mean that she's unworthy of respect. Instead of bending to Magister Meram's demands, she showed pride, knowing full well what would follow. But the girl did this consciously. Could you have accomplished this feat? Or would you have complied with the old runescribe's decision? Although, who am I asking? You don't remember anything at all. I could tell you that you tried to crawl up Karina's skirt and received a bolt to the head for it, and you'd have no choice but to believe me."

"Although there's one thing I still don't understand — how did Fardi sneak a crossbow into a meeting with the padishah? She could have been attempting to assassinate him."

"I'd like to look into that," Kimal chuckled.

"Magister Meram and Padishah Bayazid the Third have certain longstanding agreements, one of which is that neither Magister Meram nor any of his guests are inspected before their meetings. And what is the point of checking when the padishah's safety has been personally ensured by the runescribe himself? You cast *Analyze* on the padishah — would you be able to break through his defenses? Perhaps only with vyrma. But even if it reached his body, I think there are so many sigils on his body that even if the padishah was burned to the ground, he would still somehow manage to survive. So no one really took any risks. As for guests and children...who pays any attention to them? But, of course, after what happened, the relationship between the runescribe and the richest man in the world of the Light will be rendered null. What a blow to his reputation! Now anyone and everyone is talking about how the palace of Bayazid the Third is not secure."

My notebook icon began to flash frantically. I opened it and was stunned — I certainly hadn't had that many notes before. It seemed as if all the books in the world had suddenly been uploaded and organized by category.

"I see you've opened your notebook," Kimal Sarento grinned. "Yes, when you regained consciousness after the rift, we had a long talk. We agreed to cooperate on everything, and as a symbol of this cooperation, I sent you this excerpt from my personal notebook. With two integrations, mind you. Even when your book fell into the Citadel's hands, I didn't remove the integration, wishing to adhere to our agreement. Incidentally, do you remember how many integrations you had before the rift?"

"One. With Alia."

"And now?"

"Three," I frowned. Where had the other two come from? And one of them was one-sided.

"No doubt about it," Kimal said. "The Citadel and its normal bag of tricks — you have your answer as to why such a rare and valuable artifact was returned to you. Because they hope to replenish their knowledge, and quite for free. I believe it will not be possible to simply remove their integration. You will have to completely cut off all access and start the notebook over. The Citadel has covered itself well in this regard."

"My notebook ended up in the Citadel's hands? We agreed to cooperate?" I was hearing things that would be impossible to believe, even if I had imbibed recreational beverages. Kimal Sarento was clearly being disingenuous, but the huge amount of data in the notebook, as well as the presence of two additional integrations, about which I remembered absolutely nothing, said otherwise.

"Why don't you stop interrupting me, and I'll try to tell you everything that happened two days ago, alright?"

All I could do was nod and plunge into the wonderful world of fairy tales. There was no other way to describe Kimal Sarento's speech. What was saddest was that almost immediately, all the chancellor's words were confirmed by notes in the notebook, at least the *Analyze* data on people I didn't have before. And two of them turned out to be dark, including the commander. The meeting with the padishah was also reflected in the book — according to the pattern that had become a habit, I cast *Analyze* on everyone who crossed my path.

"The final moment of your previous life was relayed to me by Brother Lin. Karina Fardi got so close to you that she fell within the radius of your *Golden Dome of Protection.* For some time she showed no signs of aggression, so your ability began to perceive her as part of the interior. When Magister Meram announced that you were now the same student, Karina lost control and pointed her crossbow at you. You didn't have time to react, and you paid the price — your soulless body collapsed to the floor, and a whole mountain of artifacts formed next to it. Including, mind you, the notebook that had been integrated with mine. Fortunately, Brother Lin was present at the meeting. The head of the Citadel security service immediately stated that everything that fell from you belongs to the church and if any item goes missing, the family of Bayazid the Third will be punished. Can you imagine what it means to say such words in the house of the padishah? You have made yourself an enemy, Maximilian."

I opened my inventory and began to breathe

heavily — I didn't have a single artifact left! Not even my recipes for the items from the *Thunderer* set. Although no — there was still one artifact. The notebook that Kimal Sarento spoke of was on his belt. And in its real incarnation. I put my hand on the item and pushed it into my inventory, leaving only a flickering decoy on my belt.

"If I reset all integrations now, will you help me recover my data?"

He grinned. I almost heard him voice the phrase, *"And what do I get in return?"* but suddenly the chancellor nodded:

"Yes. Regardless of the fact that you do not remember our agreement, I intend to honor it. And I don't really want to freely offer up my knowledge to the Citadel. So, of course, I will help restore the part that I managed to take away as part of the two-way integration. But...You see, Maximilian, the Citadel will expect new knowledge from you, and its absence, even if they interfered with your artifact in such a brazen way, will be regarded by them as open hostility. Are you prepared for this?"

"A wise man once said that the only thing in this world of true value is information. If I leave the book as it is now, the information will become available to too many people."

"It's nice to be called wise." Kimal's back straightened a little. "But, besides wisdom, there is also such a thing as sanity. And sanity stubbornly insists that under no circumstances should one break off the connection with the Church of the Light. The data must flow. But it is only up to you to decide what specific data will go to the clergy.”

“The book is automatically updated as soon as some new knowledge appears.”

“That’s right, automatically. What if there are several of these books?”

I didn’t have an answer.

“Here,” the chancellor handed me another flickering artifact.

Upon accepting the gift, a message immediately appeared before my eyes:

A new notebook has been discovered. Would you like to set it as the default?

I agreed and discovered that the data from the previous book had disappeared. The new knowledge repository was empty.

“Now you will have to get used to the fact that some part of the information will need to be transferred to the clergy. To do this, you take a pencil, which is attached to the side of the notebook, and manually write down new data there. In this way, the wolves will be fed and the sheep will be safe.”

“At the same time, I won’t actually give anything of value to anyone.” I realized Kimal Sarento’s elegant solution. A funny thought flashed through my mind and I opened my old notes. This had to be done live, through the embodiment of the book and flipping through its pages.

“There aren’t any pictures here,” I said and looked at Kimal Sarento. “Two-sided integration, you say?"

"What was it you said about a wise man?" His smile was disarming.

"So all this information is just fluff?"

"Fluff? This is meticulously structured and crafted fluff. In some places it is outright falsehood and misinformation. You don't think you were the only one I had synchronized with, do you? Father Urg still believes that he has his finger on the pulse and controls my every step. You will have to learn to set aside at least ten to twenty minutes every day to fill out your book by hand. It will be annoying at first, but gradually you will get used to it. And one more thing: no more integrations. Including with Alia. Don't even tell her that you have a second book. Just fill it out manually. Remember, Maximilian, you are a doomed soldier, and the church is not going to rid you of this title. Now you play by their rules, and you have no choice. Get stronger and you can start making your own rules. But being strong doesn't mean obtaining stones of level thirty or higher. Becoming strong is raising an entire army of people with level-Thirty stones and higher. The will of one man will not be considered. It's easier to kill than to negotiate. When there are hundreds, they become more difficult to kill."

"Why are you doing this?"

"Because I believe in you." An uncharacteristically serious note had crept into the chancellor's voice. "Because I see what information and what objects you are capable of obtaining. Things that most people could only dream of pass through your hands like sand. I don't know about you, but this really irritates me. And also, Maximilian, the issue with Alia is not a joke. If you get married, the Citadel will kill both her and your child. This is the Inquisitor's price."

The doors opened and Kimal Sarento fell silent, gazing up at the newcomer. A highest hierarch of the church — they were the only ones with the righteous Light glowing in their eyes.

"Brother Lin, what an unpleasant surprise." Kimal Sarento made no attempt to hide his displeasure. "Maximilian, let me introduce you to your escort. During your presence in Al-Khorezm, Brother Lin will replace Mother Alia and her functions — your new personal attendant. Well, and he's also the cleric who was unable to save your life at an ordinary meeting. A major indiscretion, Brother Lin."

"The Citadel believes you should not expel our servants from the premises."

"So the Citadel openly admits to monitoring its guests?" Kimal Sarento was surprised. While this was happening, I put both artifacts into an intangible state, and only one book appeared on my belt. Nobody knew about the second.

"I'm not here to discuss the Citadel's decisions. Will you be present at the execution?"

"Me?" The surprise in his voice was so sincere that I even believed him. "Why? To see a beautiful girl burned, whose only blame lies in the fact that she defended the interests of her family to the last?

That she didn't flinch before the circumstances and didn't submit to you? I humbly thank you, but no. I'm not as bloodthirsty as you think. Thank you for the offer, Brother Lin, but I will decline. Maximilian will have to bear this burden alone."

"The Citadel does not dare detain you, Kimal Sarento." Brother Lin rubbed me the wrong way from the start. Not only did he wear a red robe, but there was also something so...unpleasant about him. Maybe his look, his demeanor, or just the realization that he would now be my constant companion? There were many options, but it didn't change the outcome: I wanted to avoid any long-term relationship with this unpleasant man. However, I wouldn't be able to completely evade it. As soon as the chancellor left the office and the cleric turned in my direction, I went on the attack:

"I need my artifacts. Recipes and golden plates."

"The Citadel believes that these items should be kept in the treasury." We cannot allow people in the empire to have the *Thunderer* set. Your promise to Padishah Bayazid III was declared invalid."

"Promise?" Neither Kimal nor Naira had mentioned anything like that.

"I'm not here to restore your memory. Follow me. The pyre ceremony is to begin immediately."

"I'm prepared to purchase the recipes and plates," I said. "I know where to get the essences that the Temple of Skron so desires."

"Don't try to pull one over on us. The Citadel

knows that you have a level Two *Devour* and knows what it does in the rift. We have not yet made a final decision on what to do with this knowledge. Until this time, the stone and all the resources that are in it will remain with you. As do all other stones, such as *Analyze, Praxis* and the three level Three *Amplify*s. For now, it is beneficial for the Citadel to keep these items in your possession. With their help, you may be of use to us."

"Use?"

"I'm not here to discuss the details of your future work with you. Let's go!"

The church was still somehow able to pin me down. You hide from everyone, but then a creature like Karina Fardi comes along and finishes you off, and all your secrets become common knowledge. All because you trusted an archive that you thought no one would ever be able to access. Don't make me laugh! If the Citadel demands that I provide them with *Devour*, what argument will I have, other than the banal *"I don't want to?"* No power, no connections, nothing. The chancellor was right — I needed my own army. A hundred high-level mages, loyal only to me, would be able to hold their own, even against the Citadel. I needed to return to Hearth as soon as possible. Somehow I no longer thought it was a good idea to study with Magister Meram. Runes required human sacrifice. I couldn't imagine a situation in which I could easily take someone's life so that some freak, mired in crystals of oblivion, would have a chance to escape his addiction.

The central square of the Citadel was much larger than the Fortress area. The performance was clearly of a closed nature — this was evidenced by the small number of chairs that were placed around a large bundle of firewood. The clergy approached the process with full responsibility — they even built a canopy over the fire, despite the fact that there was not a cloud in the sky. The only thing that bothered me was that I was the first to arrive at the event. All the chairs were empty.

"Your seat," Brother Lin sat me down. "The execution will begin in an hour. Wait here."

One cleric was replaced by another brother in the Light appearing next to me, wearing a red robe. It was useless to argue or object — the head of the Citadel security service had left the square. Soon new spectators began to appear, and thirty minutes before the start of the performance only a few seats remained empty. A white throne that clearly belonged to the pope, as well as twelve comfortable seats for the cardinals. Opening my notebook, I began to read. The past "me" did the right thing by entering all the data into the book through *Analyze* — while I was waiting, I got a glance at the entire top of the Church of the Light. My main notebook began to actively pump data, so I had to close the integrated notebook so as not to do anything stupid. Kimal Sarento said that most of his knowledge was complete hogwash. Why did I need this in my main book? It wouldn't take much time to restore my data. I think I could finish within a week.

Finally the ceremonial guests of honor appeared. First were the owners of golden-purple robes, and behind them was the pope himself, dressed in a colorful robe. Having sat down, the head of the Church of the Light nodded, and a voice filled the space:

"Let the execution begin!"

(Open veranda of a tavern not far from the Citadel. The same time)

"Will they let him go?" Naira Jode with concern, turned to her companion.

"Good question, my girl, very good question," answered Kimal Sarento, barely holding back a satisfied smile. Either Naira was sincerely worried about Maximilian, or Kimal didn't know how to read people at all. Still, he did the right thing by suggesting that the Conclave limit the relationship between Valevsky and Mother Alia. Even the Inquisitor liked this proposal and made it his requirement. Naive servants of the Light! They couldn't take Alia away from Maximilian completely — she made him stronger. Much stronger. But under no circumstances should they expand their relationship. Otherwise, the Citadel would begin to influence Valevsky through Mother Alia, and the stupid girl would not understand whose tune she was dancing to. No, let Maximilian enjoy his freedom while he had it. If his relationship with Naira worked out, then great. If it didn't, that was fine. Another dark one would come along with no attachments to the Church of the Light.

"What is that?" Naira's muffled whisper was heard when a huge dark cloud grew over the Citadel.

No matter how hard Kimal Sarento tried, he still could not suppress his victorious grin. What a pleasure it was to understand people, their desires, capabilities and what they were willing to do to achieve their goals.

"That, my girl, is Karina Fardi's execution. All that's left now is to determine who executed whom."

Chapter 2

I REALIZED THAT SOMETHING was wrong as soon as I saw Karina Fardi. The girl walked surrounded by churchmen, but there was no fear in the look she shot those around her. There was no determination. Rather, there was a sense of superiority there! This was how Eleanore looked down on unscrupulous builders, after which they started working two or three times more efficiently. Despite her position, Fardi looked at the clergy like pieces of garbage, and I didn't like it. When our gazes crossed, I saw complete triumph. The girl was not at all surprised by my "resurrection" and was glad that I was in the crowd.

Fardi prudently kept her mouth shut. Her hands were bound behind her back. There were numerous steel hoops around her body that blocked the use of magic. But my growing anxiety became more acute with every second. All my senses, both primary and auxiliary, screamed that something was wrong. At that moment, Fardi was just being escorted out not far from me, and when she once again threw a triumphant look at me, I realized what was making me so tense. Her face! It was smeared with blood, but it was not blood from a beating, as it might have seemed at first glance. Anyone who had not studied the symbols of the dark ones, as I had been doing for the last two months, would not have noticed anything. It was just that the constant nudges, first from Adeline, then from Naira, forced me, at the very least, to learn sigil magic. Not completely, of course, but I knew this particular symbol for sure.

The symbol is the final key of the pictogram, forming the integrity of the construct. Without a competent mentor, these were little more than a set of words for me, but it was enough to glean that Fardi's spacious robe hid much more than just her body. Some kind of pictogram was drawn on her skin, and, not being able to secretly complete the drawing, Karina had to paint her face with blood. Her own blood!

They led the girl further, but I was fidgeting. I suddenly had no desire to watch her burn. Just the news that the deed was done would be enough. Really, that would be enough. But as soon as I rose to leave, my monitor's hands fell on my shoulders. Brother Lin had not yet returned, leaving me instead to his assistant. The same stern cleric, except with normal eyes.

Should I warn him that something was about

to happen? I looked at the gloomy cleric holding me in place, turned my gaze to the other representatives of the Citadel, who were eagerly awaiting the ceremony, and realized that there was no point. It was embarrassing to admit, but Kimal Sarento was right: no one deserved a painful death. Whoever that enemy may be. Because, having destroyed even a real beast in this way, you yourself become a beast. No better than the one he destroyed. What has Fardi done to all those people who are waiting for her screams with such anticipation? Didn't live up to expectations? Killed me? Ruined the reputation of Padishah Bayazid III? So, maybe the point is not that Karina did something, but that those gathered just love to watch a person burn? Eager to enjoy her last emotions? I have great doubts that this is exactly what true followers of the Light should do.

Having discussed this issue with myself, I shifted in my chair again, finding a more comfortable position. No, I didn't intend to warn anyone. Adeline claimed that textbooks on dark rune magic were available in the Citadel and that they were being studied. So not only me, but someone else present must understand what the bloody stripes on Fardi's face meant. If this someone did nothing, not daring to disturb the highest hierarchs, the Light would be his judge. I didn't owe the Citadel anything, while it owed me a significant debt. Moreover, it wasn't so much about the artifacts, which, of course, I felt the loss of terribly, but about the unauthorized access to my notebook. They didn't even inform me, thinking that I would just close my eyes and accept the fact that this was exactly what they had done to me. The Citadel does only what it wants, considering any of its actions a manifestation of the will of the Light. So, maybe it was worth letting a little darkness in so that the Light remembered why it had appeared in this world in the first place?

I wasn't an altruist and I wasn't going to work for the Citadel for free, no matter what they came up with. Now my task was to get out of the Citadel and forget all about Al-Khorezm and urgently return to Hearth. I no longer needed any training from Magister Meram — I didn't want to become a runescribe who would easily exchange human lives for results. I needed to get stronger, and as quickly as possible. What did I have at my disposal to accomplish this? Virtually everything! All the resources provided by the rift I had in nearly unlimited quantities. The Temple of Skron would have to make an offer to me for closing a rift sometime, so the artifacts would appear sooner or later. The main thing now was to recover my old recipes or find new ones for leveling up magic stones, and create powerful mages. Then I'd get the bone armor and produce a full mithril set. For both me and my closest associates. Now I just needed to determine who I could call my closest associates. And could I even call anyone that? Three or four months was not enough time to thoroughly vet everyone, of course, but these particular people owed me everything and would do everything to continue to gain power. Alia, Gustav, Eleanor, Gimlet, Rabblerouser, Alexy Snor. Right off the bat, I could name six people who had no ties to Kimal Sarento or the church, or the emperor, or the highest aristocracy. Perhaps Viscount Kurpatsky as well, but I still had my concerns about him — he had served the Duke of Turb for too long. It needed more time. If it really came down to it, I'd take the Evil Engineer and whatever people he recommended. He was already an old man himself. Despite how he looked, he had to be well over sixty, but this did not make him weak. On the contrary, it only made him stronger. Wiser. Although sometimes I found him to be sorely lacking in the "basic humanity" department.

Once you decide what to do, life becomes much easier. Fardi was taken to the pyre and several churchmen quite deftly dragged the girl to the post. The chains clicked, chaining her in place, and her fabric gag was finally removed.

"Karina Fardi!" the herald's voice filled the square. "The Church of Light fiercely guards the human right to life. Any person who walks in the Light has this right, and only a collegial decision of the highest hierarchs of the church or empire can violate this right. You belong to none of these categories. You considered yourself above the law that guarantees a person's life. You encroached on the sacred and killed Archduke Maximilian Valevsky with your vile shot. You have tarnished the reputation of Padishah Bayazid III, who invited you into his home as a guest. You trampled on the laws not only of the Church of the Light, but also of the Shurgan Empire! The punishment for such a thing is death! Your soul is at a crossroads. It has not yet completely sunk into darkness, but it is no longer in the Light either. To save you and return you to the Light, the college of bishops has decided to purify you with fire! Burn out all the filth that has settled in your soul, and give you the opportunity to appear before the Light pure and immaculate. The same as you were when you first came to the Citadel! Let it be so!"

It was hard to maintain a cool expression while hearing this sentencing. I had never heard such hypocrisy in all my life! How quaint, eh? That bit about the right to life, and the return to the Light, the return to the camp of the righteous, white and fluffy. Almost every word that the herald shouted with such aplomb made me nauseated, but after looking at the fanatics all around me, any questions I had disappeared. They actually believed what they had just been told. That the Citadel treated every life with care, and the fact that only recently, twenty people were killed at the church's behest in order to affix Magister Meram's symbols to my back didn't count. That was different! The Church only cared about the lives of those who could benefit them here and now. Everything else was secondary and not subject to consideration. Hypocrites. What a group of big, fat hypocrites! Just let Kimal try to convince me again that the Fortress was mired in corruption, but the

Citadel was a true stronghold of Light. Yes, the place was full of religious zealots, but the way they acted was completely out of accordance with the doctrines of their own church!

Karina listened to the verdict with her head held high, looking at everyone with the same disgust with which they look at the dirt under their nails. But besides contempt, there was something else. A small detail that others may not heed. After all, we were in the place where the Light's power was most concentrated, what was there to fear here? We were surrounded by the highest hierarchs of the Citadel, the cardinals, the pope and even the Inquisitor, after all! What could go wrong? But something was wrong — Karina Fardi's lips were moving, as if she was muttering something under her breath. It was as if she was calling out to the Light to take pity on her child and grant her a quick death. But the expression in her eyes erased any remaining conviction that she might be trying to save her soul. Although I knew it was futile, I cast *Analyze* on the girl. Nothing unusual. All the same parameters as before, all the same enhancements, all the same stones, except...

There was an incomprehensible postscript in one of the paragraphs. If I hadn't *Analyze*d Karina before, I would definitely have missed this little detail, but the comparison functionality revealed everything that distinguished the current girl from the Karina I remembered. A little check mark opposite the line "Presence of status bar." I didn't even know such a parameter existed!

My thoughts began racing at top speed. Fardi had a status bar. This didn't make her dark, but it certainly didn't put her any closer to the Light. She must have crossed paths with a dark one who granted her the right to such a privilege. The final symbol of the dark pictogram was drawn on Karina's face. Her expression suggested that she was the victor and that the fire did not frighten her. And she kept on muttering...

Now I was starting to get genuinely worried. It was one thing to watch a simple execution of a person you hated vehemently, but the anticipation of realizing she was about to do something that might spare her from the stake put me on edge. Why wasn't the Citadel reacting to Fardi's behavior?

"We need..." I tried to get up, but the strong hands of the controller returned me to the chair again. "She needs to be stopped! She's reciting a dark spell!"

"Fardi is free to recite whatever she wants." Brother Lin returned to his seat next to me. "Before they sent her to the stake, she underwent an inspection. There was no darkness in her."

"There is no darkness in those who have no soul," I said, repeating the words of Father Nor as they surfaced in my memory.

"A fascinating remark." Somehow, my words amused him. "We have not yet burned anyone who has been deprived of their soul. It may be an interesting spectacle. In any case, anything she might have in mind is useless. The righteous fire will drive out darkness, even if it has settled in a body without a soul. It has begun!"

Two churchmen took up torches and began to set fire to the wood at Karina Fardi's feet. The fire flared up quite quickly, turning into a powerful flame. The heat enveloped the girl, but instead of the animalistic scream of a woman being burned alive, the area was filled with Fardi's incredibly calm and resonant voice:

"Ser mat ala fer! Ser mat ala fer!"

She repeated the same phrase, moving her gaze from one clergyman to another. Everyone was silent — the fire reached their feet and the space was filled with the cloying smell of burnt meat, but this did not stop Fardi. Completely oblivious to what was happening to her body, she continued to repeat the same phrase, moving her gaze from one churchman to another.

"Ser mat ala fer!"

"What's this? Why isn't she screaming?" It had finally begun to dawn on Brother Lin. Fardi's clothes flared up and caught flame, but this did not stop the girl, who continued to repeat the same phrase:

"Ser mat ala fer! Done! Twenty-one sacrifices have been marked! The point has been indicated! The power has been given! Open the passage!"

"Twenty-one?!" Brother Lin jumped to his feet, knocking over his chair, but the head of security caught himself too late. The clothes Fardi was wearing were completely burned away, revealing her body underneath. The spectacle was terrible — the sigils glowed red hot against her fire-blackened skin. Fardi was imbuing them with power and the dark magic splashed out, easily bypassing all the steel shackles. Over our heads, out of nowhere, a dark haze appeared, from which dark threads stretched towards some of the churchmen. The girl's voice broke off — the fire had consumed her entire body, and no matter who she really was, it was impossible to survive such an inferno. Not with her stats. But the trouble didn't end there.

The churchmen, including the cardinals, leapt up from their seats, but not all of them made it to their feet. Those to whom the dark threads stretched out had fallen to the floor and began to writhe in agony. They tried to tear off their clothes, and even their skin, as if a fire was consuming them from the inside out. It was such a strange and alarming scene that it distracted many from the obvious thought: we needed to run away. I was glad to count myself among those who slowly backed away from the blazing fire and the clergy writhing in their death throes.

"Healers! Don't let them die! We need healers!" someone shouted, but the order came too late. One by one, the churchmen froze, unable to resist the force tormenting them. Twenty-one people. I had seen so many ritualistic murders in my life. Including voluntary self-sacrifice. I managed to reach the wall of some nearby building by the time the results of Karina's dark ritual finally came to fruition.

The first dark beast let out a piercing howl, but it was immediately cut off by the flaming sword wielded by a commander who appeared out of nowhere. But after the first followed a second, third, fourth, tenth. Moreover, these were not simple kronas that could be killed by a gust of wind. Apparently Fardi had called in the dark army's elite forces. These kronas were exceptionally stronger, larger, more powerful and more dangerous than those that had torn Hearth to ruins. The crackling of the fire had died down, and the flame had been replaced by the measured blinking of the portal archway. The smaller beasts poured out in a mighty stream, filling the space, and the four commanders were utterly unable to cope with the oncoming wave. They were mowing them down by the dozens, maybe even by the hundreds, but there were many more than they could handle. The creatures broke through and immediately rushed at the crowd of churchmen, ripping them to shreds. The space was filled with the joyful howl of creatures, the hysterical screams of destroyed servants of Light, the menacing roars of commanders, the clang of metal, the hiss of magic. I turned my gaze to the white throne. It was empty. The Pope, accompanied by the Inquisitor, hastily left the square without looking back at what was happening. Several cardinals defended and covered their retreat with their own bodies, for which they paid almost instantly — one of the creatures that broke through past the commanders reached them before the crossbowmen who appeared had time to finish it off.

It seemed that things couldn't get any worse, but this was just the beginning of the Citadel's woes. Another portion of strong kronas jumped out of the portal, diverting the attention of the commanders, and at that moment the horned head of an extremely unpleasant creature appeared from the shimmering veil. The dark ones had gone all-in, summoning the incarnation of Skron to the stronghold of the forces of Light. It peered through the portal and didn't stop there, trying to squeeze through the narrow passage to display for all the Citadel to see the full glory of the creature, of which there are only nine left in our world!

The Citadel was entirely overtaken by the Wave, and this one had a leader!

(Open veranda of a tavern not far from the Citadel. The same time)

"Go to sleep," Kimal Sarento smiled, and Naira, unable to fight a sudden onslaught of fatigue, closed her eyes, instantly off to dreamland. The soporific had worked flawlessly. As if on cue, a man approached their table. Anyone, even those who didn't know Magister Elor personally, would be able to see that this man was gravely ill. An unhealthy blush on his sunken cheeks, dark circles under his eyes, tremors in his hands — he bore no resemblance to his former majesty as one of Skron's highest hierarchs, as everyone was accustomed to seeing him. But the guest's appearance could not deceive Kimal Sarento. The chancellor knew perfectly well that the dark one was just as dangerous as he was a few days ago, when he had looked immaculate.

"Dividing your soul like that will kill you one day," said Kimal, inviting the guest to sit down. Magister Elor sat down on a chair next to Naira and stared at the girl for some time.

"Sometimes I wish she wasn't my great-granddaughter," his hoarse voice said. "She would be the cherry on top of my collection. Why didn't you take her for yourself? Why did you give her to Valevsky?"

"Your other great-granddaughter is enough for me. And, mind you, I'm adhering strictly to our long-standing agreements. Adeline Jode is my wife, partner and pupil. Everything we agreed on initially. But for some reason, these agreements are observed only on my part, and I begin to suspect that you have decided to deceive me. Allay my fears, Magister Elor."

"You will get everything you require. I need time. The Temple of Skron clung to the plate as if it were a piece of Skron himself," Master Elor's face grimaced with displeasure. "Weaklings! In pursuit of amassing more resources, they lost their strength, bowed to the commanders, allowed the Church of Light to dictate their terms... For this to happen in my time? All your lands would already be on fire if the commanders decided to set their own conditions for the Temple. Times are not the same now."

"So that's why you became Orthodox? You decided that in order to rebuild the world it must first be destroyed?"

"And you're telling me this?" Magister Elor grinned and nodded towards the Citadel. "Why did the churchmen annoy you so terribly and irreparably that you decided to destroy them? I had to work hard to prepare for this. Do you know how hard it is to separate a soul, leaving the essence of the owner of the body in place? And Fardi was not mentally ready for self-sacrifice."

"That's why I helped you," Kimal Sarento grinned. "I knew that she would not resist the temptation and would try to finish off Maximilian. What I definitely didn't think was that she would succeed. But you have to admit, it turned out perfectly."

Master Elor looked at the Citadel. The howl of the dark creatures that had appeared in Al-Khorezm could be heard even there. People ran hysterically away from the Citadel, understanding nothing of what was happening, but feeling that they needed to get as far away as possible.

"Much better than if she became part of the church," Magister Elor agreed. "Will you tell me how you marked the clergy? Without this, the sacrifice pictogram would not work. I want to use this for the future."

"No, Magister, this information will remain with me. I wouldn't want you to repeat this with some other city in your thirst for destruction. As for the Citadel, they encroached on my interests.

They forced Magister Meram to draw a fixation cast on Maximilian Valevsky, they gathered in a solemn atmosphere to accuse him of all sins, punish him, even execute him, in order to later revive him and show all the greatness of the Light. The sentiment is justified, but I don't like the source. Greed. Moreover, such petty greed that I was disappointed. The Citadel decided to get its hands on the artifacts only to ensure that no one would accidentally have a complete set. I think that this cannot be forgiven. Is Fardi dead?"

"Yes, she's already gone. I am sure that her sacrifice was pleasing to Skron and tomorrow the girl will be incarnated and be back in full force. Kimal, you understand that this is where our cooperation ends forever? You'll get the plate we agreed on, but that's it. You have become too active. Too noticeable. Too uncontrollable. How long did it last? Forty years? What changed three months ago that made you decide to abruptly leave your high tower? Were you warned what would happen if you crossed the line? You were. The fact that you did not heed the voice of reason is entirely your choice. When my pupil is reborn, you will be hunted. It may not be right away, Fardi will need training, but we will make every effort to rid the world of your presence. The only thing I can promise is that I will do it personally. Await a visit and prepare some wine. Very soon you won't need it anymore."

"I'll be happy to kill you again," Kimal Sarento grinned. "Only now I'll be sure to take into account that you also have access to Magister Meram. See you soon, Master Elor. It was a pleasure doing business with you."

Chapter 3

I WAS GLAD THAT MY BACK was pressed up against the wall. When the incarnation of Skron crawled out of the portal and straightened up, the first thing it did was let out a monstrous roar, encouraging his troops and instilling fear in the defenders. The sound wave shook everyone, even the four commanders, who continued to mow through Skron's creatures by the dozens. The leader of the army invading the Citadel was a harrowing sight. A goat's head, an elongated torso with two long legs, some kind of baggy growth in the lower part of the body, similar to an inflated putrid pimple, with short powerful legs capable of holding such a carcass. The incarnation of Skron was significantly taller than all those present — I would say twice as tall. Even the commanders who stood a head above the rest seemed like insects next to this behemoth. The Citadel's defenders accelerated their pace, although this was almost impossible, and one of them found himself not far from the leader of the dark invasion.

"It's time to get out of here," I muttered to myself, knowing perfectly well what was about to happen. The commander didn't even have time to really swing before a powerful stream of fire burst out of the incarnation's mouth, instantly turning everything in its range to ash. Hundreds of dark creatures evaporated instantly. Humans as well. I was lucky — the incarnation of Skron didn't turn my way. But the commanders did not flinch. Impenetrable translucent shields shot up in front of them, which managed to protect all four from the monster's attack. The Citadel was in flames, but the battle was just beginning. A new wave of dark creatures poured out of the portal, eager to sink their teeth into warm flesh. The commander closest to the incarnation of Skron got one blow in with his sword, but immediately flew to the side as the beast waved him off with one arm. Dark mucus gushed out from the cut on the monster's body, but the wound disappeared fairly quickly.

A wheeze next to me distracted me from the events in the center of the square. Turning around, I saw Brother Lin in his last moments. He had no legs and only one arm, as several kronas clung to his body, fighting to bite off larger, juicier pieces, but the churchman fought back. He wheezed, suffered, died, but fought back, continuing to wield his only intact hand. The determination never left his Light-filled eyes for a second, although he knew the futility of his actions. He continued to do his duty to the very end. And this was the only reason he remained alive.

The invading beasts paid no attention to me, as they saw me as one of their own. I knew full well that my level twenty-five *Healing Aura*, especially with the third-level *Amplify*, would work some real miracles, at least slowing the beasts down, if not driving them out completely, but I was in no hurry to help the defenders. This was their war, not mine. Members of the Citadel made themselves out to be fighters of darkness, so let them fight, since they liked it so much. From what I could see, there were enough churchmen and soldiers on the walls to keep the Wave from breaching further into the Citadel. And even if it did break through, Al-Khorezm was chock full of powerful mages who were duty-bound to come to their capital's defense. This was not my war. However, individual heroic deeds should be rewarded. Of course, I didn't really like the head of security at the Citadel, but I was impressed by his final minutes.

Grabbing what was left of the man, I hid him under my dome from the toothy beasts. I had to use three *Heals* at once to restore the body's integrity. The dark beasts were clearly excited to fix their gaze on a new target. They began to throw themselves at the dome, striking sparks, so I had to take the unconscious cleric in my arms and leave the square, until the incarnation of Skron turned in my direction and decided to test the strength of my defense with a fiery stream. I had doubts that my shield would be able to withstand it.

Brother Lin came to his senses when we entered the main building. The kronas had already taken over this area — all the doors were broken down and everyone had been devoured. In any case, I didn't come across a single living, or even dead churchman. The Light had not vanished from the eyes of the man I had rescued, but they were missing their former brightness. It seemed that, even though consciousness had returned, the head of the security service was still in prostration before his maker. Just in case, I used *Heal* again, turned to the aisle and sighed heavily — I wouldn't be able to have a normal conversation. The creatures did not lag behind us for a second as they tried to get to Brother Lin's body. They loved it! I had to turn on *Healing Aura* again. I needed time and a calmer environment.

The wave of light swept from my body and reached almost all the way to the square. The base radius of *Healing Aura* was twenty-five meters, plus an additional thirty percent. In theory, I could cover half of the area. But the creatures refused to die. These were not runty little dark beasts that could be killed if you spit at them too hard. I had the impression that the elite troops had been reserved for this attack — those that were capable of withstanding even a blow of such force. The dark kronas fell to the ground, slowed down to the point of a snail, but still moved, and some even continued to batter my protective dome. I had to finish off those who were close to me with my hands so as not to get in the way.

Healing Aura noticeably improved Brother Lin's condition. The Light in his eyes became brighter. He even began to move and sat up by himself. The first thing my chaperone did was look at his hands. Legs. Felt his body. And only then he turned his gaze to me:

"How did you do this? Is this some kind of special dark magic?"

"Just regular twenty-fifth level healing magic. I have a question, Brother Lin. Where are my belongings?"

"Your belongings are on you!" Metal appeared in the clergyman's voice. "You must defend the Citadel! Must destroy the incarnation of Skron!"

"Alright, then, not my belongings. Where are the artifacts that fell out of me after my murder? I need them, Brother Lin."

"They belong to the Citadel!" the clergyman said fanatically.

"They belong to me, and the Citadel stole them. Where are my artifacts, Brother Lin?"

"I will petition for you to be sent to the stake, just like Fardi! It is because of people like you that the dark ones attacked the stronghold of Light!"

"Where are my artifacts being kept, Brother Lin?" Even the most serene tightrope walker walking between two high mountain peaks without a safety net would envy my calm demeanor.

"You must defend the Citadel! It is your duty, doomed soldier!" The Light in the clergyman's eyes became so bright that it became unbearable to look at him. And again they reproach me for being a doomed soldier. Once again, I owed someone something. What kind of church was this that they could not exist with others in peace and tranquility? However, it wouldn't have changed my next words anyway:

"My duty, Brother Lin, consists of returning what's mine. What the Citadel took from me. Only after that will I stand next to the commanders and, as a free man, defend the Citadel from the dark onslaught. Until that time, no Citadels that need defending even exist. You're still nothing more than a bunch of thieves to me!"

I missed the moment when the flaming sword — not even a sword, more like a dagger — formed. This symbol of the Church of the Light appeared in his hand, and without drawing back to swing, he flung a clot of flame directly at my head. Again at my head! I'd had enough! I had a lot of time to react. I could have dodged its trajectory. Could have knocked the blade aside. Could have run to the door, grabbed one of the kronas, run back and exposed him to attack. But I did what no one expected of me. Even myself.

I caught the projectile with my bare hand.

Not quite bare...covered in a mithril glove, which fit like a second skin. I didn't have the slightest idea what type of damage light weapons dealt. Was it fire? Maybe the fire was pure Light embodied in such an intricate form? Maybe even chaos, which is the essence of the Inquisitor? I acted at my own risk, realizing that I needed verification. No, not for me — my future armor. Mithril should be able to block commanders' weapons. So the order I sent to my armor was just one word: *"Adapt."*

And it did!

The short flash of pain was extinguished by *Heal,* and I found myself with a handful of living fire. It tried to break free and continue its rapid flight to fulfill the will of its master, but the tenacious grip of the mithril prevented this from happening. And the longer I held this clot of fire, the duller Brother Lin's eyes became. This continued until the Light completely left the churchman and soon disappeared with a bright flash in my hand, finally rewarding me with spots and tiny circles dancing in my vision. I looked at my palm — there was not a trace. Mithril was able to withstand the living Light of the church! This news alone was worth everything that I'd had to endure that day. I urgently needed to get back to Hearth, before I took care of any other business! A full set of armor from this material was already waiting for me there!

"But how? That was Light itself! Darkness has no power over it!" Brother Lin's whisper was as quiet as his blue eyes were wide. Which was already abnormal for a Shurganin. Both the width and the color.

"Where are my artifacts, Brother Lin?" I

repeated my question, although the response didn't come from where I expected it would.

"They are in the treasury, where they will remain until the end of time."

Two figures stepped into the room where I had dragged Brother Lin — the pope and the Inquisitor. Several churchmen, who had the same glowing eyes as Brother Lin once did, rushed to finish off the poor dark ones who fell within the range of my aura. It wasn't very fair, so I removed *Healing Aura.* Churchmen and dark ones must fight on equal terms, without using the borrowed power of a third party.

"Reactivate your aura, doomed soldier," the pope immediately demanded. "There's no need to aggravate your already unenviable situation."

"First of all, I am not a doomed soldier. Secondly, the artifacts belong to me and the Citadel has no right to take them. Third, what's wrong with my situation?"

"You refused to follow Brother Lin's orders. Or would you claim that he is dark as well?"

"Why should I follow his orders?" It was incredible, but even now, I remained as calm as a clam.

"Because you're a doomed soldier." The pope showed no emotion either. He spoke to me as if I were some kind of madman who was useless to yell at.

"And why exactly am I a doomed soldier?" I continued to question him.

"Because you're dark."

"Why am I dark? After all, I was born in the Zarak Empire. In the Light empire."

"Because you went through initiation by fire through a dark stone."

"So now I'm not dark anymore?" I asked, expelling my *Golden Dome of Protection*. I had been planning to do this for a long time, as soon as the opportunity to remove my stones arose. I wanted to see what would happen to me if I removed this stone. Finally, I had a reason. An unpleasant feeling came over me, as if I stood naked in front of a huge pack of kronas, but it was too late to retreat. The status bar didn't go away, my inventory remained with me, the mithril gloves continued to work, so what else did I need? Yes, the dome was useful, but I could change it to *Magic Armor* and forever forget this "dark" period in my life. Except that now I would have to behave more carefully around converts — from now on they would be able to influence me. And not only them — that beast in the box, as well. Placing the shining gold stone on the floor so that even its presence would not raise unnecessary questions, I looked at the Inquisitor.

"Answer me, Embodiment of the Light, am I still dark? I won't pay for your reply."

"There is no darkness in this man. He is not dark." The thunderous voice rang out, causing goosebumps to erupt all over my body, but I didn't fall to my knees. I was no longer dark, and I was not under the influence of the Inquisitor's voice.

"Let's go back to the original issue, shall we?"

I turned my gaze to the pope. "Why should I follow Brother Lin's orders? No, not even that. Why should I, the light Archduke Valevsky, a subject of the Zarak Empire, the head of the autonomous city of Hearth, carry out the orders of the Citadel of the Shurgan Empire? Is it really all about this shiny gold rock?"

"How did you extract it?" the pope asked, and at that moment a howl of dark creatures was heard from the corridor. "Reactivate *Healing Aura...*Archduke Valevsky."

"I want my artifacts," I said, switching my aura back on. As I picked up the golden stone, I could hardly refrain from frantically stuffing it back in my magic field. The feeling of defenselessness was infuriating.

"Can you stop the Wave?" The pope said, ignoring my words. Magister Tarra taught me that this was also an answer that should be accepted and somehow responded to. Okay, I'd respond.

"Without this stone, no." I held up the eight-faceted gem.

"Can you return it to your magic field?"

"Yes, but I won't. Because this will turn me dark once again and I will become a doomed soldier. And that is something that I do not need. This war is between the Church of Light and its stronghold in the Shurgan Empire. The battle with the dark ones has nothing to do with Archduke Valevsky. I have never been dark, the Church of the Light knew this very well, but it was only concerned with formal indicators. Since the stone made me dark, it means that I am completely dark. This won't happen again. I honor and respect the Church of the Light, but I have no right to interfere in its fight against darkness. Because there is only one punishment for ordinary people who do. Death!"

"You are not an ordinary person."

"The Inquisitor just said otherwise. I'm not dark. I'm not part of the church. I'm an ordinary person."

"We can walk in circles for millions of years, but it will bear no results. While we are sitting here, people are dying over there. And it is in your power to help them."

"Through my own sacrifice? No, Your Holiness, I can't do that. You have commanders, you have an Inquisitor, you have a huge army of servants of the Light who are capable of destroying any dark infection of this world. They can handle it, no doubt."

"Is this really all about the artifacts?" the pope asked after a pause. "Are you prepared to let an entire city die because of simple greed?"

"It's not about the artifacts, Your Holiness. It's about your attitude. I'm not sure why, but I was perceived as less than human. As an object, bound to perform its functions. Closing the rifts, the Fog of Pharapho, looking for converts among the highest strata of society. Not a person — a function. They didn't even rescind my status as a doomed soldier, although the Church of the Light understood perfectly well that I had nothing to do with the darkness. Why? Because it was convenient. Because all they had to do was lift a finger, and their boy would immediately rush to carry out their order, not daring to refuse. I don't understand the reasons for this behavior. After all, it's much easier to come to an agreement. But no, the Church of the Light is not used to negotiating. They're used to giving orders. But the Inquisitor has just shown that you have no right to order me around anymore — the emperor of the Zarak Empire returned me to the world of the living. Me, the light Archduke Valevsky. And once again, instead of coming to a civil agreement about shutting down the Wave, which threatened not only the Citadel, but also all of Al-Khorezm, the servants of Light started giving orders. You must! You must! It's your duty! No, Your Holiness, my duty is not here. My duty is to protect my city and the people who live there. The fact that I am now in the Citadel is a monstrous mistake, which I mean to remedy in the very near future. As you can see, there are no artifacts involved. They are a different story. I still consider them my property, which the Citadel unlawfully took from me, but I have already been told that my items will remain in the treasury until the end of time, so there is no point in discussing this issue anymore. I just want to say that I don't work with those who stole something from me."

"You dare to threaten the Citadel?" For the first time, emotion appeared in the pope's voice.

"I dare to tell the Citadel the truth, without

hiding it behind the fear of losing everything."

There was an explosion and the pope swayed. The head of the Church of the Light looked in a bad way, and he had to lean against the wall to avoid falling. The clerics, but not the Inquisitor, rushed to his aid. The Inquisitor stood still as a statue and continued to stand. Except that he never took his eyes off of me. Suddenly, he said:

"One of our commanders just died. The remaining three cannot push back the Wave and the incarnation of Skron. The help that is rushing here as fast as it can won't make it in time. The Citadel will fall."

I didn't hear anything that sounded like a question or request, so I remained silent, waiting for him to make a move. And he did — in the blink of an eye, he was next to me. Eyes blazing with Light penetrated into the very depths of my soul, but this time there was no darkness in it. I managed to survive and withstand the pressure of the powerful beast. The only sad thing was that *Analyze* once again proved useless. I needed more *Amplify*s.

"There is no darkness in you. You have anger, rage, disappointment. You have confidence. What do you require in order to save the Citadel and the remaining survivors?"

"Official acknowledgement that I am not a doomed soldier, even with *Golden Dome of Protection* involved, all my artifacts, as well as everything that the Citadel has on the first emperor. Information, objects, archives, rumors.

That's it!"

"Why the first emperor? He's not the only one who has wielded a *Devour*."

"I want to understand how he did what he did. How did he close entire rifts and come out completely unscathed? How did he unite the people? How did he liberate these lands? How did he found the Church of the Light? For five months now I have been poking around in the dark, bumping into the same rake. Sure, my superiors can tell me much more clearly than information from textbooks, but sooner or later it will kill me. I need knowledge, but the Citadel has a vice grip on it, as if it were something that could topple the very foundations of the Church of the Light.

"You've made yourself clear concerning the knowledge. What are the items for?"

"They are an integral part of the knowledge. You cannot learn to use a conventional crossbow without having a conventional crossbow."

"Return the stone to your field and go to the square. You will get everything you want."

"Is this the Citadel's decision?"

"It is the decision of the Light!"

"Is there a difference?" I couldn't help but ask.

"There is. Uphold your part of the agreement, Archduke Valevsky."

The Inquisitor fell silent and teleported back to the pope's side. The pope looked like his condition had improved, although the pallor did not leave his face. A moment later, the stone was returned to its rightful place and a protective dome formed around me. I almost gasped at how nerve-wracking it had been to stand there completely defenseless. The dome, as practice had shown, was also not a panacea for all ills, but at least it gave me some confidence in my future. I'll need to add *Magic Armor* inside the dome and also make it an eight-faceted stone. The two defense stones would complement each other perfectly.

"Barricade yourself and don't let anyone in to see the pope. I'll be quick," I said and ran back to the square. There was no point in running after every individual krona. If I destroyed the portal, the Wave would be suffocated. I needed to tackle the main inferno and not concern myself with putting out small fires.

When I ran out to the square, the first thing I did was look around. Only a few defenders remained on the walls. And there were almost no walls left to speak of. A huge avalanche of dark creatures had broken through the defenses and rushed from the Citadel into the city. Somewhere behind the wall, there were flashes of magic from those who came to help, but for some reason I had the firm conviction that the mages of Al-Khorezm did not pose any particular threat to this Wave. Because it was unique. It was immensely powerful. The three commanders who wielded their fiery swords looked exhausted. Their movements were not as deft and swift as they had been thirty minutes ago, and the beasts were no longer dying in droves, but rather one at a time. The Citadel's best and brightest had taken too many bites and, judging by their melted armor, the fiery spit of Skron's incantation. The goat-headed creature stood stolidly within the portal, as if guarding it, and the flow of creatures did not subside for a moment. My appearance improved the situation a little: *Healing Aura* reached the commanders and the portal, completely blocking the effect of the kronas. The Forces of Light immediately took advantage of this. They were not concerned with the kronas; their goal was the embodiment of Skron. All three rushed forward, as if in a final attack, but it immediately choked in a fiery whirlwind. The Skronbeast made no misstep and certainly had no intention of being skewered. It defended itself, and quite well. The commanders had to stick their swords into the stones so as not to be carried away by a powerful stream of fire, and when the flames subsided, the goat used the long prongs on its head to send two commanders flying. But the third remained standing. He jumped towards the incarnation of Skron, and a moment later he stuck his fiery sword into the thick, festering pustule of its body.

The pope must have felt the blow again as an unpleasant green rot poured out of the pimple, spilled over the commander and instantly transformed him into a scalded skeleton. The armor dissolved, the flesh decayed, only the bones proved immune to this poison. Even the stones where the commander's remains fell were scorched. Skron's incarnation knew how to defend itself.

Three *Dash*es brought me close to my target before it even realized I was there. A blast from *Heal* only aggravated it. It began to draw in breath to envelop me in fire, but didn't make it in time — another *Dash* threw me into the air, and, finding myself in close proximity to the creature, I used my only remaining weapon. The mithril glove slammed into the chest of the dark creature and easily tore out its heart. No, not a heart — a huge entity that immediately went into my inventory. *Devour* remembered its purpose and, while I was flying back to earth, dismantled the monster into its component parts. All that was left was the goat's head, from which, apparently, nothing could be extracted. Upon landing, I found myself near the portal. The kronas froze under the influence of *Healing Aura* and quickly blocked off the passage.

There was no trace left of the original fire, but Fardi's body was still somehow intact. It was this that acted as the foundation of the portal, formed without any stone arches. The charred body was a terrifying sight to behold, let alone touch, but *Dark Thorn* wouldn't have any effect on the portal. The *Durability* bar did not appear. Turning around, I saw the staggering commanders. There was nothing remaining of their former greatness. Now they were nothing but exhausted soldiers. They couldn't even find the strength to destroy the frozen kronas, let alone help me destroy the portal.

"Alright, apparently I have to do everything myself," I muttered and, throwing back several dark beasts, made it to the source of the portal. I didn't see the point of sticking my glove into the body. The source of magic was on the surface, not inside. The portal was held in place by the glowing red symbols. For the first time since I had put it on, the mithril glove met resistance, but I pressed, making my way to the body, and squeezed one of the symbols. It shook so much that the remaining walls almost fell! The bodies of the silenced creatures fell on top of me, and when I raised my head, the portal no longer existed.

"I hope you're dead for good," I said, watching as Karina Fardi's body crumbled into dark ash. However, stubborn logic insisted that, having made this sacrifice, Karina remained alive. Skron had accepted her into his army, and our battle with her had just begun.

Chapter 4

"YOU COULD HAVE STOPPED IT in the first few minutes, but you didn't?" It seemed that the commander would grind me into powder. His expression darkened and he loomed up, glowering over me like a mountain.

"I could have. But I didn't. That's your job, not mine. If you're bad at it, maybe you should consider finding a more suitable position?" I retorted, holding his gaze. I was honestly sick and tired of these constant grilling sessions! Only a couple of hours had passed since the portal was destroyed, and before they could even get all the details, both surviving commanders had almost crushed me into dust. I was saved from lightning by the huge crowd of innocent bystanders surrounding me. Only later, when both warriors of Light came closer did I rise to my feet, ready to repel their attack. The flaming sword was no small weapon, of course, you couldn't just hold it with your hand, but I wasn't going to retreat either. If necessary, I would rip out the commander's essence and sell it to the Temple of Skron! No! I'd just give it as a gift! Let them rejoice.

"Commander, business awaits you," came the voice of Brother Lin. The Light had returned to the head of the security service's eyes and, together with the surviving brothers in the Light, dragged the wounded to me from both the Citadel and Al-Khorezm. There were many victims. A terrible number. At some point, I even began to worry that I would have to ask for a mana elixir and display my weakness. But now that I had managed to return a man deprived of limbs to his normal condition without the help of elixirs, my actions looked like the will of the Light itself.

"We're not finished, dark one!" the commander said with hatred. Both warriors of the Light turned around and quickly left the square.

"Should I start worrying?" I looked at Brother Lin.

"The Citadel will have a talk with them. Commanders are considered the Light's strongest warriors. They learn to battle the most powerful dark beasts, but today, all four commanders were unable to resist one incarnation of Skron. In addition, two brothers in the Light were mercilessly killed. However, you and your dark mirror dealt with this monster quite easily, although you have not been preparing for this your entire life. They are emotional, Archduke. We are people too, although many people may think differently. The Citadel apologizes to you for the inappropriate behavior of its children. They will come to their senses."

"That doesn't look like a krona bite." I stopped near one of the survivors. The man was on the verge of death, but not due to lacerations or missing limbs — a kitchen knife had been stuck into the poor wretch's chest.

"A victim of the looters," Brother Lin said after a pause. "Despite the threat to their lives, not everyone left their homes when the dark ones broke through the perimeter of the Citadel. They were afraid, and their fears were not in vain. Many vagabonds, taking advantage of the situation, staged house-to-house raids. The capital is home to all sorts."

I cast *Heal* on the poor man, and the knife jumped out of his wound and clattered on the stones. Turning back to the cleric, I decided to determine the extent of the Citadel's impudence:

"And how many more such victims are you planning to bring to me? I suppose all those who lost limbs or other body parts in faithful service to the Shurgan Empire will also be dropped at my feet? Or those who had a finger lopped off in a drunken bar fight? Brother Lin, maybe I'm unaware of the Citadel's rules surrounding healing magic, but I do know that it costs a lot of money. Yes, I volunteered to help the Citadel and raise up as many brothers in the Light as possible. Because I see what the dark creatures have done to you.

But you decided to go further and began dragging townspeople to me. I turned a blind eye to this — I know the townsfolk were ravaged by kronas. But this...this is too much."

The church really did lose a lot of men — I witnessed a conversation between Brother Lin and his group that was exploring the Citadel. About sixty percent of all the brothers in the Light were completely gone — the ravenous omnivores didn't even leave a scrap of tissue behind. Including the cardinals — all thirteen chairs were now unoccupied. Approximately ninety percent of those who survived had injuries of varying severity. If it weren't for my *Healing Aura,* which radiated out in all directions, regardless of obstacles in the form of stone walls, there could have been many more victims. You could say that I saved the Citadel twice today. I destroyed the monsters and cured the churchmen. And everything for free, purely out of the kindness of my heart. And they had started taking advantage of this kindness in the most brazen way.

"Are there any clergy among the remaining victims?" I looked around the square, where there were about a hundred wounded, and the vast majority of them were lying prostrate, unable to hold themselves upright.

"No. These are residents of the city."

"When will my things be returned to me?" I turned away from the victims. I felt sorry for the townsfolk, who were suffering, but I wasn't an altruist. I had already pulled a hundred people back from beyond the veil. At one time I had to give up an *Amplify* to save the Evil Engineer, so I knew very well the cost of treatment.

"The Citadel is ready to make a proposal." An incomprehensible tone appeared in Brother Lin's voice. I couldn't identify it. It was like resentment and disappointment and anger. Maybe all of this at once.

"I will not leave my artifacts with the church!" I warned, just in case. Who knew what they would offer?

"If you save everyone who is in the square now, you will receive three missing recipes from the *Thunderer* set."

"The church knows full well that this set is useless to me. I need recipes for elixirs, and of all levels. Starting with a mana elixir, ending with something unprecedented, with resources that do not even exist in nature. My priority is facet elixirs. I need to strengthen my stones.

"The Citadel has made its offer, Archduke," Brother Lin said gloomily. "We are ready to allow you to create a full-fledged set, but not turn your city into a hotbed of unauthorized elixirs."

"You know, let's go about this a different way. The Citadel knows all about my magic stones. About my magical field. Besides that, you know the basic principles of my work. Dark mirror, vyrma blades, healing. Over their long history, the brothers in the Light have probably created several ideal sets of stones that can significantly enhance your attack, defense, and auras. Give me a description of these sets. With connections, support stones and minimum levels. Aside from that, I know for certain that *Thunderer* isn't the only set that exists. Surely there are others, and some of these sets may be useful to me. Strengthen my *Heal*, help me pass through rifts or adapt to darkness, or something else. In the Caliman Empire, there are two rifts where metamorphs rule. These chasms must have already delved down further than level Fifteen — for as many years as those rifts have existed, they must be at least level Thirty. In order to pass through them with peace of mind and not turn into a skeleton again, I need to update my items. Meet me halfway, I will meet you halfway, and the vast territory of the Light lands will be freed from darkness.

"The Citadel is ready to discuss your demands," Brother Lin answered after a pause, but I just chuckled:

"Then I am ready to discuss my participation in the treatment of these unfortunate people. I can stand on the sidelines and moan with their relatives. Brother Lin, I am not asking for anything that is impossible or forbidden. Moreover, I propose to increase the power of the Church of the Light and demonstrate our strength to the entire dark world. The fact that you and I are on the same side means that we are ready to provide each other with all possible support. But now, for some strange reason, I'm the only one who is providing any support."

"There are no sets that can help you conquer rifts or make it easier to adapt to the darkness," the pope's voice rang out. Turning around, I saw a whole procession entering the square. The pope, with the Inquisitor on his heels, stepped aside, revealing a line of clerics with objects in their hands. Glimmering gold plates, shimmering scrolls, several figurines and unidentified notebooks. All the objects that fell out of me after my murder in the house of Padishah Bayazid the Third had been returned to me. I accepted them and immediately hid them in my intangible inventory. What was the point of hiding my ability when everyone already knew all about it?

"The Church of the Light has fulfilled its promise. Your items have been returned," the pope announced when the last artifact had vanished. However, the procession of clerics did not end there — there were still several others standing behind the first row. And their hands were clearly full.

"If you help these unfortunate people, regardless of the nature of their injuries, you will receive insights about the ideal sets of stones for all types of magical fields. This is classified Citadel information, but for the sake of the townsfolk, we are ready to part with it. Will this payment satisfy you, Archduke Valevksy?"

"Including the three missing recipes for the *Thunderer*?" I asked. If I was going to be bold, I might as well go all the way.

"Including those," the pope replied after a

pause.

"What's all this?" I nodded toward the ten clerics holding scrolls, journals, and other items in their hands.

"Everything that the Citadel has on the first emperor. We are honoring the agreement. You can pick up the items to study them, but the books you will have to read here."

"I need time." I turned toward the square. There were even more people now — the churchmen continued to deliver the victims of dark beasts or looters.

"No rush. The townsfolk are the priority." The pope nodded, turned around and went to the main building. I wiped my face wearily, assessing the work I had cut out for me. My aura was constantly on, but all it did was prevent death from taking the victims with the worst injuries, and was unable to heal their terrible wounds. Looking back at the line of clerics holding the treasured information, I returned to healing. The sooner I started, the sooner I'd finish.

I had to hand it to the Citadel representatives: they limited the number of victims trying to enter the territory and fall under the "manifestation of divine will." Rumors that something impossible was happening in the Citadel instantly spread throughout Al-Khorezm. Someone under the auspices of the clergy was treating people for free! And not just colds or bad teeth — he can restore limbs! Naturally, people gravitated towards us, but the servants of the Light filtered out those who suffered during the attack from those who simply wanted to improve their physical condition. Nevertheless, it took several hours before the flow of wretches dried up. By the end of the work, I was already exhausted, like after a good workout with the Evil Engineer! Sitting down on the stones, I watched as the churchmen finished dragging all the kronas into a huge pile. They were planning a huge bonfire, which I hoped to avoid.

"Today will go down in history," Brother Lin said, approaching me. "For the first time, the dark ones have opened a Wave inside a densely populated city. A Wave was opened for the first time in the stronghold of Light. For the first time, all the cardinals of the Church of the Light were destroyed at once. This day will definitely be written in the annals of history. The day when the Light began to plot its revenge after its defeat. A note of protest has already been sent to Kerux. What happened will not go unpunished. The light will strike back, and this day will go down in history, and not just in the light empires."

"Karina Fardi was dark. We need to find the one who made her like this. There is no point in exacting revenge on everyone."

"She was light. She was checked before her execution."

"Brother Lin, why don't you just believe me? She was dark. Light ones do not know how to form portals from their bodies. They do not disappear into dark dust. She's not dead, Brother Lin. Karina Fardi is alive or will be alive in the very near future.

I have already encountered creatures similar to her. They called themselves "soulless" and obeyed Magister Elor. They were the ones who opened the Gate under the magical academy of the Zarak Empire. What was the point of killing everyone if the perpetrators go unpunished?

"The Fortress still has not provided a report on that event, although plenty of time has passed," Brother Lin thought. "You have been given a room that you can occupy for as long as you want. The books and records about the first emperor must not leave the Citadel."

I was taken to a separate room, devoid of windows. A red robe sat down next to him. Apparently he was there to carefully watch me and make sure I didn't get my hands on anything. But I didn't want to. Opening my notebook, which was connected to too many people, I took out a pencil. Kimal Sarento was right — a half-truth was always worse than a lie. If you want to hide something, put it in the most visible place.

The first emperor. A legendary man, whose very existence was considered fiction by many people. Amazingly, the emperor had been born into a family of ordinary peasants. The first mention of him dated back to the hundredth year after the moment Skron appeared in the world — incredibly, a simple peasant fought back against the dark creatures that attacked the village. Gathering his assistants, he moved deep into the forests, where he found a rift. This was the first rift that anyone was able to close. Of the twenty people who went with the man, none returned. And the future emperor himself returned a different person — he had become a mage. The next five years were very eventful for the young man. He united all the surrounding villages into one, formed a separate city, not subordinate to the then ruler of those lands, and also founded the first Church of the Light. The one hundred and fifth year from the coming of Skron was considered the date of the official appearance of the Church of the Light.

Flipping through the notes, I frowned more and more. The Citadel gave me about ten books, ancient and dilapidated enough to be feasibly authentic, but the information they contained was just a greatly expanded version of the tales of the first emperor. No specifics or features — only general words about how a simple peasant became the first mage, then the ruler of the surrounding lands, then a mentor and teacher for hundreds of future mages and clergymen, then a leader who led his troops into battle against dark creatures and those who decided that it was easier to join Skron than to fight him. Battles and skirmishes, the construction of the Wall, clearing the lands, determining the principles of separation of dark and light, the formation of three independent empires, united by a common principle: they were all light. After his death, the body of the first emperor was burned, as he himself demanded. Everything that remained after this process was placed in a tomb, over which numerous descendants fought for a long time. Over the more than hundred-year history of his reign, he sired about five dozen children alone. Subsequently, they founded their own clans, which have survived to this day. And in fact, that was where the Citadel's records ended. No adaptation mechanisms, no methods of destroying the dark ones, and not a word about mithril. There were also several portraits made during the life of the first emperor, from which a frail man, gloomy and clearly dissatisfied with life, looked back at me. That was how I looked after I crawled out of a rift.

Putting the books aside, I began to examine the objects, and here, too, complete disappointment awaited me. Some hats, daggers, incomprehensible things, which even *Analyze* defined as "a device requiring more clarification." They didn't even fit into my inventory or artifact storage! What kind of madness was this?! If this was all the Citadel had on the first emperor, then they essentially had nothing! I didn't even know how to react. It looked like they had an abundance of information, and so many books, but in the end, I found I didn't learn anything I hadn't known before, which was virtually zilch.

The only thing that interested me was the pauldron, which was clearly part of some kind of set. This was indicated by several fastenings on the inside. Visually, the pauldron was quite adorned. It was made of soft gold, painted and decorated with all kinds of designs, and the weight seemed consistent. However, it was an item owned by the first emperor, and Kimal Sarento repeatedly said that all his things were made of mithril. What if the pauldron was also mithril, but frozen into useless gold? I had to check, but I really didn't want to do it in front of my monitor. And regarding the mithril, next time I saw the chancellor, I'd have to prostrate myself at his feet. The information he added to the notebook was so wild that the truth was simply lost in the background. I could fly with the help of my gloves, and breathe underwater, and snatch essences from my enemies, and sense the movement of underground phantoms at a distance of three hundred meters. How could I identify important things among this nonsense? Moreover, some of them looked quite reasonable, and were even true. But not the whole truth.

"I need to study this item separately, everything else can be taken away." I showed the pauldron to my monitor. He nodded, and soon a chain of clerics cleared the room of materials.

"The Citadel thanks you for your help and reminds you that its doors are open for you at any time," Brother Lin said as he entered. He didn't even notice the fact that I kept one item for myself.

"My carriage?"

"Waiting at the entrance. So are your people. They have been informed that you have been released. And what are your plans now?"

"Return to Hearth. Nothing special."

"Don't you need to train with Magister Meram?" Surprise slipped into the clergyman's voice.

"All that I need to do is return home. Magister

Meram warned me that he would not allow me to study with him for five years. I'll try again in five years. A little advice for the future: when you decide to burn a dark one who is painted all over with various symbols, try wiping the symbols off first. It could save a life."

"I have information that Padishah Bayazid the Third wants to see you. Very much."

"I'll be happy to meet him in Hearth. That's it, Brother Lin, I ride no further. If anyone has questions, suggestions or comments for me, you are welcome to visit me in Hearth and we'll discuss it. The most I am now ready to do is to attend several events in Turb, and only if the emperor is there. To ensure that the level of security is appropriate. I plan to ignore everything else for a while. It's time to process everything that has happened to me over the past weeks."

"You won't be able to hole up in Hearth, Archduke Valevsky. The infected rifts won't just go away. This is a problem that also needs to be solved."

"I'll await the Citadel's offer to pay for my services. It's one thing to send weak-willed doomed soldiers into a rift, another thing to send the Archduke of an autonomous city. The payment, as you understand, must be commensurate. When you know what you are ready to offer me, come to me and we'll discuss it. You have a full month and a half to respond."

"How were you able to hold the flame of the Light in your hand?" Brother Lin asked suddenly.

"No human can do this. Neither light nor dark."

"I still don't have any amulets against lethal damage or blocking *Analyze*," I replied. "I deliberately did not remind the church that I came here completely naked. I thought you'd figure it out yourself, do something nice for me, earn my trust with your generosity. However, nothing of the kind happened, so I have no moral right to talk about how I did it. You just won't understand."

"Won't understand?" Brother Lin frowned. It was funny to watch as mistrust flooded his Light-imbued eyes.

"Only complete selflessness and faith that I was doing the right thing helped me handle the fire. No matter how strange and stupid it may sound. But how could the Citadel know anything about complete selflessness? After all, you're always trying to benefit in all matters, without considering others at all. While I, please note, have treated the servants of the Light with complete selflessness. Sincerely. Just as a true follower of the Light should act. And what do I find? That they try to take advantage of my selfless behavior, slipping not only ordinary servants of the Light into the line for healing magic, but also ordinary citizens who could have turned to the services of other doctors. Selflessness and faith in my actions, Brother Lin, is what really helped me handle the fire of Light."

"Is this some kind of particularly sophisticated joke that is popular in the Shurgan Empire?"

"I told you, you won't understand. But try to understand my words. A miracle will happen and all will suddenly make sense. All the best, Brother Lin. I hope we never meet again. The head of the Citadel's security service is not someone one wants to regularly cross paths with."

Gustav was already waiting with the carriage in the square. The horses were noticeably anxious, as they were standing close to a huge pile of dark beasts, and Gustav had to make an effort to calm them down. Naira sat inside the carriage and tried not to stick her head out too much. Which, given the churchmen's penchant for waging global war against the dark ones, was not without reason. The Citadel has lost too much today to look kindly on any darkness within their walls.

"Anything useful?" Naira asked when I sat down opposite her and threw my pauldron next to her. If I was going to work on the mithril (if that's what this really was), I'd have to do it away from her company.

"I need to study it. Nothing special yet. You can see for yourself."

"Where to, Your Radiance?" Gustav asked, looking through the cabin window. Naira took the armor into her hands and began to turn it, as if she was trying to find a secret message. But it wasn't there. Even *Analyze* did not reveal anything unusual. But it couldn't detect my gloves either. I needed to test it, but I would do it all at home.

"Home, to Hearth. It's time for some rest and relaxation."

Chapter 5

"MAX, ARE YOU SURE?" Alia looked incredulously at the bone armor.

"I agree — the idea seems rather strange," Eleanore agreed. "If everything were so simple, this transfiguration process would have become popular long ago."

"Before popularizing it, you need to make this full set of armor," I said. "Which is a pretty tough process in itself. Then you need to find mages with level 20 stones and make them work hard. The process itself is simple, but it requires too many conditions. Shall we begin? Alia, you first!"

A fireball flew from the girl's hands, then a second and a third. They were joined by Gustav's lightning. Eleanore's spike. Gimlet's water jet. Rabblerouse's stone chips. I had to put in the most effort — because of the fact that I could split my abilities, I sent dark spikes into the bone armor, adding a sixth type of damage, and to stabilize the entire process, I cast *Heal* on top of it all. My group was burning through mana elixirs by the dozens, but no one gave up, pushing through at full force. I'd conveyed to them the importance of continuing to give it their all, no matter how stupid or strange it seemed to them.

"Stop!" I cried, and all five lowered their arms in relief. Only Eleanore and Gustav remained on their feet, and they were noticeably swaying. The others fell to the floor with a groan. Despite their level Twenty stones, they hadn't been prepared to channel such an intense stream of magic. It was an issue of experience, which none of them possessed. But no matter — the more mithril we crafted, the easier it would become. But that was enough for today. Kimal Sarento and three other "pie slice holders" of the Zarak Empire could have created four mithril orbs in succession without incurring any damage. For those who had only just become mages, more time was needed.

But the result was achieved — an orb swimming with all the colors of the rainbow hung in the air in front of them. I approached it and held out my hand, allowing the orb to flow onto me. Moments later, a plate appeared on my body that covered me from my waist almost all the way up my neck. My back, sides, and neck itself were exposed — I'd need the subsequent pieces of armor for that. Whatever mechanism was holding the plate to my body was a mystery to me. It hung there as if magnetized. I could easily tear it away from my body, and replace it just as easily.

"And all that struggle was just for this?" Gustav came closer and knocked on the plate.

"Do you have a vyrma bolt? I have my shield down — shoot the plate. Try not to aim at the heart, in case it does pierce through."

"Shoot? With pleasure, as always," he replied, taking a few steps back to avoid getting caught by the ricochet, and after calculating for a moment, shot a vyrma bolt, capable of piercing straight through any armor, defenses, or magical shields. But not mithril! The silver lightning bolt hit the plate and ricocheted off, nearly hitting Rabble-rouser. The short man not only managed to dodge, but also managed to intercept the bolt midair, shooting a reproachful glance not at Gustav, but at me. But I was no longer paying attention — I removed the plate again and examined it from all sides. There was not even a scratch left at the point of impact, but most importantly, there was no transfer of inertia! Somehow the mithril plate managed to dampen the energy of the crossbow bolt.

"That's enough for today," I said, returning the plate to my chest and allowing it to assume the shape of my body. The amulets hanging around my neck nestled under the mithril, which covered them entirely. Now they wouldn't "accidentally" disappear in the rifts. It would be difficult for anyone to access them at all.

Two weeks had passed since my return to Hearth. No one had bothered me — neither the church, nor the dark ones, nor the empires, which permitted me to consider and construct my future completely calmly. Above all, I was concerned with setting up my entourage. The first five mages were determined automatically — they were those to whom I could entrust my life, because I had repeatedly held their lives in my hands. I'd needed to transform Gustav and Rabblerouser into mages, but fortunately I had all the necessary resources and two level-fifteen altars at my disposal! Count Shub had already determined the winner of the first auction and we were waiting for the gold to arrive. Until then, why not utilize them? They would be restored in a week anyway. Who won the first auction? The Temple of Skron, of course! The Dark Ones could not allow anyone to have an altar that was superior to them in level. They had not yet rolled out their proposal for the destruction of the infected rifts, but I was in no hurry. I had things to do.

Having identified my main group and turned them all into mages with hundreds of enhancements (thank you gallo crystals), I distributed magic stones among them and sent them to the Fortress for integration. The Citadel had provided me with the universal "builds," as they had called the sets of magic stones, so I had no problems filling in my magic field. The only thing they couldn't do was find a decent "build" for me. None of the options they had included *Golden Dome of Protection.* And I couldn't turn this stone down. It had proven its worth on multiple occasions. So I'd have to develop my build on my own while referring back to the Citadel's work. Although that was a bit disingenuous — I hadn't developed anything on my own. It had been a group effort, a brainstorm between me, Alia, Eleanore, Gimlet — everyone who was in any way connected with magic or just had a sound mind helped me become stronger. In the end, it all fit into place quite well, but there was a problem: there were some I simply lacked. I should have gone to see Kimal Sarento, but I did not want to leave Hearth. Here, for the first time in a long time, I felt safe.

The pauldron I had taken from the Citadel which supposedly belonged to the first emperor turned out to be a simple piece of iron. Not mithril. In any case, I never managed to find its properties, no matter how much I put it on and tried to adapt the item to my body. So after a week I had to send the item back to the Citadel by caravan. But what I was really proud of were the two sets of *Thunderer* that I made for Alia and Eleanore. There weren't enough resources to make more yet. All the crystals mined from the rift went to upgrading the stones to level Twenty for all five of my new mages. My first army, which suddenly transformed Hearth into a force to be reckoned with. In my notebook, which had far too many subscribers, a description of the properties of the full set appeared, so it was not surprising that a couple of days later a request came from Kimal Sarento to create him a set. For those with lightning as their main ability, it increased their strength several times over, not to mention their defense. It wasn't mithril, of course, but it seemed equally as impossible. I did not make a third set, but rather replied to the chancellor that I was awaiting his proposal for what he would be willing to offer for a thing of such value. There was no reply, but I was in no hurry. I lacked the necessary resources anyway.

"We couldn't stop him, sir!" The doors swung open, and an unpleasant old man appeared on the threshold. Behind him, there were maids and even a few guards, but they really couldn't do anything about the uninvited guest. This new guest to Hearth had "god syndrome," as Alia called it. He believed that he had the right to behave as he wished, regardless of any rules or conventions.

"Welcome to Hearth, Magister Meram." I gestured to a chair and dismissed the guards. Viscount Kurpatsky had been ready to shoot the runescribe with his crossbow.

"Valevsky, let's do without all these courtseys and platitudes." The old man swept all my papers off the table and laid out a map. "That's it, I've got it all. You have half an hour to prepare for the campaign."

I sat back in my chair and looked at the map laid out in front of me. It was of an unfamiliar location. From what I could gather, the terrain was a nasty swamp, and the path marked on the map allowed us to bypass the most flooded areas. Judging by the way the path twisted, there were many impassable areas. The route ended in the very center in some kind of palace, if the map was to be believed. Ensuring that the map had been copied into my notebook, I turned my gaze to the old man. He looked as if he had just crossed the finish line of a lifelong race and was eager to share his joy with others.

"What is this?"

"What does it matter? Our task is to get to this point and figure out what's there."

"I'd like a little more detail."

"Valevsky, don't test me. Have you decided that your shameful escape from Al-Khorezm frees you from your obligations as a student? Well then, I'm here to disappoint you, young man — for the next two years, you will be my pupil. With all the duties that entails. Such as accompanying your teacher on campaigns."

"When did I become a pupil? I thought the matter had already been decided, and not in my favor. Especially after I failed to show up on time. I have to wait five years, as you said..."

I suddenly fell silent, as two symbols appeared before my eyes. One was responsible for casting a curse, the second for acceleration. These two symbols flew into the wall, where they crashed into an invisible man. One of the main issues of my palace was that *Phantoms* kept poking their long noses where they weren't wanted. I even had to inform the Temple of Skron that I'd like another bracelet for identifying these invisible bastards. Unfortunately, I didn't even have any vyrma boxes left! The trip to the infected rift had taken its toll on my items. From now on, I only had three boxes hanging on my belt that the local blacksmiths had made, but they contained no dark beasts. I'd need to go back to the rift to get more, and there were no suitable rifts near Hearth.

The symbol crashed into the invisible person and stripped him of his flesh in a matter of moments. His garments fell to the floor with his bones, stones and amulets inside. Even a few vials of green poison rolled out, untouched and ready for subsequent installation. But what I liked most of all was that the remains were dry as they hit the floor. No bloody stains, flesh or other unpleasant consequences for the servants to clean up. There was not even a smell of entrails. The two symbols had dealt with all the organic matter in a matter of moments, without leaving a trace. I remembered the symbols, all that was left was to learn how to form them. The first I could do, but not the second. True, I didn't have any attempts left.

"I can't stand them," Magister Meram muttered discontentedly, gazing at the remains with hostility.

"Me too. How do I identify them?" I tried to use the opportunity to gain additional knowledge, but to no avail. Magister Meram just waved me off:

"Start your training and find out for yourself. So, what was I talking about? Oh yes — our journey. You and I, my pupil, are going to the lands of the offworlders!"

It was unpleasant to realize that my heart

began to beat faster. From the moment I learned about the existence of another force that the dark ones were messing with, I wanted to see it. To find out what it was and how to get rich from it. But emotions and desires were one thing, while giving in and following them was quite another.

"No, Magister, we are not going anywhere. I do not plan to leave Hearth for the next few years."

"Well, I'm not asking you." A look of sheer astonishment was painted on his face. "I'm just informing you of the facts, Valevsky. We are setting off on a campaign. You, me, one more of my pupils and three converts for the trip back. I won't accept no for an answer."

"And yet, you'll have to accept that answer." I wasn't giving in. "I refused your training, I refuse to follow you now. Will you also put a curse on me?"

"Valevsky, don't make me disappointed in you!" The old man's face twisted with displeasure. "If I wanted, I would have subjugated you long ago, and you would follow me like an obedient dog. I need a competent student, not a soulless machine. But you will still have to follow me. If only because you owe me a favor. Or have you already forgotten? So let me remind you: when I taught you the symbol of remote communication, you almost jumped out of your pants, you were so eager to offer me anything. It's time to pay up. Or do you intend to go back on your word?"

Damn! After all, I really had promised the runescribe a favor!

"Young man, have you forgotten? This is not good, not good at all. When you throw around such words, it's strictly forbidden to forget. I'm actually upset. So, are you betraying your word? No favor?"

"I'll grant you a favor," I said begrudgingly. "I need details. What, when and where?"

The old man had finally pinned me down.

"Well, that's another conversation." A satisfied grin broke across Magister Meram's face. "You and I need to make it to that point on the map. It's called the 'Lair of the First Moon.' I'd like to rip the arms off of whoever named it, but there's nothing to do about it now. Here, in the Lair, a rupture occurred, through which the offworlders entered our world six hundred years ago. At first, the dark ones rejoiced — 'Wonderful, a bunch of new resources and materials running towards us' — but after a few battles, they lost their former appetite. Standard magic doesn't work there. Stones begin to behave strangely and lash out at their wielders. Converts completely lose control and open portals. It's a treacherous place. But it's not all doom and gloom — the offworlders couldn't touch rune magic. Or they brought rune magic with them. Thanks to our runes, the beings were contained and clear boundaries were drawn. The offworlders have tried to penetrate further into our lands, of course, but the Temple of Skron has stopped them. You already know what essences are used for, right? So, by creating creatures that are uncoupled from Skron, the dark ones learned not only to defend themselves, but also to cause trouble for the offworlders. At one point, the dark ones even managed to reach this location. The place where it all began. This was two hundred years ago. The dark ones had to retreat — they lost too many, and they were unable to gather another army. Inter-clan conflicts broke out and there was no time to pursue it. But the Lair hasn't gone anywhere. It is still in the middle of this island, waiting for us. So why not go and take what belongs to us? All the wealth that has accumulated there over six hundred years? Sounds like a perfect plan to me."

"Let's say it's a great idea. Still, why am I needed? You could walk the world alone and no one would say a word to you."

"The road is long, and anything could happen along the way. You're a mirror who closes level Thirty-One rifts. I still don't understand why the Temple of Skron didn't buy you out right away. They certainly have something to offer you. I know. My pupil can't go too far — I need to ensure the transfer of my knowledge. And you'll get plenty of good practice. Or did you think that once you got the alphabet down, you'd be a runescribe? The alphabet is the base, Valevsky. It's useful, but just a base. All the most interesting things are formed later, through combinations of symbols. I'll teach you this on the road. There are no portals in that area, so we'll have to do it the old-fashioned way. On horseback. I despise it, but what can you do? Such is life. How long do you need to prepare?"

"A week?" I cast the line, determining the

limits of the old man's patience. He scoffed at my impudence.

"I'm talking about hours, Valevsky! Hours! Two, three max! That's all I can give you!"

"Three hours, then." I took as much as I could get. "I need to warn my estate manager of my absence. Incidentally, how long will we be gone?"

"Two months, no more."

Now it was my turn to scoff.

"Two months? Where did this time frame come from? You know about the infected rift near Al-Khorezm! What will it become of it two months from now?"

"Nothing will become of it. I've put another seal on it. It'll last for ten years, and then you'll run around and close them all. Your three hours have begun. Pack light, the caravan is already loaded, I've taken care of the essentials. Alright, I'll be back in three hours. I'll go and see what you've done with Hearth. The last time I passed through here, it looked completely different..."

"Come see me, Eleanore," I said. "I have news. And I can't say I'm thrilled about it..."

The news that I was being whisked away for two months was received rather calmly. She merely suggested that we make another piece in the mithril set before I go. Everyone could deal with the consequences later, and it would be useful for me. Especially if this time I managed to create a helmet or a second piece of armor covering my back. It seemed like a good idea, so an hour later I was absorbing another mithril orb. No luck:

the mithril embodied the form of a belt and something resembling a loin-cloth-like skirt. Looking down at the bodies on the floor and panting heavily myself, I didn't dare try again. This time, even Gustav and Eleanore could not stay on their feet, and Alia completely lost consciousness. That was something I definitely did not need.

However, I quickly learned the undeniable advantages of my new garment. First of all, it had a system for organizing my mana and recovery elixirs. I brought the vials to my belt, and they immediately dissolved, passing into the immaterial world. While before, I could barely squeeze ten vials onto my belt, which then made me much wider and heavier, now even twenty vials in no way affected my appearance. It was a similar story with the vyrma cubes — the mithril belt perceived them as part of me, hiding them from the eyes and grubby fingers of strangers. The only thing that the belt refused to transfer to the immaterial world was my purse with gold and silver. Everything else was hidden, even a knife in its sheath! And it was all somehow attached to the new belt, for when I removed my old belt, nothing fell out.

Heal was of little help in restoring my mages — they had given up part of their life force, and a thorough restoration was required. Alia and Eleanore assured me that nothing terrible had happened to the children — as mothers, they sensed this. Although I was still seriously concerned. Evidently I'd have to find two other mages for next time. I wasn't about to risk the children.

"Ready?" Magister Meram returned exactly three hours later. "Then let's go. The Temple of Skron is already waiting for us."

"The Temple of Skron?" I was taken aback.

"Of course. It makes no difference for me, but my pupils need permission to move freely across the clan lands. Only the Temple of Skron can grant that. Plus, we need to shake down these tightwads a little. The offworlder problem is much more acute for them than it is for us. The fact that I'm interested in studying this topic doesn't change the fact that they'll have to pay us a lot. And it wouldn't hurt to build you up a little. Anyway, first we'll go to the Temple of Skron, then further. If you're worried that you..."

Magister Meram was unable to finish this sentence as at that moment, the door nearly flew off its hinges. A maid ran in, and from her appearance one could tell that something extraordinary was happening.

"Your Radiance! Your Radiance! There! There!"

Two symbols appeared in the air and immediately crashed into the distraught woman. She calmed down so abruptly, as if she had lost all emotions at once.

"Speak," ordered Magister Meram, and in a monotone, the woman replied:

"Two minutes ago a procession of churchmen entered the city. According to Viscount Kurpatsky, who went to meet the guests, the pope has come to Hearth.

I exchanged glances with Master Meram, and confusion flashed in his eyes.

"The pope?" The runescribe asked incredulously. "Who never leaves the Citadel? Kurpatsky wasn't mistaken?"

"There can be no mistake," the maid replied, still in a strange state. "The carriage bears the banner of the head of the Church of the Light."

"Valevsky, what did you manage to get into this time?" Magister Meram clearly felt out of place. "Or is it me? I don't think so — it seems we parted on good terms. No, I definitely can't let this pass. We're staying. We need to find out what the pope needs that made him crawl out of the Citadel and come all this way? Why are you just sitting there? Go and greet our dear guests! If the pope is here, then the Inquisitor should be with him. Do you have any converts in the city? Dark ones? If the Inquisitor sees them, he will destroy them. Immediately. After the Wave, the clergy are extremely aggressive towards the dark ones."

As I left the palace, a painfully familiar carriage pulled by huge oxen was entering the central square. It was accompanied by a couple of smaller carriages, several dozen horsemen, even one of the commanders was present. The carriage stopped nearby. The door opened, and the Inquisitor stepped out onto the central square of Hearth. Alone. Without the pope.

The Embodiment of Light immediately headed towards me, ignoring the assembled group. Magister Meram took a few steps back, acknowledging the guest's authority. It was embarrassing to admit, but I wanted to retreat too, although there was nowhere to retreat. This was my city, and I had to be the first to meet such guests.

"Archduke Valevsky, how good that you're still here," said the Inquisitor, and Magister Meram's curses flew from behind me. The runescribe was gray, and the words of the embodiment of Light weighed on him as heavily as on me. I even had to urgently remove the *Golden Dome of Protection*, because it was only by a miracle that I managed to stay on my feet.

"Welcome to Hearth, Inquisitor. Why are you here?"

"In the eight hundred years that the Church of the Light has existed, only three have managed to hold the fire of pure Light in their hands. The first emperor, his eldest son, and you. The first emperor is dead. The eldest son disappeared four hundred years ago, and no one knows his fate. Only you remain. I had to wait, hoping that you would die a terrible, drawn out, agonizing death. But you are not dying. And, as I see, you do not intend to die."

"Can you get to the point? Why are you here?"

"To give you power. He who can hold the fire of pure Light is Light himself."

With these words, the Inquisitor extended his arms towards me, and a thick stream of Light hit me in the chest. The last thing I remembered before losing consciousness was the phrase "adapt" addressed to the chest plate. If I survived, I would smash the Inquisitor into tiny pieces! I was tired of higher beings doing whatever comes into their heads with no consideration for those around them!

Chapter 6

"AND HOW DO I REMOVE this Skron-damned thing?" I looked in the mirror, again to no avail. Pure, blinding Light beamed back at me, washing out all detail. But even without the mirror, I could tell that the Inquisitor had set me up well — my eyes now shone bright with the Light. At one point, I had yearned to know what having Light or darkness instead of normal eyes was like. What else can I say but be careful what you wish for! One day they may come true. What did the Light in my eyes grant me, other than making it impossible to look in the mirror? Many things, and not all of them pleasant! First of all, from now on the dark ones could not influence me, as if they had been able to before. And it didn't apply to the rift. Things were different there. Next, any curses will bounce off me like a wall. The Light eyes granted complete immunity to various kinds of curses, which automatically protected me from Magister Meram. The old runescribe did nothing but cast curses on everyone and anyone he did not like. In just the last day, which I had spent lying in bed, he destroyed two more *Phantom*s. I even felt sorry for them — the runescribe did not leave them the slightest chance of survival. Another positive aspect was that none of the ordinary churchmen had the right to even look at me funny, for I was the embodiment of the Light itself. There were few who actually did have the right to request (not demand) anything of me: the pope, commanders, any sort of Brother Lin-type. I didn't think there were many people with eyes like mine. But that was where the benefits ended, and the other side of the coin was worse.

First of all, I didn't gain the ability to form a sword of pure Light, like a commander, or even a small knife like Brother Lin. Either the Inquisitor was being greedy, or the the mithril plate was protecting me from such an irrational expenditure of my energy. But worst of all was that from now on, I could not communicate normally with anyone dark. Even the gray ones constantly winced from the unpleasant sensation. A certain force had appeared behind my voice that weighed on worshipers of Skron like a steel vice. Moreover, the force pressed equally on everyone without exception, with no heed for status, strength or position — both Naira and Magister Meram. Both gray magisters felt uncomfortable when they talked to me. But even this was not as bad as the fact that the *Golden Dome of Protection* was now closed to me! After I opened my eyes and asked what the Skron was going on, my brain almost exploded! The power in my voice affected not only those around me, but myself as well! I had to suffer a lot before I managed to understand the reason for my terrible state. I was able to speak normally only after I pulled the stone out of my magical field. I immediately wanted to find the Inquisitor and rip him a new one, but was disappointed. He left immediately after he drove the pillar of Light into my chest. The bastard did his job and left, just as much of a bastard.

Although that wasn't entirely true. I had to admit that my Light-filled eyes did have some sort of effect on my own people. Everyone in my presence (aside from the grey ones) felt an unprecedented lightness. Their strength was restored, their minds were cleared, their will to live, create, and do impossible things was restored. Alia assumed that this was the effect of some invisible aura. Moreover, this aura acted on the entire city — Eleanore had already reported that the workers no longer needed to be spurred on. Everyone rushed to perform their duties at triple speed, as if the prosperity of the city depended only on them. No one shied away from work, and everyone was striving to do their best. There was no need to even supervise anyone.

"Do you need to remove it?" asked Alia. As I had already been informed, she'd had an unpleasant conversation with the Inquisitor. Not even a conversation — the Inquisitor spoke and my personal attendant listened. The general idea was that after Alia had a child, she would have to return to the Fortress and continue her service, because there was nothing left for her to do near me. There was no talk of any wedding. When Alia mentioned that she would leave the church, but stay with me, the Inquisitor said that this was impossible. One could only enter the Church of the Light, not leave it. The punishment for this was death. Basically, not a very productive conversation. The good news was that we still had six months ahead of us, and anything could happen in that time. Up to and including the Inquisitor vanishing. Or I could come to an agreement with the pope. I wasn't letting Alia go anywhere. And if Mr. "I Am Chaos" ever came to my city again, I would meet him fully armed. I would win back my woman by any means necessary.

"I do," I said without a second thought." The Church of the Light had put their stamp on me, marking me as one of their soldiers. I was deprived of my right to choose, my right to communicate with the Temple of Skron. There are some things you can never abide by, even when done with the best of intentions.

"Max, look at your notebook," said Alia. I'd already had the opportunity to discuss with her the fact that from now on, I'd have to keep two books, since the old one had too many prying eyes peering in. There were no demands that I share my information. When Alia was told that she would have to return to the Fortress, she was glad that we had not set up another integration. However, now the notebook proved its worth — information from Kimal Sarento appeared in it. Alia described the current situation with the Inquisitor and what he had done to me, to which the chancellor, noticing the update, added the following:

"Similarly to the influence of Skron, there is the influence of the Light. It makes no difference what is in a person's eyes — darkness or light. What is important is what can be done with it. The dark ones become gray, leaving the influence of Skron. What happens to the light ones, and is there such a possibility? A question, the answer to which will give an understanding of what is happening..."

The chancellor didn't say directly what to do, but I understood what he was getting at. Crystals! I had two of them in my development model. While one had been used up entirely, the other still had three facets free that gave me unnecessary key abilities. I had once crafted *Dark Indifference* on this crystal, but it didn't make me grey. I had to give up this key skill, since with it, it was impossible to get fragments of various stones and essences. Following Kimal Sarento's train of thought, one could draw the reasonable conclusion that if you could get rid of the darkness in your eyes, you could get rid of the light as well! What would this key parameter be called? Something like *Light Indifference.* The only question now was what would be the cons? If this, too, made it impossible to receive fragments, then I'd have to think twice before agreeing. In any case, I'd need to find it first. As far as I could remember, I'd never come across such a key parameter before. Which was not surprising — how would I have found it when I was dark? Surely the only ones who could receive a stone that blocked the Light's influence were those who walked in the Light themselves. As I did now.

The development crystals were easily extracted from the development model, so after adding it to my special inventory, I began to test Kimal Sarento's theory. I had plenty of stones to cut, I was not going to sell them, at least not now, so the only limiting factor was time. Eleanore had already said that Magister Meram wanted to see me.

The cutting stones vanished one after another, but the key parameter I was searching for never appeared. I had key parameters for all other skills, just not the one I was looking for. But I wasn't giving up that easy — I was ready to spend everything I had obtained thus far to protect myself from the Light. True, I had to go to the treasury and replenish the empty inventory, but I continued systematically going through all the cutting stones, carefully poring over the text that popped up. Nothing. All wrong.

You have used 900 cutting stones. You have been sent to the *Fog Stalker* portal.

The notification was so unexpected that I didn't have time to react. The treasury in which I was sitting suddenly filled with a thick fog, hiding everything within arm's reach, and when the fog cleared, I found myself on the edge of a huge round platform that hung, as it seemed to me, in the middle of a void. Turning around, I saw a sharp drop. Beyond it — darkness. Leaning over the platform, I barely stopped myself from recoiling. The platform, which had seemed solid enough, was only a hair thick. Below, as above, there was nothing. Darkness. Lanterns loomed over the entire circle, filling it with light. I leaned over and touched the surface; the material felt soft, but at the same time quite dense and solid. Opposite me, on the other edge of the platform, there was a strange creature. Dark and foggy, it hung in the air and looked like a ghost from a scary children's fairy tale. It wasn't human — when I approached, significant differences became visible. An eyeless face, a mouth like a Tarkatan, strange multi-jointed arms that could turn in different directions, and there were four of them. The creature wore clothes made of mist, which hung in patches, covering an unpleasantly blanched body. It clearly saw me — wherever I went, the monster's head turned to follow me. As I got closer, I used *Analyze* to figure out what I was dealing with.

Fog Stalker. A being outside of time.

What exactly could I glean from this information? Nothing at all — no stats, no properties, as if they didn't exist at all. Only the name.

"Alia?" I put my hand on my thigh where our

shared communication symbol was, attempting to contact her, but there was no response. Our connection didn't work in this area. Even sound here behaved rather strangely. It felt like I was in an empty room and every word was reflected a hundred times from invisible walls.

"Greetings, traveler!" an unpleasant voice rang out. In my imagination, it sounded like a huge monster who had suddenly learned human speech. Low, resonant, filled with something metallic and clearly not belonging to a human throat. Humans don't talk like that.

"Greetings, being of this unknown realm!" It was impolite to remain silent when someone greeted you. Stopping a few meters from the hovering creature, I waited for him to continue. From what I could tell, escape from this area was impossible.

"I'm the Fog Stalker. The one who sits below Pharapho and allows those who distinguish themselves to play roulette with death itself. You will be given a choice. You can leave this site, and if so, the way here will be closed to you for a long time. Until you collect a key again. This is the first way. There is a second. You can take part in battles with copies of creatures from your and our worlds. The world of humans and the world of Pharapho. The battles will come in waves. Easy at first, so that you understand the principle, but the more waves you want to go through, the more difficult the battles will become. One day, you will come face to face with Pharapho himself. Also a copy, but possessing all the power of the Lord of the Fog. After each wave, you will receive a reward. The quantity and quality will improve as the waves grow. The battle is not endless — there are only forty waves. Pharapho begins to spawn in every second wave after the twentieth, and in every wave after the thirtieth. After the thirty-fifth, another copy of the fog lord is added. But the reward for victory will be much greater. Incommensurately greater."

"What is the reward?"

"Anything you might need. Gold, jewelry, magic stones, equipment sets, artifacts, resources from rifts, development crystals and much more. Everything that can be mined in your world."

"Including resources from the offworlder lands?"

"Yes. Offworlders, phantoms, undergrounders, creatures of Chaos, Skron, Light, mechanoids — everything that can be obtained from creatures currently in this world can be obtained from the Fog Stalker platform. The higher the wave level, the better the riches."

"How do I leave the platform?"

"You may leave at any time, even during battle. Just come to me and ask. Say: "Fog Stalker, send me back" and you will be sent to the place from which you were summoned."

"You said that my opponents will be copies. Does that mean I am also a copy?"

"No. You are the only living being in my arena. You are granted the right to receive a reward for the deeds you have performed in your world. Deeds related to the Fog of Pharapho. If you die in the arena, you die once and for all. Both in this world and in all other worlds in which you were or could be."

"You said that Pharapho is a being from another world. Why did he appear in our world? For what purpose?"

"Answered questions are also a reward for clearing waves. I see you have a notebook. You can choose not only material but also immaterial subjects as a reward. Knowledge. Information. But integration with other books will be carried out only after you leave my arena. If you leave."

"So I can leave your arena right now and I won't face any consequences?"

"Other than losing the key that brought you here, none. This area was created to reward those who distinguished themselves in the fight against Pharapho. Distinguish yourself once more, and you will be allowed to enter here again."

"You said I could leave the arena at any time. Even after the first wave? Who would I have to fight?"

"You can leave the arena at any time, even during the first wave." The Fog Stalker had plenty of patience. "The composition of the first wave is determined each time the battle starts. It's impossible to find out in advance. The only thing we know is when Pharapho begins to appear. But even here, there are limitations. At first, the fog lord is weak, as if he had just appeared in your world. By the fortieth wave, he reaches his current form. Mighty and deadly."

"What do I need to do to launch the first wave?" I'd finally made up my mind. Even if monstrous creatures appeared that cannot be destroyed, there was always a chance to escape.

"Touch me and say: 'Wave.' To leave the arena, touch me and say: 'Fog Stalker, bring me back.' That will be sufficient."

Sighing heavily, still unsure of what to do, I put my hand on my belt, and *Golden Dome of Protection* stone immediately appeared in my palm. For all the time that I was working with the development crystal, I had to remove it from my magical field. Because it was impossible to talk with this stone. I had the feeling that if there was a way to adapt to darkness, there was a way to adapt to light. In other words, I needed to stick the stone back in my field and talk, talk, talk until the Light came out of my ears. Only the excess of Light would allow me to be able to exist calmly. But this wouldn't work with other dark ones — my aura would still have a negative influence on them.

Alright, whatever! No one had taken my dark mirror from me, so if the creatures from the rift appeared, I'd just finish them off. If there were fog spawn, I'd throw them off the platform. Let them explode somewhere below. I couldn't resist trying the first wave, especially since the path back to the ordinary world was so clear. Sticking *Golden Dome of Protection* back in place, I approached the Fog Stalker, reached out to touch it, and said:

"Wave!"

My body immediately gave into pain — the sensation of hearing my voice was dreadful. The Fog Stalker's eyes turned red, and he raised his arms to the sky. The space echoed with the sound of an unfamiliar language, something that didn't even remotely resemble our language or the dark tongue, and the platform filled with fog. No matter how I braced myself, I still wasn't prepared for the first opponent. It was a Pharapho soldier and it appeared to my right. My dome sparked, reflecting a dark orb — the soldier had barely materialized before it launched into its attack. *Dash* delivered me to the target, and the mithril glove easily tore out whatever the creature had instead of an essence — a heart or some important organ. But it melted before I managed to tear my hand out of the body of the Pharapho spawn. Then the soldier itself vanished in a puff of fog, but its place was immediately filled with other creatures. Kronas, lurges, rapses, Pharapho soldiers, broxies, and even humans! Although it was hard to call them human — it was as if someone who had never seen humans but had heard stories about them had molded them from clay and breathed life into them. Jerky, unnatural, they nevertheless wielded sword-like objects quite well. They too, remarkably, were made of thick fog.

I went all out, filling the space with *Dark Spikes*. What could a level Twenty magic stone do to the first wave of fog creatures? Everything! The monsters flew apart, torn into tiny pieces that immediately evaporated into fog. The fragments of the explosions pierced the creatures, returning them to their creator. At some point, I hit the creature that appeared next to me, and the explosion of *Dark Spike* rolled across the Fog Stalker. Or rather, across the place where it stood. My abilities did not affect the arena master in any way, as if it existed in another plane. At some point, I remembered to turn on *Healing Aura,* and things only got more fun. The fog creatures died before they even fully materialized. The light that filled my eyes significantly increased my healing ability, turning it into a formidable weapon. I walked to the center of the area and just stood there, watching the green stripe above the Fog Stalker's head fill up. It was hard to see it up close.

When the green stripe filled the last millimeters of the strip, it began to blink and soon disappeared. The sound of breaking glass was heard, the platform shook, and the wind swept all the fog to Skron, returning the arena to its original state.

"You've passed the first wave!" The Fog Stalker proclaimed. "What do you wish to receive? A material or immaterial reward?"

"Knowledge!" I answered immediately and almost fell to my knees. My stupid voice! It would finish me off one day. I was not interested in anything that could be obtained in our world. The information that could be obtained in this closed location was much more important.

"What do you wish to know?"

I nearly bit my tongue to stop myself from asking how Pharapho appeared in our world. What difference did it make now why the fog lord had arrived? He was here, and that was enough. Personally, something else was important to me now: I needed to somehow get rid of the Light in my eyes. Return myself to human form. I needed this knowledge like air. Pulling out the *Golden Dome of Protection*, I approached the Fog Stalker so that he could understand exactly what we were going to discuss.

"I was given these Light-filled eyes against my will. How can I turn back into a normal human? How can I turn off the Light at will so that I may speak to the dark ones? Those who worship Skron."

"Your question is clear," the Fog Stalker answered after a pause. "However, it is impossible to answer it after the first wave. The knowledge you seek will become available to you after the twentieth wave. Now, all I can say is that the ability to turn off the Light exists and you have everything you need to accomplish it. Why you don't utilize your tools now is a question for you or your training. Apparently, you don't have the slightest idea what you possess."

What did I possess? I looked at my palms. The only thing the Fog Stalker could be talking about was the mithril. The episode with Brother Lin immediately popped into my head, when I managed to block his fiery blade with my glove. Mithril had absorbed all the Light, turning Brother

Lin into an ordinary person. Could I somehow perform this trick on myself? But how? Damn it — I simply lacked the knowledge!

"Do the rewards roll over from level to level?" I asked. "So that I can get an answer not at the twentieth, but much earlier?"

"That could be possible," it replied. "You may receive an answer after the twelfth wave if you don't demand any other information."

"Another question. Will you just tell me how to use mithril to short-circuit the Light as it hits my armor, or will you tell me about mithril's other properties?"

"You will receive an answer to your question on the ninth wave," it replied immediately. "And the answer will only concern blocking the Light with your chest plate. Information on the properties of mithril will only be available from the twentieth wave on."

I returned *Golden Dome of Protection* to my magic field and activated it. The evening ahead was starting to look a lot more exciting! I desperately needed knowledge, and I finally found a place where I could obtain it. There was only one small thing left to do: I needed to prove to the Fog Stalker that I was worthy of this knowledge.

"Wave!"

Chapter 7

PHARAPHO...MASTER OF THE BLACK MOUNTAINS, who had settled in its depths and sent his fogspawn throughout all the ancient ruins not blocked off by rifts. I didn't even know how to describe him — a huge mountain of flesh, resembling everything and nothing at once. The one who controlled the fog was not unlike fog himself — he had no single form. He easily transformed from a massive lump capable of withstanding a blow from *Dark Spike* to the thinnest of threads that engulfed my *Golden Dome of Protection.* If I had given up my stone and exchanged it for the classic *Magic Armor,* it would have been the end of me.

My attempt to attack with mithril was blocked. Pharapho proved the only being that could not be pierced by my glove. Vyrma — yes, but mithril — no. The highly adaptable metal was ineffective against its creator. I had to remember my katars, crossbow, and *Heal.* In fact, it was thanks to this last weapon that I won this horrendous battle — I healed the beast to death. A few times, I was nearly pushed off the edge of the platform, the creature's blows against my shield were so strong that I was simply blown away. If not for the lampposts that I managed to grab on to, it would have been disastrous. That being said, the fight itself turned out to be quite simple — the small fries were taken out by *Healing Aura,* and Pharapho himself I silenced with *Heal.* But I knew at that moment that I wouldn't summon the twenty-first wave. I'd seen the clear limitations of my magic stones. Even with a level-three *Amplify,* my aura was no longer enough. The creatures of the twentieth wave suffered, but did not immediately turn into fog. In order to move on, I'd have to pump up *Healing Aura* to level thirty or affix several more *Amplify*s.

"You passed the twentieth wave!" said the Fog Stalker. "What would you like to receive? A material or non-material reward?"

The Light in my eyes went out — the process of transferring Light through the mithril was getting easier every time. By the twentieth wave, much had been revealed to me — the nature of mithril, what it paired well with, and how to customize my items. For example, the chest plate not only protected against all sorts of nastiness flying into the chest, but also participated in the process of oxygen generation. Now, of course, this function was unavailable to me, but a little later, when I got the other pieces, it would become quite difficult to kill me. Not impossible, however: mithril did not protect against darkness. For some reason, Pharapho couldn't adapt to it. Light, no problem. It could block, and absorb, and give it back. But Darkness, no. Steel could handle this much more effectively than mithril. At the same time, mithril was able to cope with the rot that appeared at the twenty-fifth level of the rift, the invert that seeps out at the fortieth, the twist at the sixtieth and even the filth at the eighty-fifth.

"What is invert and how do I fight it?" I asked. No one else had information about what went on in the lower levels of the rifts. Because there were rifts out there that were seventy-one levels deep, I would definitely need this information sooner or later. For me, any rift, and especially the deepest, was a source of resources.

"Invert is a state in which the inner essence of a being comes to the forefront and forms a shell around them. It is impossible to destroy invert creatures in the usual way. You must completely destroy their shell. Both the external, represented by the essence, and the internal, which is the basis of their existence. Mithril is the ideal weapon for this task, as it is capable of absorbing the external essence, or products made of edriel, amethyst crystals mined from the thirty-fifth level of the rift. Weapons made of edriel can cut through steel and vyrma, are immune to rot, and can also damage invert beasts. I can't tell you anything more after the twentieth wave. Do you want to launch the twenty-first wave?

"No. Fog Stalker, send me back."

"It will be so. Your result: twenty waves out of forty. This is the seventh-best result in the entire history of the Fog Stalker waves. Information about your success will be recorded in the logs and passed on to interested parties."

"What parties? What kind of logs?"

But there was no one to respond. The space around me filled with fog, hiding the platform, and a few moments later I found myself in Hearth's treasury. In front of me towered shelves containing all the wealth of the city. In fact, everything that I had managed to obtain up until that moment. There were no other sources of "wealth" in Hearth yet.

"Max?" Alia's worried voice appeared in my head. "Where are you? Are you okay?"

"Seems like. What's all the fuss about?"

"The connection seal became inactive, there was some kind of empty spot in its place. As if you had died. And now, all of a sudden, it has been imbued with power again. Are you sure everything is okay?"

"Yes, I just ended up paying the Fog Stalker a visit. And I wasn't exactly formally invited. How much time has passed since I disappeared?"

"Almost five hours. Everyone was worried. Magister Meram was ready to drag everyone in Hearth from their houses and send them out looking for you."

"I'll come out now. I'm in the treasury."

"Maximilian, we have guests." Eleanore was not as emotional as Alia, but there was some tension in her voice as well. I'd heard enough of this phrase lately. It was always accompanied by extremely unpleasant consequences, which had to be sorted out by me.

"Who?"

"Dark ones. Three misty servants of Skron all showed up at once."

"Take them to my office. I'll be there in five minutes."

The Temple of Skron had suddenly sprung into action. Why? I already knew the answer: a certain log, in which information about my passage through the Pharapho site had been recorded. But I didn't like how quickly they had arrived, and in numbers. Usually they traveled alone, but there were three here at once. Just like the meeting at which Four had made decisions about our further collaboration.

Despite the fact that I had guests waiting, I was in no rush. Calling the treasurer who kept the register of the treasury's contents, I unloaded all the low-level resources that remained after leveling up the stones. I had no way of using them anyway, and I shouldn't be carrying them around. If I did get back into a rift, the full slots would clog up my inventory and I'd be unable to turn a profit.

"The Temple of Skron has finally matured enough to make me an offer on the sealed level Thirty-One rift?" I entered the office and sat down in my chair. The three servants of Skron stood, unwilling to settle into the guest chairs, but heeding such strange behavior from the mist men was absurd. Logic was often absent in the actions of the dark servants.

"The Temple of Skron has been informed that you have been to the Fog Stalker Arena." As usual, pleasantries were not the Temple of Skron's forte.

"Twenty waves," I confirmed. It was foolish to deny what was already on the record.

"The Temple of Skron wishes to receive the key to the Fog Stalker Arena."

"The Temple of Skron may wish as it pleases," I replied. "I have no right to forbid or permit you anything."

"Are you in possession of the key?" the one in the middle demanded, and the other two took a barely noticeable step forward, as if to encircle my desk and grab my arms. What, again? Why did no one ever negotiate, and everyone immediately resorted to force?

"It seems to me that the servants of the Temple of Skron came to Hearth in vain. The topic of the Fog Stalker Arena will not be discussed here," I said, returning the Light to my eyes. My voice was filled with a force that pressed me into the chair, but I overcame myself and rose to my feet, ready for battle. I was a little unsteady, but I still couldn't let my protective shield down. The dark ones behaved too irrationally.

The way the three of them recoiled from me almost made me forgive the Inquisitor for his gift.

There was no longer any talk of holding me down. Huddling into a tight group, the misty servants began to back away until they ran into the door. I sat back down and demonstratively removed the Light, returning my normal voice.

"When can I expect payment for the infected level Thirty-One rift?"

"I am Four," the figure in the middle said after a pause. The other two left my office without even saying a word. He sat down in the guest chair as if nothing notable had just happened.

"I am Archduke Valevsky," I said, unable to refrain from sarcasm.

"The Temple of Skron is saddened by the fact that you have become a servant of the Light."

"Does the Temple of Skron wish that I would become a servant of Skron?"

"Yes," said Four, not pulling any punches. "By siding with Skron, you could gain power, authority, and wealth beyond your wildest dreams."

"I'm not interested," I replied. "I am not a vain person, I am content with what I have now. Or what is gradually coming my way. Why force things?"

"If you join Skron, you will gain access to all the information obtained by the Temple of Skron," continued Four. "You will become one of the most important figures in Kerux, and the Bartolomeo Clan will lead the council for many years to come."

"Does the Temple of Skron wish to buy me off?" I asked, surprised.

"I am just describing a hypothetical situation that may occur if you accept."

"Are you saying that the Light in my eyes doesn't deter you?"

"On the contrary, it is encouraging. You were given a piece of Light, and you managed to survive. This means that you can accept a piece of Skron and survive too. We are ready to give you this gift."

"No need," I replied and returned the flame to my eyes. I would rather remain silent for the rest of this frustrating conversation than allow the Temple of Skron to experiment on me.

"You shouldn't worry, Archduke Valevsky. We are not here to destroy the Light in you," said Four. "The Temple of Skron understands that we arrived too late. We thought that in your hunger for the reward promised to you, you would come to the Temple of Skron, where we could offer you something you would never refuse. And then you would become one of the dark ones. A true dark one, imbued with the power of Skron. But you have shown patience, and now we must admit our mistake. The Church of Light reacted before we did. We have come to you to negotiate."

"About what?" My head was instantly covered in cast iron, but I still wouldn't remove the shield.

"The key to the Fog Stalker. According to an agreement that has been in effect for hundreds of years, the Fog Stalker informs us of everyone who passes through. Since the beginning of the Fog, only twenty-three keys have been received. Twenty-three times, the best of the best went to the Fog Stalker Arena to try to get as far as possible in the terrible battles that ensued. To understand how to destroy Pharapho. You stopped on the twentieth wave and decided to leave the arena. Why?

I had to remove the Light from my eyes once again.

"Everything that happened in the Fog Stalker's arena is between me and it. I don't understand why I should share anything with the Temple of Skron, which still has not fulfilled its obligations to me. The infected, level Thirty-One rift, in which I lost everything I possibly could lose, requires payment, and yet, I haven't seen it. The hoop for identifying *Phantom*s, protection amulets that block lethal damage and Magister Meram's powers. Rings of adaptation. My ousel boxes. I lost everything, but I got the job done — your territories can rest easy. A lot of time has passed, and the Temple of Skron is slow with their payment, although I even sent a request saying that I needed to identify invisible people. There was no answer. But as soon as the dark pyramid needed something, its representatives immediately ran to my city. They even tried to threaten me. Bribe me. This is not right, Four. I will not do business with those who do not fulfill their conditions. I can surmise why you would want to go to the Fog Stalker — you can get answers to your questions. All other sources of information have probably died or are inaccessible to you. But I don't understand why you want to get it at my expense. I also want to get to the Fog Stalker. I also need answers, because the Temple of Skron does not want to fulfill its agreements."

"The Temple of Skron believes that you can get answers to all the questions you may want to ask in the dark pyramid. Three and Two are ready to meet you there."

"Four, we're going in circles. You're talking about something I can get later. Someday. If the Temple of Skron deigns to accept me. While you wish to obtain the Fog Stalker key here and now. The Temple of Skron knew perfectly well that I could easily destroy the Pharapho spawn. Knew that sooner or later I would have the key. Why didn't you strike a deal with me in advance? To explain what this arena is and what it is for? Nothing of the sort. Right now I don't have a key to the Fog Stalker, but I know how to get it. If the Temple of Skron is interested in learning something, it can ask its question through me."

"Why did you only pass through twenty waves?" Four repeated his question.

"Because I came to the arena unprepared. Once I killed the Pharapho copy, I was told that the strength of my opponents would grow with each coming wave. There are six who have gone farther than me. On what wave did they stop?"

"The farthest any of our members have gone was level thirty five. When faced with two fully fledged Pharaphos at once, our man didn't return. But a record of his journey appeared in the logs."

"Did any of the other six return alive?" I was

getting the picture.

"Only the one who bears the name Two. He passed through thirty-two waves. A lot of useful resources and knowledge were obtained. Two wants to go back through the Fog Stalker Arena again. All clans in Kerux are aware of the fact that any key to the arena must be handed over to the Temple of Skron. Including the Bartolomeo Clan."

"I do not belong to the Bartolomeo Clan," I reminded him. "I have outlined my stance. If the Temple of Skron wants to receive information or resources, they can do it through me. I cannot provide any other offer at the current stage of our relationship. Because the Temple of Skron does not fulfill its obligations."

"Your payment for the thirty-one and eight-level rifts is currently being processed through the Hearth portal. We will pause here to give you time to personally appreciate the generosity of the Temple of Skron. We have never neglected our obligations."

"Eleanore, do we have more guests?" I said, contacting my estate manager.

"We have absolute mayhem!" came the response. "Max, I have no idea what to grab first. The dark ones arrived and brought...everything! Fabrics, metal, gold, artifacts, resources, a bunch of elixir bottles with mysterious contents. I need time to structure and sort it all out. Great Light, they keep coming!"

"Where are you?"

"In the treasury. Don't worry — I can control

myself, I won't go into a frenzy. Converts won't be allowed in, and I won't seek them out to kill them myself. Stop!"

"Eleanore, what's going on?"

"We've got trouble, Max! More than half of the bone armor is missing! I'll contact you later!"

Half the bone armor? I had almost a hundred Pharapho sergeant armor pieces lying around in my treasury, and if someone had stolen half my stores...There were only four people in this world who weren't among my trusted confidants who knew how to use the armor. Kimal Sarento and Counts Vyazemsky, Kuzmin, and Shub. None of them had access to the treasury, but that didn't mean anything. All four had the resources and manpower to get into places that were completely inaccessible.

"The Temple of Skron senses that something has happened."

I looked over at the misty man. In fact, another suspect was sitting in front of me. The dark ones were also hunting for the contents of my treasury — development crystals, cutting stones, raw materials, essences. Even though I hadn't removed the latter from my inventory, this didn't mean that they didn't check every shelf of my supposedly well-guarded and inviolable treasury.

"I've been robbed."

"No surprises there. When you built your treasury, you didn't care to put in a proper security system. The friend-foe system. The Temple of Skron has seen this problem and will provide a security system for you. It is part of our gift."

"What security system?" I was starting to get worried. There was no point in panicking until Eleanore reported back. Maybe the treasury keeper had simply moved the bone armor to another location.

"Once installed in your treasury, it blocks the passage of any creature that does not have a special pass issued by the owner or their legal representative. A mark that is implanted into the very essence of a person. It cannot be forged. It will not be possible to enter the treasury without a mark — they will be blocked. This system is not only possessed by all clans in Kerux, but also in the Citadel, Fortress and Stronghold. All who care about the safety of their belongings install such a security system."

"And the Temple of Skron remains the main operator of these systems? That is, the universal key that opens the treasury is possessed not only by the owner, but also the Temple?"

"Only for security's sake. If something happens to the owner or his legal representative, the heirs will know where to go to gain access to the treasures of the family, clan, lineage or church. The universal key is tied to One, which guarantees the inviolability of the treasuries. The Dark Pyramid is static and unchanging."

"And you are now sharing this system with me?"

"This is one of many rewards for destroying

the level thirty-one infected rift. The friend-or-foe system is an extremely rare and expensive security measure. It is currently installed in only nine locations. Hearth will be the tenth and only the fourth location in the light empires."

"Max, trouble. We need to take a full inventory, but it's already clear that half of everything you had is missing, and some items have disappeared completely. There are no development crystals. Many elite pieces of dark beasts have disappeared. Elixirs, amplifiers, magic stones...The guards are already being interrogated."

"I understand." An unpleasant pressure hung over my chest. I wanted to kill someone, but I didn't yet know who. Looking back at Four, I clarified:

"Can only the Temple of Skron install a security system in the treasury?"

"Only the Temple of Skron has this capability. We don't allow anyone else access to this system."

"Is it just the entrance that is blocked? Or the entire treasury along the perimeter? Is it possible to dig through it from below?"

"The block applies across the entire area. Thanks to this protection, the treasury can be located anywhere. There is no point in hiding it in deep basements or high attics. The Temple of Skron believes that the treasury should be quickly accessible, without needing to walk or climb for hours."

"Does the Temple of Skron have specialists

that can determine who robbed me?”

“Summoning creatures of such power requires payment. Significant payment.”

“The Interrogator?”

“Yes. Only he can determine how the thieves got into the treasury. Those he interrogates cannot hide information. But they will not survive. They will become converts.”

“No, that’s not an option. Not yet,” I said. “Start installing the security system. The treasury is in this building, we will not change its location.”

“The Temple of Skron wishes to return to the original conversation. The key to the Fog Stalker Arena. We need it. You were interested in the first emperor of the light empires. You were given information already, but we can go further. Many centuries ago, the Temple of Skron participated in the unearthing of the first emperor’s tomb. According to agreements made with his descendents, they took the magic stones and records, and we got the armor. Over six hundred years, the Temple of Skron conducted many experiments with these items, some were irretrievably destroyed. The material from which this armor is made belongs to the creatures of Pharapho, and we were interested to know where the first emperor got this metal from before the master of the Black Mountain appeared in our world. This adaptive substance was called mithril and is considered one of the most expensive materials in this world. The method of obtaining it is still unknown. Perhaps there was something about this in the records of the first emperor, but they are irretrievably lost. They disappeared together with their eldest son. However, the Temple of Skron is ready to give you the armor of the first emperor in exchange for the key to the Fog Stalker Arena. We know that this is not an unequal exchange, but we are ready to make it. However, we understand that you are to go with Magister Meram to the lands of the offworlders. The Temple of Skron is interested in ensuring that these creatures leave our world. They are diverting too many resources."

"The armor — now that's interesting. Bring it here, I'll look at what you have, and then we can discuss the subject further," I agreed after a pause. "But that's not all. I have two requirements. First, I need the stones *Augment* and *Mentor,* both level two. Second, I need a rift that has reached down to the forties, preferably forty-one or forty-two. All the resources that I can extract from this rift are mine."

"The Temple of Skron is interested in the high-level dark essences that you plan to obtain from the rift."

"That's negotiable. First of all, I need to pass through this rift, then we can talk about essences. First, I need to figure out how to destroy invert beasts."

"You gained much knowledge in the fog arena." Four did not ask — he stated. At the same time, there was a note of respect in his voice. "The Temple of Skron respects those who strive for knowledge and ignore material rewards. You will get what you want. In our lands, there are some forty-level rifts that are becoming a problem. The Temple of Skron has a counter-offer. After you return from the lands of the offworlders, we propose that you conduct an expedition to the Black Mountain. The question we want to ask the Fog Stalker is simple. We are interested in how to destroy or expel Pharapho from our world. The Master of the Black Mountain must leave."

"Max," Eleanore's voice sounded. "The situation has cleared up a bit, but I can't say it has made it any easier. One of the treasury guards has disappeared. He was my man, whom I trusted. He couldn't have stolen anything. The other guards said that he had been acting strangely for the last week. He wasn't himself. He had become somewhat harsh. Alia once told me about one of your adventures and..."

"You don't have to continue. Our treasury was robbed by one of the Faceless. And I bet I know who they were working for."

Chapter 8

"VALEVSKY, HOW MUCH LONGER? I'm tired of sitting in one place!" Magister Meram almost kicked the door down. No one could stop the old man. Those who resisted his will in any way were rendered speechless for a day. If that wasn't enough, the runescribe would immobilize the poor fellows. I had to have a word with him on several occasions about how it wasn't right to treat people like that. Especially my people.

"My treasury has been robbed. Until I find everything that was lost, no one will go anywhere."

"Find it? Any leads?" Interest flashed into Magister Meram's voice.

"They stole fifty of my bone armor shells from the Pharapho sergeants. That's not exactly a trifle that could be tucked into the hem of a coat and taken out of the city. Whoever did this has been working on it for a long time — almost a month.

"

The armor was not taken out of the city — each cart undergoes double inspection. Both by the city guard and the clergy. They couldn't throw it over the wall either. Destroying it is not an option. Therefore, somewhere in Hearth, there is a room in which fifty one-and-a-half meter-wide shells are stored. My people are currently systematically going house to house, so sooner or later we will find the loss. However, whoever did this deserves punishment. As does their patron. Does the word 'Faceless' mean anything to you?"

"Changing one's appearance? Yes, quite an interesting solution," the old man calmed down and sat down in the chair. "Let's say you find the missing items. Who will stop the Faceless from breaking into the treasury again?"

"The Temple of Skron will install its own security system. No one else will be able to enter the treasury. Not even a Faceless."

"Is that so?" This time Magister Meram did not hide his surprise. "The dark ones are betting so much on you? Amazing. It seems I will have to teach you not only how to pick your nose, but also more serious things. I do not want to gain a reputation as a talentless teacher. Well, if I find you the Faceless one, can we finally set off on our journey?"

"Destroying the perpetrator is one thing. The one who considered himself brave enough to rob me also deserves punishment. I am one hundred percent sure that Padishah Bayazid III is involved in this matter. This is his revenge for everything that happened to him."

"Nonsense!" the old man waved his hand. "Robbing the treasury for a few measly items? Bayazid wouldn't do that. Killing you — now that would be interesting. Stealing the bone armor of the Pharapho sergeants, and in such quantities — that's not like him. No, pupil, some other hand is involved here. Definitely not Bayazid's. Whose path have you crossed?"

"Better to ask whose path I *haven't* crossed. Wait. Pupil? Not 'Valevsky' anymore?"

"Don't be persnickety. Have they found the bodies yet? If a Faceless is involved, there should be bodies."

"Why do we need them?"

"I will teach you an important lesson! Any corpse is first and foremost a source of information. Who killed him, how he was killed, why he was killed. Although it will be impossible to determine why at the moment, but we can find out everything else. You have the skill unlocked, right? In that case, let's start training. Today we will study words and how to form them!"

"I'm not really in the mood for studying right now."

"Which is a great shame!" Magister Meram's voice was filled with enthusiasm. "You need to learn in any situation, regardless of your moral or physical condition. As far as I remember, you destroyed Bishop Zwat's estate. What did you see there?"

"A Riftmaster."

"That's not what I'm talking about. Did you see my creations?"

"The living dead who slumped around cleaning the house? I saw them. If I understand correctly, you raised them with the *Live* symbol. It was a disgusting sight."

"There! So you do know something! That's right, *Live* is cast on a dead body and grants it mobility for a short period of time. The body can even perform the simplest actions, but this symbol does not solve the problem of decomposition. After three or four days, these servants must be replaced. But! We are not going to return the corpses back to service, right? We need them for something else."

"*Live* can be combined with another symbol to form a word?" I guessed and opened the syllabary. Magister Meram stood nearby, pleased as a cat that had eaten its fill, allowing me to come to a solution on my own. "Let's say we were able to raise the corpse. Now we need to make it speak. Let's use *Verb*. But speaking does not mean speaking intelligently. The body requires some kind of intelligence. The symbol *Think*? Three symbols in a word... I can't even imagine how to do it. I can't even do two."

"Four," said the satisfied runescribe. "We also need the control symbol *Us*. It's easy for a dead man to deceive. We can't let him do that. A dead man must tell the truth and only the truth."

"That's impossible. Four symbols isn't just a word. It's a whole sentence. I can't handle that."

"You don't need to exaggerate. First, you have to learn to operate with two symbols. You have some brains in your head, as I can see. As well as an understanding of the basic principles. What's missing is practice and knowledge of the basic combinations. They all exist and have been described for ages. And you'll have to remember them all — I'll be strict with you. I can't give you the book now, as my other pupil has it, and I'm too lazy to get a new one. But as soon as we unite, you'll start studying right away. Where's the corpse, pupil?"

"Eleanore, have any bodies been found?"

"Just a second, let me ask...Yes, they found the body of the keeper. What was left of him."

"Order everyone not to touch it. We'll be right there."

"We?"

"Magister Meram is helping me find out who killed the keeper."

Eleanore didn't argue, she just told us where to go. Soon we found ourselves near one of the buildings under construction. Like all the buildings in Hearth, this one had undergone major changes. It had been completely demolished, a basement was dug, it was connected to the city sewer system, and the walls were already in the process of being rebuilt. The body was found in the basement. When we arrived at the crime scene, it became clear that the body had been dragged here from somewhere else. And it was done by one person — traces from a lone wolf were left in the dust.

"So, forming several symbols at once," Magister Meram used every opportunity to demonstrate his superiority and to teach me, an illiterate. "When you're only drawing one symbol, the process is quite simple: make several passes with your hand, hold the symbol, saturate it with energy and send it to the target. But when it comes to several symbols, everything becomes much more complicated. You need to keep the entire drawing in your head and, without being distracted for a moment, form it in one single movement. The transitions between symbols are formed like this."

The runescribe made some imperceptible movement with his fingers and gave me a pointed look so that I would repeat it.

"Don't tell me you've forgotten it already," the old man grimaced when I didn't respond.

"To remember, you must first see and understand. Not only did I not understand, I didn't even see it."

"Almighty Skron, who have you brought me?" Magister Meram rolled his eyes to the sky, begging the dark deity for an explanation. There was none, so the runescribe sighed and once again, this time slowly, demonstrated the motion, commenting on each individual gesture.

"Repeat it!" Magister Meram demanded. He paid no heed to our surroundings. So there was a thing that used to be a person lying on the floor, big deal. It'll stay there a bit longer. Teaching this amateur to form the space between symbols was more important.

I managed to move my fingers correctly on the third try. My constant practice activating the katar and crossbow had had an effect. But even this result seemed unacceptable to Magister Meram. Judging by his face, I should have succeeded on the first try. Even while writing three or four symbols.

"Now combine the first two symbols," the old man demanded. "You must hold them in your mind and not be distracted for a moment while you form them. Raise the corpse and make it speak."

A muffled whisper was heard — the onlookers had begun to understand why we had come here. Some even vomited at the mere thought of what we were going to do. However, I was not backing down now — I needed to be able to combine two symbols with my eyes closed. Otherwise, I did not feel protected from the machinations of the old man, who today was good and kind, but tomorrow, might feel the reins hit his hindquarters and start running rampant. As long as he was the only one who held knowledge about multi-letter runes, he would have to be reckoned with.

So I kept trying, losing concentration time after time during the transition. Magister Meram's snide remarks did not add to my positive mood, and several times I wanted to give up and admit that I had no talent for runework. I could draw a single symbol — and that was it. However, every time such a thought crept into my head, I looked at the old runescribe and returned to training again. If I failed, then I would have to acknowledge someone else's power over me. And not just anyone else — a specific person who is standing next to me, sneering. Is that what I wanted? Never!

"Finally!" Master Meram was delighted when, after half an hour of fiddling around, two symbols began to flash in front of me. I aimed them at the corpse, but for some reason I couldn't hit the target. Everything went dark before my eyes, my head started spinning, and I staggered and couldn't stay on my feet. I couldn't even use *Heal* on myself, it was so bad! The symbols dissipated into the air, and I, lying in the dust, tried to figure out who I was and what I was doing here.

"And now, you have finally encountered the main problem that keeps my number of pupils so low. Writing individual symbols is child's play. Any talentless hack can do it. But as soon as you need to transition to the next level — two, or even three symbols — then the problems begin. In addition to the standard payment for the work, be it savory ink or human souls, the runescribe must pay with his own life force. And there is no way to reduce this fee. That is why there is no place for the skinny or frail among my students. And I myself, as you can see, have not acquired a respectable plumpness in my many years. All my energy is spent on connecting symbols. And the more runes in a sentence, the harder the toll it takes on the scribe. You must be prepared for this. Nevertheless, you managed. Even if not on the first try, even if it took you nearly two years, you still did it. I have been teaching neophytes for two hundred years. During this time, I have had both geniuses and complete mediocrities. You, pupil, are closer to the first. I think you will definitely be in the top ten. Closer to the top. This makes me happy. I have not had a pupil such as you for a long time."

"Two hundred years?" My voice came out as a wheeze. It felt as if I hadn't slept, eaten or drunk for a week or two, and had been running around that entire time. My body had reached the limit, but couldn't cross it, hanging somewhere between life and death.

"Why are you surprised?" chuckled Magister Meram. "A true runescribe lives as long as he wishes. And no deft pupil who has torn out his mentor's heart is able to prevent this. For your information, pupil, I will turn three hundred and twenty years old next year! Among all the people currently existing, I am the second longest lived."

"Second? Who's the first?"

"Isn't it obvious? My mentor, who taught me after the Temple of Skron. The one who taught me to follow my own path, regardless of all conventions. The one who learned all the secrets of this world."

"So somewhere in this world there is another high-level runescribe?"

"Of course. He abandoned his work long ago — I don't even know where he is right now, but even after all this time, our shared communication symbol hasn't lost its power. He's alive, and that knowledge is enough for me. Of course, I won't get involved with him. Our last meeting didn't go so well. He wanted to kill me, and I resisted in every way possible...Ah, those were good times! Mages ruled the world, the church remained part of the fold, traveling through the light empires was much easier. Alright, we've gotten some rest, that's enough. Get up! You, bring your master some food. Lots. Onward!"

The man that Magister Meram pointed at with his long, crooked finger ran as if all the dark creatures in this world were chasing him.

"We've already made a decision about you — you need training, training and more training. As well as strengthening your constitution — the more you invest in development, the easier it will be to handle fusing symbols. It is impossible to completely rid yourself of the consequences of forming two or more runes. Your life force will always be drained. But you can make it so that this deprivation does not greatly affect your well-being. I will make a list of skills that you will need to pump up first. Now watch what I do. Remember every movement. In two years, you will have to repeat all this. Otherwise, I will be disappointed in you. And I will kill you. I do not need talentless competition."

I just grinned — another potential assassin. Wherever I looked, there was someone who wanted to finish me off. Two years...I couldn't even see that far ahead. Living through today was always a victory!

Nevertheless, I did not slack off and carefully watched what Magister Meram was doing. In the end, I would also need to finish off this multi-centenarian. Someone who could easily destroy hundreds of people for the sake of his symbols did not deserve to live. For now the old man was useful, but later he would need to be disposed of. The main issue was — how? Ripping out his heart again would be useless. I'd need a more serious weapon. I'd need to consult with Alia — she had been able to craft all sorts of inventions. The clergy were specialists in this.

"Great Light!" A frightened cry was heard, and in a matter of moments the runescribe and I were left alone. The escorts ran away, frightened by the sudden twitching movements of the corpse. There was no point in lying — I also felt such a repulsion that it made me want to turn tail and flee. It was so frightening that my knees shook. It was one thing to see the raised dead performing simple tasks, and another to be present at the revival.

The keeper's body rose to its feet and froze in an unnatural pose, inspiring further horror.

"Can you hear me?" asked Magister Meram.

"Yes, master," the voice also barely resembled a human one. I wasn't even sure that it was the corpse itself speaking.

"Who killed you?"

"The one who called himself Faceless. He stole my image."

"When was your image stolen?"

"Thirty-two days ago. He kept me locked up all this time."

"Where were you locked up?"

"The eighth house down on the third street over. There is a secret room in the basement, fenced off with a panel."

"Do you know the name of the person who gave the order?"

"Yes, master. The Faceless One said several times that his master would be pleased with the result. The stolen items are in the same room where I was held."

"What did the Faceless One call his master?" Magister Meram had almost lost his patience. The corpse answered, and a satisfied grin broke across the rubescribe's face.

"I told you so! I told you that Bayazid the Third is not interested in such hullabaloo. That's it, pupil, get ready, it's time for us to move. The offworlders won't drive themselves from our plane!"

"Without catching the Faceless One?"

"Why do you need him? You've secured the treasury, if one of your comrades gets killed, you'll find new ones. What else can the Faceless do? He's a scoundrel, nothing more. A trifle that shouldn't be paid attention to."

"And leave the one who gave the order unpunished?"

"As if you can do anything to him now," Magister Meram chuckled. "I can. You can't. Accept this fact and get ready. Time is money."

There was a clamor as the body fell to the floor, losing its strength.

"First, I want to catch the Faceless. Would you be happy to know your house was run by miscreants?"

"Let them try!" Magister Meram frowned for a moment. "Okay, you've convinced me. It really isn't good to leave the city to any sort of riffraff. Either the *Phantom*s or the Faceless — they're both irritating. And you'd essentially be leaving this Skron-forgotten place to them. Let's go. First, we need to have a look at the premises."

A secret room...in a city under construction. And this room was planned in advance, fenced off from prying eyes, built, and all this without our control. It was worth seeing Eleanore's eyes when she entered the room. No one had seen her like this, even when she was a countess. Taking out a book, the city manager quickly determined which of the teams built this house, after which she called Kurpatsky and handed him the list of names.

"Leonid, you know what to do."

The head of security nodded and left, allowing us to admire the builders' creation. We had recruited teams from all over the empire, delighted at how cheap some of them were, and no one could even imagine that the builders would be working for more than just us. Now the question was, how many of these secret rooms are there in the city? This one, apparently, had been built by the Faceless One's client. But there were other interested parties who were conducting such disgraceful activities under our noses.

"Max, this is my fault." Eleanore saw no point in passing the blame. "I should have known in advance that the other 'pie pieces,' as you've put it, would be interested in Hearth. "In our rush to meet deadlines, this slipped through our security measures. I'm not sure that a total inspection of all the buildings would yield results. If you didn't know that there was a room here, you'd never guess what to look for."

"First, we need to interrogate the builders and their foreman." I turned my gaze to one of the guards who was standing not far from us. My *Analyze* was running constantly, so I knew full well who was standing in front of me. But knowing does not mean acting. I didn't need an explosion from level-twenty magic stones in the center of the city. I remembered how that turned out last time.

"Mentor, I need advice." I turned to Magister Meram. "If I needed to capture a mage, how would I do it? I am especially concerned about the issue of protecting myself from exploding magic stones. What if the mage is so mad and reckless that he decides to take this step?"

"What an interesting question." The old man looked at me quizzically. I had to nod, confirming that the Faceless was nearby. "Perhaps I should give you another lesson, student. A single symbol won't do the trick here. Even a double one won't be effective. Three symbols. You need to maintain control over the victim and not allow him to act willfully. Look at the alphabet and think."

I was taken aback. Since I was the person that posed the question, I'd have to find the answer myself. I had a description of all the symbols, but none of them even came close to the task that was required. Maintain control? I couldn't imagine how to do that. Nevertheless, I began to reason:

"One of the symbols is *Us*. I need information, and mages love to lie. But *Us* is the third symbol, installed over the finished structure. First, you need to block...*Ground* and *Peace*? The first symbol delays, the second grants some semblance of control, imposing the curse *Dessicate*. With an *Us* on top."

"Almost to a T, except for one thing: you didn't arrange for the mage to speak the truth in the first place. With *Truth,* it's four symbols. Yes, you should use the two you listed, but they won't work without the control symbol *And.* Four symbols, a whole lot of headaches, and you'll have thirty minutes to talk to your mage. Where is he?"

"The guard by the door. That's Faceless."

What happened next took a matter of moments. The guard tore off with such speed that he was smeared in the air like a dark bolt. A knife appeared in Magister Meram's chest, but this did not stop the old runescribe — first the symbol *Ook* appeared in the air, significantly slowing the Faceless man down, and then a whole sentence of four symbols grew before my eyes. Magister Meram turned white, but did not stop, directing his creation at the Faceless man.

"He's yours." The runescribe's evil grin as he pulled the dagger out of his chest did not bode well for the guard. Neither did mine. I approached the future corpse:

"Who is your employer?"

He resisted for a long time. He sweated, growled, tried to use the poison built into his body, but all to no avail — he had lost control. I asked the same thing tirelessly, sweeping away his defenses. After about ten minutes, his mind began to give in. No matter how hard he fought the obsessive desire to tell me the truth, he was unable to overcome Magister Meram's runes.

"Who is your employer?"

"Count Vyazemsky! He sent me to Hearth to bring back the bone armor from the treasury. I was to deliver twenty bone shells minimum, but everything I could get my hands on. Magic stones were a priority."

"How many houses with secret rooms belonging to Count Vyazemsky are there in my city?"

"Two! The team that built them worked for Count Vyazemsky. The foreman is one of his trusted servants. His real name is Viscount Ourite!"

"Where are these houses located?"

Faceless resisted, but once he started talking, he couldn't stop. I got the addresses of not only the hidden houses of Count Vyazemsky, but also Counts Shub, Kuzmin, and even General

Khabensky. Each pie slice of the Zarak Empire had his own brigade, and because of the unique service he could offer, Faceless had been tasked with visiting each one, supervising the acceptance. But most unpleasant of all was the fact that the Nocturnal Guild also had their own, separate residence. The hired assassins had settled in Hearth, building their lair in the very center of the city. Right by the city square, next to my palace.

Two symbols that Magister Meram actively used when punishing invisibles came to mind. Realizing that this was going to sap my life source and that it would be best to use the mithril gloves, I nevertheless resorted to this method. The space in front of me swayed, my vision darkened, I suddenly wanted to fall, close my eyes and never get up again, but I forced myself to stay on my feet. This was my city and only I had the right to rule here. Faceless' eyes widened in horror and pain, and a moment later the guard's armor filled with bones and magic stones fell to the floor. The body had rotted away in a matter of moments.

"You passed!" Magister Meram said, satisfied. "Now we can move on to triple symbols. There's no longer any use in training you with two. But you must remember them all! Otherwise, I'll kill you dead and say that I found you like that!"

"Eleanor, seize and interrogate all the construction teams. There is a possibility that the Faceless One did not list all the houses. Execute Viscount Ourite after the interrogation. I am not going to bargain with Count Vyazemsky for this man's life. And also — I need detailed information on what Count Vyazemsky does. Where does he make his profit? What does he value most? The time has come to strike back. The Zarak Empire must understand once and for all: no one will ever dare to rob me with impunity. I will return in two months, by which time everything should be ready. Magister Meram, I am ready to go to the lands of the offworlders. Let us settle this issue."

Chapter 9

"NO! NO!" OUR SIMULTANEOUS CRY of indignation filled the Temple of Skron.

"Yes, my pupils, yes!" Magister Meram was reveling in the effect he had created. "You, Fardi — either moderate your temper or forget forever that you want to acquire the skill of a runescribe. As for you, Valevsky, you have no choice. You owe me a favor and are obliged to comply. If, of course, your word can be trusted. Again, if you refuse, then you will go home and wait for me to come for you. Because I can't abide by those who don't keep their word. I come and kill them. As soon as we finish with the offworlders."

I looked at Karina Fardi, barely holding back the urge to cast two symbols on her and turn her into a pile of bones.

"This beast tried to kill me!" I blurted out.

"You started it, scum!" Karina wasn't backing

down.

"We were in the arena, you crazy fool! We fought one-on-one! There was no trickery there!"

"And you deserved nothing less! As soon as I get the opportunity, I will definitely take advantage of it! There's only one place for creatures like you: the grave!"

"Do you think that just because you managed to escape to Skron, that will save you? I will scorch you through with Light!"

"Are you two finished?" Our mentor was clearly amused by the back-and-forth. "Now, you'll listen to me. From now on, you are one. You will eat together, sleep together, train together. The failures of one will be the failures of the other. If one of you fails to cope with something, I will punish both of you. I do not care about your personal problems. Upon becoming my pupils, you left all prior difficulties between you in the past. If you do not want to obey, you can leave right now. If you stay and I see you act aggressively toward one another, I will punish you. And in such a way that next time you will think thrice before acting...but what am I saying? Why tell you what awaits you when it is easier to just show you?"

Two words with three symbols each appeared in the air, and before I could jump back, one of them crashed into my chest. I didn't even have a chance to return the Light to my eyes. Although it would have been useless. What Magister Meram used was not a curse. It was pure pain, multiplied by suffering. My mind left me in a matter of moments — there was nothing left but insane pain, twisting every cell. I couldn't even scream, because I simply didn't have enough air. I didn't see or hear anything that was happening around me. The monstrous pain swallowed me whole. When it was all over, I lay on the floor for a long time, unable to find the strength to get up. What the mentor used against me was beyond good and evil. He would die for this. I'd kill him!

"I used only ten seconds for the demonstration," the rubescribe said. Ten seconds? It seemed like an eternity that I had lay there on the ground. "If one of you disappoints me, I'll increase it to thirty seconds. Then to a minute. And so on, until you go mad from the pain. The longest a person has managed to maintain their sanity was six minutes and thirty seconds. Are you ready to test your strength? If so, I'll ask again: will you remain my pupils or will you decide to run away in disgrace? You know the consequences. Fardi?"

"I'm staying," came a wheeze came from my side. Gathering all the strength I had, I turned my head. Karina was lying next to me, looking like a broken doll, her position was so unnatural. She couldn't even find the strength to rearrange her limbs into a more comfortable position. Let her suffer.

"Valevsky?"

"I'm staying." The decision was easy for me. In fact, there wasn't much choice, and Magister Meram had just clearly demonstrated how much stronger he was than any person operating with magic stones. The symbols ignored any protection or blockages, and if I refused to become his pupil, I would be killed in two months. And did I need any of that? No. I had no desire to feel those symbols again. So I would have to commune with Fardi temporarily, whether I wanted to or not.

"Magnificent!" Magister Meram rejoiced. "Alright, I'm going to negotiate payment for our services. We don't get a free ride, now, do we? Fardi: the dark ones want to conduct several tests on you to determine the degree of your commitment to Skron. Valevsky, Four is waiting for you. We'll meet here in two hours. Anyone who's late will be punished."

"And if you're late?" Fardi asked. The darkness that poured from her eyes was frightening in its intensity. I've only seen such pure black in the gaze of the Interrogator.

"A mentor is never late, stupid pupil. A mentor always comes exactly when he needs to! Now I will pretend that I did not hear this question, and next time there will be punishment. For both of you."

The doors to the room moved aside and one of the misty servants of the Temple of Skron appeared on the threshold, where Magister Meram and I went immediately after overseeing the execution of Viscount Ourite. The foreman had tried to explain, said that his life could be bought, that Count Vyazemsky would avenge his loyal vassal, but I did not listen to such stupid speeches. This man had illegally entered my city and I had every reason to punish him. Moreover, to punish him myself: I decided that it was impossible to force Eleanore to carry out the order to kill an aristocrat. In the eyes of the Zarak Empire, my city and estate manager was an ordinary woman, deprived of her title, so the public may be outraged, even despite what this Viscount had done. However, it would be more difficult to present a case against me, Archduke Valevsky. I was fully within my rights.

"Four is waiting for you," said the temple servant and stepped aside, allowing me to pass. The old runescribe had already run off to his business, so Fardi and I were alone for the first time.

"Magister Meram's training lasts two years. I need it. And so do you. I propose a truce. I give you my word that I will not attack you first and that, if necessary, I will protect you from external dangers. But only while we are training with the runescribe. As soon as we pass the final exam, I will do everything I can to finish you off. You and your entire family. And I will do it by my own hand, without any middlemen. I give you my word!"

"There can only be a truce on one condition, Valevsky," Fardi's voice was filled with unmasked hatred. "As soon as we finish training, right after the exam, we have a duel. You and me. One on one. No restrictions, no rules. We use everything the runescribe teaches us or that we receive within these two years. Only then can I promise you that

I will train by your side. Do you think pain will stop me? Pain has become my kin! It will become a part of me! A minute, two, five. How much can you endure? You'll go mad first!"

"We'll battle after our training. On my word!"

"I will fulfill Master Meram's demands and become one with you, as he wishes. If you need help in these two years or if your life needs to be saved, you can count on me. We will go through training without looking back at each other. But then you will die, Valevsky. You, all your whores and whatever little flecks of pondscum they produce. I will finish what my father started! On my word!"

I left the room, trying to figure out when Fardi had become such a fanatic. Karina had never been particularly tolerant of others — she was a real bitch, in fact — but deciding to suffer immense pain just so that someone else would suffer was too much. And she could actually withstand it! What madness!

"Archduke Valevsky, the Temple of Skron is happy to see you within its walls."

"My mentor left me no choice. He wanted to visit you, so I had to follow him. Are you ready for the exchange?"

"Did you bring the Fog Stalker key?" Four even twitched slightly.

"Have you prepared the First Emperor's mithril armor?"

"The armor is ready. I hope you have already familiarized yourself with the information that was provided to you. We see that you are already wearing the amulets and bracelet."

"Not yet. I leafed through several books and realized that they need to be read carefully. Your books contain more information than those in the Citadel."

"The Citadel has a full copy of our information on the first emperor," said Four, to which I only grinned. The churchmen had deceived me once again. It was becoming so commonplace that I was tired of being surprised by it. They gave me fairy tales about how the great man grew up, but about his feats and how he achieved them, which was described in the books of the Temple of Skron, the servants of Light for some reason decided to keep silent. They pretended that they had nothing.

"I will discuss this matter with the Citadel separately. Your key," I embodied one of the five keys to the Fog Stalker Arena available to me and placed it on the table. "Where is my armor?"

"You will be led to it." Four's voice quivered and he didn't take his eyes off of the key. It was annoying not to be able to see the other person's face. After some hesitation, I left the key on the table and left the room, but all my negative thoughts instantly vanished when I was let into the next room. There was nothing here except a rack holding the armor, but what a suit of armor it was! My throat even went dry when I saw it — not every high-ranking aristocrat had the right to wear something so fine! Forget aristocrats — not even all emperors would have the right! The

Founder of the light lands had exquisite taste. He'd made a suit of armor so superlative that it would cause envy in anyone who saw it! So that it would provoke anyone who coveted unique items and make them commit rash acts.

I was left alone, but somehow there was no doubt that my every move was being closely watched. The Black Pyramid wanted to know how the mithril was being used. If the misty servants were telling the truth, then the absence of the first emperor's journal prevented the Temple of Skron from figuring out the true value of this set. They knew it was an adaptive material, but the adaptation itself was inactive. Would they really just let me take such a valuable thing? This would be the biggest failure in the entire history of the Temple of Skron!

I walked closer and touched the helmet. It was plain metal. Just like the pauldrons the Citadel had given me, with one small exception — when my fingers made contact, one of the strangest messages I had ever seen appeared before my eyes:

Integration is not possible.

The current owner of the Mithril Set helmet is still alive.

Similar messages popped up when I touched other parts of the armor. None of the mithril items came under my control, time after time reporting that their owner was still alive. Which was impossible in itself — the first emperor was officially considered dead. They had even taken his

Devour! How could a man who died six hundred years ago still be alive?

I took the helmet and put it on my head. Nothing happened. The first emperor's head was larger than mine, and the helmet hung on me like a mannequin. An attempt to adapt the object and force it to at least take the form I needed was not successful. The mithril did not want to recognize me as its master.

"The Temple of Skron sees that you have encountered the same issue that we could not solve," one of Skron's misty servants appeared in the doorway. Judging by the timbre of his voice, it was Four. Apparently, he had already managed to give Two the key to the Fog Stalker Arena and had come back to jeer at me.

"I was informed that the current owner of the set is alive. How is this possible? The first emperor is alive?"

"No, he is dead. When the body was removed from the tomb, the eldest son of the first emperor of the Light lands took control of the armor. The Temple of Skron realized this too late. Attempts to find the one who deceived us were unsuccessful. The eldest son of the first emperor of the Light lands disappeared. However, he is still alive, as you could see just now."

"That must have happened many hundreds of years ago!"

"The Temple of Skron knows the exact dates of when he came into possession of the now useless set. Runescribes have the ability to extend their own lives at the expense of the lives of others. The Temple of Skron believes that the eldest son of the first emperor of the Light lands takes advantage of this opportunity and kills two hundred people every five years to live through another era. Just as your mentor does."

"Two hundred people?" I was taken aback by this news, but I immediately pulled myself together. "The Temple of Skron knew that I would fail. They knew that I was not the owner of the set, but they did not warn me about what I would have to face. Four, I am a kind, sympathetic person, but when I'm treated like a cash cow, I start to feel sad. Do I need to tell the Temple of Skron that I am not interested in trading with the source of my great sadness? Now it turns out that you deceived me and took the key to the Fog Stalker Arena from me for free. Partners do not behave in such a way."

"The Temple of Skron knew that this news would disappoint you, so we offer you a reasonable price for the key to the Fog Stalker Arena. You cannot use this mithril, but we can provide you with an identification system for your city. The Temple of Skron knows that you organized a hunt for the Faceless in Hearth, found him and executed him. As well as many other people who did not work for you. The Temple of Skron welcomes a ruler who personally defends his lands. Archduke Valevsky, we want to return the stones that allow a person to be faceless, and in exchange, the Temple of Skron will provide you with a city security system that will inform you of all illegal visitors. Anyone who has not passed through the control system and has not received a universal key will be detected. We will help set up the identification system — only people with the appropriate access will be able to go to certain places. You will know exactly who your guests are at all times, be they illegal immigrants, citizens or trusted friends. Complete control over a city of your size."

"Where did you get such a system?" I asked in surprise, assessing the proposal. From the description, it seemed ideal.

"It is the legacy of the mechanoids."

"That's the second time I've heard that word. Who are these mechanoids?"

"Guests in our world, crafted from living metal. They appeared at almost the same time as Skron. We established trade with them, but the sudden appearance of offworlders prevented this. The mechanoids disappeared, and we still have not been able to find out whether they left our world for good or hid, like the eldest son of the first emperor of the Light lands. However, the old systems that we received in exchange for resources are still active and can be used. The magic academy in Kerux contains such a monitoring system, and a number of other institutions not inferior in size to Hearth. The Temple of Skron understands that the mithril did not recognize you as the owner and offers an equivalent replacement. We believe that the key to the Fog Stalker Arena and the faceless stones are a worthy exchange."

"Agreed," I said after a moment's thought, but added: "Before installing anything, my city manager and I need a description. We need to know how to use it and how to set it up."

"The Temple of Skron will provide the necessary training to as many operators as your city requires. The description has been prepared and will be given to you and your manager after our meeting. The Temple of Skron values partnerships that can benefit everyone."

"Nevertheless, I have some vague doubts about the level of access. Yes, we will ensure control over the illegal presence of representatives of the light empires. What about the dark ones? Will the servants of the Temple of Skron pass into Hearth just as easily as before? The beastmen? The Dark Orthodoxy?"

"The security system that will be installed in the Hearth only works for the followers of the Light. It was configured by the mechanoids for our cities to ensure their safety. In the old days, the servants of the Light caused too much trouble in Kerux. In order to guarantee there are no dark ones operating illegally under your nose, you will need a different system. One that the Temple of Skron does not have access to. However, we will try to keep the Orthodox out of Hearth. The Temple of Skron knows that you destroyed the incarnation of Skron when the Wave in the Citadel was destroyed. According to the unspoken law of Kerux, there is only one punishment for such an act: death. However, we take into account what happened in the Citadel and what consequences it led to. Twelve cardinals and two commanders were sent to the Light, which can be considered a worthy exchange for one incarnation of Skron. The Church of the Light has never received such a heavy blow."

"Is that why Karina Fardi is part of the temple now?"

"Skron singled her out. He gave her strength and abilities unheard of in any human. He made her a true weapon and conductor of his will. Sooner or later, the light empires will be dealt a crushing blow, and Karina Fardi will stand at the forefront of this attack."

"The Temple of Skron openly admits this? Even knowing that I am one of the warriors of Light?"

"You are different. The Temple of Skron does not fully understand who you are. How did you appear? How have you managed to close rifts so deep that the last time one of their kind was closed was seven hundred years ago?"

"The first emperor of the Light?" I clarified.

"Correct. That's why we gave you the mithril armor. It is considered one of the main treasures of the Temple of Skron, yet you were given access to it. One believed that you were a descendant of the founder of your empires. However, now we understand that this is not so. The armor did not recognize you. Which makes you even more strange and mysterious, but at the same time, detached from the forces of Light. Even though you can light the Light in your eyes. The empires of the Light will not be completely destroyed. The Temple of Skron wants to destroy the Church of the Light. They anchor you in one place and do not allow you to flourish. It is time for you to return, Archduke. The meeting between Magister Meram and Three has just ended. The parties have agreed on payment for the expedition to the lands of the offworlders."

After warning Eleanore that a brigade of dark ones might show up in Hearth soon and that they shouldn't be killed — at least not right away — I headed back to the main waiting room. Fardi was already there, and from the gleam in her black eyes it was clear that she had been given something. Something that made her even stronger.

"That's no fun!" Magister Meram appeared in the room and grimaced with displeasure. "Couldn't you have given your old mentor a few kicks and showed up late? Alright, let's move on — they're taking us to the Gourfan Clan, who will provide us with transportation. Fardi, give Valevsky the book. He'll have a couple of days to learn it by heart. I hope you've already done so yourself? There are only a little over one and a half thousand combinations. A mere couple of hours of study!"

Fardi's face twisted for a moment — she clearly hadn't fully memorized the descriptions of all the combinations. The runes themselves were easy enough to remember: two symbols from the alphabet in all possible combinations, but it was necessary to remember not only the position, but also the description, because two identical symbols placed from different sides gave different results.

"I'll test you on the material in a week," Magister Meram warned. "If either of you fails, I'll punish you both. But I'll punish the one who fails more severely. So that they don't do it again. Do you understand? You have one book, learn to use it together."

"Mentor, can I ask a question?" I couldn't help myself.

"Go ahead, while we are in the Temple of Skron, I give you this right. But as soon as we leave, any question will be punished. You either grasp everything the first time, or you figure it out on your own, or you suffer and get an answer. Any lukewarmness in your studies is unacceptable. What did you want to know?"

"Why do you want to unite us? You know that Fardi and I, to put it mildly, don't like each other. I almost killed her, she succeeded in killing me. And yet you stubbornly insist we live as one, as if you enjoy the way we squabble with each other."

"A runescribe, Valevsky, must have perfect control over his body and emotions. Many can form one, or even two symbols, but when the time comes for true art, speech, as you understand, which occurs with three runes and above, then any loss of control is fraught with consequences.

Do you remember what happened to you? If you do not fortify yourself and you instead lose control, even runic magic will not be able to revive you. Because your very essence will die. If you cannot restrain yourselves in each other's company, then you will never be masters, no matter how hard I try. Because sooner or later you will break. This primarily concerns you, my girl. You have not yet received the punishment you deserve for your stupidity. Killing Valevsky when I ordered you not to do so...Only the fact that Skron accepted your sacrifice and exalted you gives you the right to stand in my presence. Neither Magister Elor nor Kimal Sarento could convince me that you need to be trained.

"Kimal Sarento?" I frowned. The old man fell silent so abruptly that everything became clear as day. "So he's involved in this too?!"

"That's it, enough chit-chat. Pupils, you're in charge of the luggage. Since we will be unable to travel across the lands of Kerux in my cart, you must carry everything to the portal. The cart is near the inn. I'll give you two hours. If you can't handle the task, I'll finally be happy. It's not good to start training without punishment. It's already been two hours, slackers! What are you sitting around for? Chop chop! My suitcases won't grow legs and walk to the portal on their own!"

Chapter 10

"AGAIN! FASTER! Why are you flapping your arms around like a drunken housefly? Faster, I said! Valevsky, what are you grinning at? Get off the cart and run next to me! If there's nothing in your head, at least your legs will work! Fardi, may you explode, what are you doing? Why are you turning your hand like that?! Almighty Skron, why did you give me such talentless pupils?"

I jumped off the cart and ran alongside, quickly adapting to the horses' leisurely pace. We had been on the road for four days already, and during that time I realized one thing: training with the Evil Engineer had been a fun and joyous time. The way Magister Meram had mocked us deserved a separate chapter in the textbooks for church executioners. The runescribe quickly realized that curses did not work on me, but this did not stop him. In addition to the usual arsenal of weakening or strengthening symbols, the mentor had added something of his own. Words of two, and in some places three symbols that did not leave my body, forcing me to suffer. It got to the point that I even began to order the mithril to block the actions of the evil old man, but it was all in vain — the chestplate could not withstand the symbols' influence. Either the mithril did not know how to handle it, or a whole suit of armor was required, and not a pathetic semblance of one, like mine.

In the end, I returned the Light to my eyes so that I wouldn't fall under the old man's curses and silently carried out all his orders, gradually approaching the peak of my current abilities — a word of three symbols. I was still far from achieving the desired result. While I could more or less write two-symbol words, as soon as I started to form the third, something extremely unpleasant happened that knocked me out of training for two hours. My body simply started to die. I'd need to fully pump up all my stats so that I wouldn't turn in a vegetable every time, but knowing and doing were two completely different things. I had more than enough gallo crystals, enough for half of Hearth, but the crystals required an altar, and that posed certain problems. The one in Hearth was being restored, the Temple of Skron did not grant me access, the Gourfan clan refused to even discuss the topic with me, and we did not encounter a single solitary rift along the way. Why was I on the hunt for rifts? To destroy them and make the Pharapho fog appear. I wanted to get an altar my own way. But alas, this was not meant to be. In the end, I continued to torture myself, consuming food in huge quantities in order to somehow recover. At some point, Magister Meram even reprimanded me not to eat so much, because at this rate there would not be enough food to last us until the end of the journey. In the end, my mentor ordered me to train only twice a day. I had already successfully screwed up the morning training, unable to withstand the pressure of even beginning to form a third symbol, and another torture session would follow in a couple of hours. All I could do was continue running toward it.

However, all my suffering was nothing compared to what Fardi had to endure. In contrast to me, Karina had been buffed to the max, raising her stability, endurance and constitution to astronomical heights, so Magister Meram didn't restrain his "creativity," forcing Fardi to form one symbol after the other. *Analyze* demonstrated that the girl's words about how she could "kill me with pain" were not just empty talk. Now Fardi surpassed me in everything. Both physical and magical development. The Temple of Skron and Magister Elor had invested heavily in her development, turning the once-ordinary girl into something terrifying. I had no desire to engage Fardi in combat now. Not only did she now have a crossbow with vyrma bolts, but her armor was also made of this expensive material. And she never removed it! The only way I could win was with the mithril gloves, but I needed to get close. This proved rather difficult, as Fardi had an analog of my own golden dome that had been pumped up to level twenty. This was despite the fact that she also had Magic Armor. The only thing she didn't have was a vyrma-blocking stone. I believed that at the reception with Padishah Bayazid the Third, Karina could have killed me with her bare hands, but she didn't because she was afraid she wouldn't have time. She was afraid that Magister Meram would stop her, so she took the less risky option. It wasn't a fantastic feeling to be so near a person who was so much stronger and hated you so deeply.

However, in the midst of all this madness I had once again immersed myself in, there was a bright spot. And it was that Fardi, no matter how she tried, could not form a dual symbol. No way! Magister Meram was furious, yelling, punishing, but it was all useless — Karina could not maintain control over the two letters of the mysterious alphabet blazing in the air. Which gave me hope for success in the upcoming duel. I needed to learn to work with four-symbol sentences. This was the only way I saw my salvation and the opportunity to destroy both Fardi and Meram. The old man had definitely stayed in this world too long.

"Halt!" Master Meram commanded, and the three supreme converts rushed to set up camp. The angry mentor jumped to the ground and looked at me: "Valevsky, why can you do what your partner cannot?"

"Her concentration. She gets distracted and tries brute force where smoothness is needed," I suggested. Each time, it became easier to speak when my eyes were filled with Light. Now, for example, I even managed to stay on my feet. It was bad, of course, but already quite bearable. As for my response, I had established through experience that when addressed, I needed to respond. Otherwise, the runescribe started to get angry and throw pain symbols. And I no longer evaded them, even despite the amulet. I also came to this through experience. Two days ago, when Magister Meram realized that I was avoiding his symbols, he completely flew off the handle. In a frenzy, he almost killed me on the spot, and after consciousness returned, he warned that if I pulled another prank like that, I would be in trouble. Blocking any symbols imposed upon us during our apprenticeship was simply a bad idea.

"It's easy to make up for a lack of concentration," Magister Meram looked at the cart where Fardi lay. She didn't have the strength to crawl out. "But it won't do any good. Something's holding her back. She needs to think. Okay, now let's figure out what to do with you. Do you see the forest on the horizon? It's about fifteen kilometers away, no more. Get a move on. I'll be expecting you back in the morning."

"Magister?" I was surprised by this order.

"'Magister' what?" There's a rift in the forest. Didn't the Temple of Skron provide you with maps of the area?"

"It did. No layers." I tried to speak in as few syllables as possible, to avoid traumatizing myself further.

"Do you know how to transfer information from one dark one to another?"

"Just theory."

"Amateurs. Amateurs, everywhere! They've left these blockheads on my doorstep and now I have to suffer with them. Both of them. So, open the section you want to transfer. For example, maps. If you want to transfer only part of the map, zoom in to the required size. Turn on or off the layers that the other person doesn't need. Basically, you should see in front of you whatever you want to transfer to the other person. And only that. Then lean your forehead against the person you want to transfer to. A new icon will appear on the status bar: *Exchange.* Press it and stand there, resting your forehead against the receiver, until the progress bar is full. Keep in mind — the more you give, the more pain it will be for the person receiving the information. You can burn out your brain like this. Although in order to do this, you must have a brain in the first place. From what I can tell, neither you nor Fardi are at any risk. Come here! I'll give you a map of all the rifts. This is balderdash — the only person who can close rifts without difficulty doesn't even have a basic understanding of where to find them!"

"If possible, I'd also like a map of the Black Mountain," I said, causing Master Meram to frown.

"Why is that?"

"I want to pay Pharapho a visit."

"You're still too weak for that." Was it just me,

or did something like concern flash in the runescribe's voice? "But I'll give you a map. Especially since there are plenty of rifts there too. Keep in mind, student, if you stick your nose in there before I give you permission, I'll kill you."

"The Temple of Skron wishes to send an expedition there," I said, ratting the dark ones out.

"Boundless is the madness of the brave!" The old man snorted. "What good does it do you? What can the dark ones offer you that you can't get yourself? No, pupil, the Black Mountain is captivating enough, I would go there myself, but later. In a year, when you both learn to form three or four symbols and I assign you the title of Senior Pupil, we will finally do really serious work."

"So four symbols isn't serious?" I was surprised. "What is your limit, mentor?"

"Four symbols is the threshold for the next stage of apprenticeship. Only the untalented do not reach this level. My limit should not interest you. You should only care about your training. And about Fardi. If she fails, neither of you will succeed. Even if you start scribbling full sentences, you will still be kicked out in disgrace!"

"One more question, mentor. Why are you sending me into the rift?"

"Because without your cubes where you keep your ousels, you're nothing, Valevsky! You were spared solely because the Citadel liked the way you could identify the dark ones. What are you? A runescribe? Far from it. We'll go with that for now, but it will be at least thirty years, no less, before I can even begin to call you a master. Governor of an autonomous city? Don't make me laugh! If it weren't for Eleanore, Hearth would have died two months ago. During the design stage. A powerful warrior or mage? Even Fardi could knock you down with the little finger of her left hand without breaking a sweat. Do you have some sort of special knowledge? You were just on your hands and knees, practically begging the Temple of Skron for a drop of information. It was hard to even watch. Maybe you have your own army? Trusted confidants? Those who depend on you? Those for whom you have once done a favor? Something tells me, young man, that you do not have any of this. So it turns out that the only thing available to you is to be an errand boy. To close rifts, to stamp out the fog of Pharapho. And you're never even asked whether or not you want to do it. They just inform you that you must. If you naively think that the ability to close rifts and fogs is something so unique that it will make you a welcome guest at any party, I have some bad news for you. Nobody gives a damn about you. Rifts aren't in danger of destroying our world at this moment, so there's no need to think about them. Because they're an old and familiar evil, and you, little lap dog who jumps at the emperor's bidding — you are God knows what. The only reason that you haven't been killed yet is that the infected rifts have suddenly started popping up. That's the only reason! The Temple of Skron has already consulted with me and asked if it would trouble me terribly to start closing the infected rifts again. Because you'll be gone soon. I had to protect you! If it weren't for the fact that you easily cast two symbols, I wouldn't have given it another thought. I haven't had a pupil such as you for a long time. So they left you alone. Temporarily. Until they make sure that no more infected rifts appear. But even in the task that you perform better than anyone in the world, there are limitations — without your ousel cubes, you are nothing and no one. A complete zero. We're going to a place now where your skills as a rift conqueror may come in handy. For some reason, the offworlders don't react well to Skron's darkness. That's why I am sending you to the rift. Have I described the motive behind my actions in sufficient detail, or do I have to dumb it down for you? Alright, get going. The sun's about to set and you still need to reach the rift."

A minute later, I was staggering back from the mad old man, gasping for air. Magister Meram had been true to his word and gave me his entire map, including the rift levels, all at once. The transfer process was so horrible that I threw up. The old man grimaced in disgust and retreated, ordering the converts to clean up the mess and pull Fardi out of the cart. Her next training session awaited her.

As I opened the map, I gulped at how large it was. Kerux, which enveloped the light lands from all sides, stretched out before me in all its glory. The lands of the offworlders were only a few days' journey — luckily, the Gourfan Clan could not oppose the will of the Temple of Skron. But what struck me even more than the size was the sheer number of rifts. If we assumed that each of them sat on top of ruins, then in ancient times these lands were thoroughly populated. For some reason, even before Skron arrived on our planet, the ancients had vanished, leaving behind only ruins, where Pharapho had settled several centuries ago. The Black Mountain, incidentally, was also marked. It was surrounded by several dozen level Fifty rifts. Moreover, from the offworlder's side, under the auspices of the Black Mountain, I saw the infected rift that no one else could close. level Seventy-One. The huge empty space next to it indicated that all the nearby rifts had already been absorbed, but it wasn't developing any further. The reason why was simple: it had run up against the border of the Black Mountain. At this point, it was essentially frozen. A level every six months to a year was nothing for this monster. Apparently, before destroying Pharapho, we'd have to resolve this issue, otherwise the entire planet would perish as soon as the fog was gone. The rot that would crawl out of the rift alone would destroy everything and everyone.

I saw this all while jogging towards the twenty-seven-level rift. I would have to go through the last two levels wearing only boots and body armor. I'd have to take everything else off, otherwise the rot would destroy my items again. I'd have to kneel before the Temple of Skron once more...Damn it, what a terrible way the old man had put it! After all, I really would have to kneel down, ask, beg. Do anything just to get information. Was this bad? It was horrendous! But I had no other choice. Because the alternative was even worse. I would have to bow not only for information, but for no reason at all, simply because I had a master. He wouldn't call himself that, of course, but everyone would understand perfectly well who I was. An obedient dog to a master.

The rift didn't cause me any problems. I didn't initiate the metamorph ring — I only needed one from an invert, which started at level forty. The miniature storage container on my belt accepted the ring, placing it next to the exclusive amulet. Now, if I got down to the right level in the rifts...Damn again, I really only did think in terms of rifts! How to get deeper, grab more resources, upgrade *Devour* to level four. An errand boy...

When I reached the Rift Master, I stopped a meter away. A twenty-seven level normal, uninfected rift was easy enough. On the last two levels, there was even a minimal amount of rot. When I returned to Hearth, the first thing I would do was pump up the magic stones of my loved ones to the twenty-fifth level and make them train to acclimatize to channeling such a huge stream of magic. As practice has shown, being suddenly gifted with enormous power doesn't mean you can use it if you haven't had training. But all these thoughts faded into the background as I gazed upon the Rift Master. Some terrible creature was forming next to it, but I paid no attention. As I mentioned, this was the first time I'd reached the Master on foot, not on my hands and knees, gasping for air. I started to wonder about the nature of the Rift Master. Why was it a Master? What was it master of? How did it feed? How did it transfer energy to other beasts? And the ousels that I had kept in my cubes — how did they feed? After all, their Master was dead, they had no source to draw energy from, and yet, the little yellow orbs remained alive and operational. Why?

I walked around the Master, peering down at it from all sides. The difference between this beast and the one I found on the top floor of the dark estate was immediately obvious. The one at the estate had been a pruny, dried-up runt, while this was a monster, brimming with power as it spawned other beasts.

But was it really a monster?

I waited until the creature fully spawned and, grinning viciously, rushed out of the cave. In its place, a new projection immediately appeared — one of the many kronas that I mercilessly mowed down. Once again, there were many essences, as well as stones, but I had to leave most of my loot at level twenty-five. I was afraid of losing the heaping pile of elite and exclusive stones to the rot. So Kimal Sarento was accusing me of completely destroying the market for magic stones? It was time to roll out a whole bunch of gems for auction and declare that from now on, anyone could buy them. An errand boy? Well, I'd turn around and transform this world of clerics into a world of mages! Magister Meram was right — I needed people to depend on me. And magic stones would be an excellent outlet. If Kimal Sarento disagreed with this, it was his problem. I had already fortified my defenses against lightning.

Returning to the Master, I was about to destroy it, but I hesitated. I was now standing behind it, if this horrendous cube of ribs and flesh could even be divided into a front and back. It was nearly identical from all sides. However, from this side, I noticed something strange — some kind of energy channel was branching off from the lower rib. It looked like static lightning and buried deep into the stone. It would be easy to miss, if you weren't specifically looking for it. Bending down, I activated the katar blade and peeled aside the rot that had accumulated over the long years of this rift's existence. I tried not to touch the strange lightning. Who knew what it was and where it came from? Clearing away the extra rocks, I assessed the picture and frowned. It was not lightning. Most of all, it looked like a fog that was collecting along the entire lower rib, concentrated in its center, filled with strength and energy and transmitted this very energy into the stone floor. There was no humming noise like electricity. There was nothing at all, except for the visual effect.

Crouching down, I began to carefully cut a hole in the stone floor near the entry point of this hazy energy channel. The stone resisted, as if my katars were not made of vyrma, but of ordinary steel. I tried hacking at it from several places to try and break a piece off. Strangely, my blade could still pierce the stone a meter away from this point in all directions without any problem. I checked all around to make sure. Finally, throwing all caution to the wind, I began to chop at the stone with all my might, trying to carve out the device. Where did the Master's energy flow?

At one point, I began to feel like the Evil Engineer in the mines. Stone chips flew in all directions, but the energy channel delved deeper and deeper, causing me to hack into the stones with renewed vigor. I stopped only when I realized that I could stand up in the hole and my head didn't reach the edge. The hole was so deep and wide that I could turn around completely, but my efforts had been fruitless. The channel continued lower and lower. as if mocking my efforts.

I didn't stop there — time was still on my side. Deciding that I could spend another thirty minutes on this futile exercise, I made a few cuts and pulled out another large piece of stone. Throwing it out of the hole, I bent down to cut out the next one, but stopped. I'd finally made it!

A crystal the size of my fist and as black as Fardi's eyes lay in a small niche that had appeared in the stone. The crystal hissed and bubbled as it was exposed to the air. I heard a noise from above and saw a flickering light, but nothing came down into the pit. Making up my mind, I bent down and grabbed the crystal, having set the *Adapt* task for my gloves prior. And they adapted. After tearing the dark gem from the stone, I saw the energy channel disappear and the surrounding space went dark. The blue crystals that had lit the rift were extinguished. It became hard to breathe, as if the air had suddenly been sucked from the room and heaviness rolled over me, as if several dozen bags of sand had been thrown on top of me and pressed down from above by an elephant. Several elephants. But even all these circumstances weren't as strange to me as the message that appeared before my eyes:

level 27 rift has been destroyed.
You have entered the Abyss.

Chapter 11

THE GOURFAN'S LIGHT CRYSTAL was of little help. I took it from my belt and the surrounding area lit up, but to little effect — it was difficult to light what didn't exist. There was nothing below my feet, as if I was falling. Although there was no sensation of falling. I simply hung in the middle of absolute nothing. Panic set in for a moment, but I got over it quickly. Since Skron had informed me that I had ended up in an incomprehensible location called the "Abyss," it meant that someone from the humans or beastmen had already been here and managed to return back. It was unlikely that one could learn about the *Abyss* if there was no way out of it. All I had to do was figure out how to get out of it. There really weren't that many options. Either sit and wait, or actively try to move. Swim, no matter how stupid it might sound. I decided to go with the first option — I could always move later. Just in case, I put my hand on my thigh to check my contact with the main world. There hadn't been any connection in the Fog Stalker Arena, for instance.

"Alia, are you there?"

There was no answer. The Abyss was another completely separate location, unconnected to our world. Taking a deep breath and closing my eyes, preparing to wait, I decided to check the second symbol. Just on the off-chance —

"Eleanore, you there?"

"Here. Is it urgent? I have a meeting right now, can I call you back in ten?"

"Wait! What's going on with Alia?" My insides went cold. "She's not answering."

"With Alia?" Eleanore sounded surprised. "Isn't she with you?"

"…"

"She hasn't been in Hearth for four days. Everyone was absolutely certain that you went on a trip together…Where are you now?"

"The Abyss!"

"Very funny. You know, they usually say 'Up your ass and around the corner…'"

"No, I'm actually in a place called the Abyss. But screw me — find Alia! She was there when I left Hearth. We haven't been in contact over the past four days, there was no need. I tried to call her now, but she didn't answer."

"I understand, Max. I need time to reconstruct the sequence of events. The dark ones are installing an identification system for us, and the city is in total disarray right now. Everyone is on edge. And it will be like this for another week or two. Do you need help?"

"I'll figure it out. Reschedule your meeting. Find Alia!"

I spent about twenty minutes trying to contact her, but to no avail. She did not answer. I immediately dismissed the possibility that my personal attendant was dead. If I was to believe what she had said, the connection symbols had begun to behave rather strangely. Everything was standard, except for the fact that Alia, who had been enhanced, buffed and equipped to the gills with level-twenty magic stones and a full set of *Thunderer* armor, for some strange reason, was out of reach. And she wasn't just asleep — being called through the symbol automatically woke you up. The only option left, which I was extremely uncomfortable with, was that Alia was unconscious. And someone was deliberately keeping her in this state.

Who?!

There were two possibilities off the top of my head: Padishah Bayazid the Third or Count Vyazemsky. These were the only surface-level options, but there could be others. The Citadel. Kimal Sarento. Anyone, really! I'd kill them. I'd find and kill them all! Then I'd learn to raise corpses and kill them again!

Rage flared up in my chest. The Abyss no longer seemed so scary and menacing. Just another location from which I needed to find an escape. So that I could return to Hearth. The offworlders had been waiting for several hundred years, they would wait some more. I stretched my arms out in different directions and fired *Dark Spike*. They immediately disappeared, but I was noticeably shaken. Shaken? Stretching my arms forward, I repeated the shot and immediately began to gasp convulsively — there was a feeling of motion. Free fall. It stopped rather quickly, but I bared my teeth victoriously. I could move in this "nothingness." If so — I needed to act! I had no time to watch black paint dry. Alia was gone!

Every time I fired, it took my breath away, but I wasn't slowing down, releasing two spikes every second. With each shot, my speed increased until I was accelerating so quickly that the wind began to whistle in my ears. There was something to this "nothing" after all! I continued nonstop — my mana stores were more than sufficient. I was even glad that I'd kept *Dark Spike* for myself, instead of exchanging it for a more classic stone. I didn't think that lightning would be able to propel me like this.

I managed to track the moment when I suddenly left "nothing" and was back in "something" — after my final shot, the space around me suddenly contracted and exploded, turning into a dark, but spacious room. The light crystal immediately started working happily, finally able to cope with its task. The wind in my ears stopped, there was not even a hint of acceleration. I simply found myself in the center of a dark room, and in front of me lay the broken white body of some creature. Something similar to a shtryk from a rift, a spider with a humanoid torso. Only the body was not so dense, had four arms, and there were only four legs, not eight. Otherwise, it was an ordinary, nasty looking shtryk. I never liked to encounter them in rifts — they always caused problems.

I looked around. The space bore an uncanny resemblance to a standard rift cave. The differences were in the details — there were no light crystals, resources, anything at all. There were even minimal rocks lying on the ground, as if the cave had been thoroughly cleaned and processed. Taking a step forward, I stopped short — the echo that resonated around the room was astounding. The body of the white monster twitched, drawing my attention once more. *Analyze* did its thing, providing a short description:

White Seraphim. Spawn of the Abyss.

It didn't have any particularly special stats. No stones, no enhancements, it didn't even have the standard five-parameter development foundation — *Strength-Stamina-Speed-Constitution-Mana*. At the same time, it did have its own system of some sort — progress bars, incomprehensible symbols. It gave me the same feeling as when I first saw textbooks in the dark tongue. Now I could practically read them, although my knowledge was still insufficient to independently form pictograms. The symbolic magic that the orthodox used was quite non-standard in relation to magic stones, but at the same time it had practically no limitations. You could do anything you wanted. The whole question was only how to translate your desires into pictograms.

Here, when looking at the white seraph, the situation was similar. Another incomprehensible language, which had nothing in common with what existed in our world. At the same time, it seemed quite coherent, and if I spent enough time, I could figure it out. The creature began to wheeze and twitch, and the space around me again began to blur and turn into "nothingness." It was not difficult to put two and two together — the strange place I had found myself in was being generated by this creature. Apparently, *Dark Spike* had managed to break through the defenses and deprived the creature of consciousness. But now it was trying to recover and return me to nothingness again. If so, it was its own fault. I came here in peace, and all that.

Dash pulled me right up to the moving body, and the mithril gauntlet easily pierced the creature's torso. This was not a spawn of Pharapho — the spawn of the Abyss had no defense against my weapon. The creature twitched one last time and froze, and a strange object appeared in my hands:

Abyssal Gem. Unidentified item.

A perfectly round ball the size of my fist shimmered purple in my palm. I was even taken aback when I saw the new aura. Regular items did not shimmer. Magic items with one or two properties shimmered blue. Elite ones with three or four glowed gold. Exclusive ones, which had special features and five or six properties, glowed red. Everyone knew about these three colors. I had once believed there to be no other auras. Even artifacts obeyed the same scale. However, quite recently, I had seen a number of new items emitting a green hue. It existed in certain sets, such as *Thunderer.* Now, apparently, I was to learn of another aura color. Purple. And it surrounded Abyssal gems, whatever those were. **Would you like to identify the item?**

I didn't delay — I needed everything I could to help me escape. If necessary, I'd even identify the ring and the amulet. I needed to get back to Hearth!

Abyssal Gem. *Description: Integrates into an Abyssal nest or a development model slot. Available properties: Immune to burn damage up to 1000 degrees, +20% damage for each Abyssal gem integrated onto you, gives you immunity from the influence of the white seraph, allows you to adapt to the aura of the Abyss.*

A new pictogram appeared on my status bar: *Abyss.* Opening it, I saw the already familiar symbols that still carried no semantic value for me. The only comprehensible thing was the progress bar: it was filled to some minimal percentage. Apparently from killing the white seraph.

Closing this tab, I looked back at the gem. I had no idea what an Abyss nest was. I knew what a development model nest was, since I had two of them open at once. They currently contained development crystals, but I could remove one of them. Yes, this would slightly reduce my defense, make me dependent on stunning, but I, in turn, would start stunning again with *Dash.* Overall, removing one development crystal would not affect me much. True, before that, I tried to bring the Abyss gem to the gloves and asked to integrate, but nothing happened. The mithril refused to touch such items.

Pulling out the development crystal, I added my new find to the model and it felt as if a mountain had been lifted from my shoulders. Only now did I realize that all this time something incomprehensible and strong had been pressing on me. *Healing* myself several times, I looked around again. The room had changed once more. The walls had become lighter, colors had reappeared. But most important was that I saw a passage ahead.

I'd found a way out of here!

Turning around once more to make sure I hadn't forgotten anything important, I left the first room. The differences from the rift were immediately apparent — the corridor system was predominant here. There were no more caves or rooms similar to the one I had ended up in. Just in case, I put my mirror up and pulled out the twenty-fifth-level ousel. If even one of those bastards came near me, it would be in trouble.

But my perfect plan was ruined as soon as it was conceived. I stepped out into the corridor and ran into several dozen small creatures that looked like dwarves. Ugly, toothy and extremely aggressive. This entire group rushed towards me and, despite the active ousel, and chomped into my shield. *Golden Dome* coped well with their aggression, and a few moments later I went on the counterattack. The Abyss spawn did not react to either the Light from the eyes or the darkness of the high-level ousel. Moreover, they handled the vyrma bolts with ease. I shot one of the creatures with a crossbow, but the bolt ricocheted, unable to pierce through the dwarf's body. The mithril glove, on the other hand, worked real miracles. But I did not come across any more Abyss gems. *Devour* merely shrugged its virtual shoulders to inform me of the bad news — the dwarves dropped no loot.

A second group of monsters came after the first, then a third and a fourth. I inched forward as if going through a rift for my first time. I had to fight for every meter of the corridor. If it weren't for the level twenty-five protective dome and practically unlimited mana, I definitely would have been in trouble. My progress through the Abyss was also slowed by my need to *Analyze* every new creature, of which there turned out to be an incredible variety. At one point, it even seemed that every new mob was a separate kind of monster, completely unlike any of the others. And none of them even came close to giving me another

Abyss gem. As if the white seraph that had almost locked me in a world of complete "nothingness" was something unique.

Eleanore contacted me several times. Alia was indeed nowhere to be found, but she had not left through the portal or the gate. The city had announced another wave of searches. And this time the clergy had gotten involved — one of the Fortress bishops had disappeared. Of course, this could have been outright hypocrisy, to cover up their tracks. The situation had thrown me off track so much that I periodically forgot to update the database.

As for any answer as to what the Abyss was, I had nothing. In order to understand the essence and nature of this location, I'd have to go to the Fog Stalker Arena. I won't lie — I tried to manifest the key right then and there in the middle of the corridor. I needed answers. But the Abyss turned out to be a particularly vexatious place — I couldn't activate the key. I had to put up with the inevitable, continue recording every little thing in my notebook and move forward, exterminating the creatures that were becoming stronger and stronger. Eventually, I was spending up to five minutes on each group, as the beasts proved too fast and strong. My protective dome even started to eat up my mana, with no time to absorb the attacks.

But even victory over the strongest opponents didn't bring me much, other than raising my morale. The mithril gloves pierced through the fastest monsters time after time, but only pulled out useless chunks of flesh. Obviously vital flesh for them, since they died instantly, but useless for my purposes.

"Max, I have new info. We found a strange note. An unknown person offered Alia a unique item that would surprise and delight you. You have a birthday coming up, and a gift like that would be incredibly valuable and demonstrative on her part."

"What birthday, by Skron?! It's in six months!" I almost shouted.

"I disagree with you here. People whose attention you value get birthday presents long before their birthday ever arrives. I, for instance, have been working on this task for over a month now. I am not surprised that Alia is also concerned about it. The stranger who passed her the note suggested that they meet in one of the houses that is still under construction, so as not to arouse suspicion and not to give rise to unnecessary rumors. This house was checked — judging by what we saw, a battle occurred. Scorched walls all around, traces of lightning. It was not possible to disguise this, although someone clearly tried to do so. Alia was indeed captured and carried out of this house unconscious. Or killed. But they carried her out, she did not come out on her own. We are operating under the assumption that the first is true. If she was killed, they could have simply buried her anywhere, and we will never find her again, no matter how long we search for her."

"She is alive. I feel it. Our communication symbol is still active, although she can't respond."

"That's a plus. It's hard to leave the city, but it's possible. Even while carrying such a heavy load. As I said, everything is in complete disarray, everyone's running around like chickens with their heads cut off, it's total chaos, everyone's dragging something somewhere, and that's probably why Alia was kidnapped. Now the question is, did she stay in the city, or has she already been taken away?"

"Who would need to take my woman away, anyway?" I muttered to myself.

"Not her. You. Taking control of Alia, who is carrying your child, is an effective measure to take. You will do anything to save them. Max, my advice is that you do not need to go back now. If Alia was really kidnapped and taken out of Hearth, you can't do a thing. Until the kidnappers show up and make their demands, you have nothing to do here. Deal with the offworlders, we will try to get down to the bottom of this."

"Are you kidding me? How are we talking about offworlders right now? My girl was stolen!"

"She was. Do you know who did it? No, you don't. I have at least four suspects. The padishah, Vyazemsky, Shub, Fardi. And there's also the Church of the Light and Kimal Sarento, but these two are still working for us. You can't rule out the forces of darkness — they could be trying to conduct experiments on your child. What if they show the same gifts as you have. Max, there are just too many possibilities. Whatever force at work here is extremely powerful. Don't forget, I also have a *Thunderer* set, I know what I'm talking about. Alia never took hers off either. Nevertheless, she was still kidnapped. So someone managed to neutralize the armor. How many people are there in the world who can do this? And who among them visited Hearth? Until we have their demands, you should mind your own business. Talk to your mentor. Maybe the runescribe will be able to suggest something."

Eleanore ended the connection, leaving me alone with the creatures of the Abyss. Me. Angry, irritated, ready to tear apart anyone and everyone who encroached on my woman. As soon as I was free of this expedition, I'd never leave my city again! They wanted to use me and my abilities? Let them pay and provide protection to my people. The errand boy died today. The person who returned from the Abyss would be a free man.

But how could I return when this corridor seemed endless? It twisted and turned like a mad hare, but never branched out, forcing me to choose each path. Like a huge, winding intestine. But I knew it had to end eventually. As I finished the next mob off, I turned the corner and stopped, finally encountering something different from what I had observed in the previous few hours. Another expansive room, in the center of which stood the main force behind all the ugliness that surrounded me. Or so it seemed. It was a white seraph, except that it was twice as big as the one that I'd met before, significantly exceeding me in height. The creature spread its arms to the sides and hummed, hoping to immerse me in nothingness, but the Abyssal gem, which I had, thankfully, equipped in time, prevented this. *Analyze* didn't reveal anything new — this beast operated under the same vague symbols as all Abyssal spawn.

I entered the room and the passage closed behind me, as if marking the beginning of a battle. But there was no battle. Either that, or it was being fought on levels inaccessible to me. I stood and looked at the shaking creature, deciding what to do. My first thought — that I needed to attack and kill — was too obvious. Even in my current state, I realized that this was too banal. Killing was always easy and simple. Understanding and sorting things out was much more difficult. And more interesting.

"I am Archduke Maximilian Valevsky, human!" I cried, approaching the white seraphim. "I do not yet understand what this place is or how I got here! I am prepared to trade. I have resources, essences, artifacts. Everything that the creatures of the Abyss might need to strengthen themselves! Can we talk?"

There was no answer, as expected. The white seraphim continued to cast its magic toward me, forcing me to act. But my actions were in no way forced. The room I found myself in was different from all those I had already visited. The walls were covered with the same strange and incomprehensible symbols that meant nothing to me now. But they definitely held some sort of information, so I slowly began to back away along the walls, managing to keep both part of the wall and the central creature in my field of vision.

Yes, there was something written here. And in some places there were some pictures depicting the white seraphim that I already knew. The depictions also stood in the center of the room, spreading their arms to the sides, as ordinary creatures brought them gifts. I walked around half the room, observing the various gifts they would receive. Starting with human-like bodies, ending with stones and even round things that looked very much like essences or Abyssal gems. The monsters offered all sorts of gifts, and in return...what they received in return was still incomprehensible to me, even as I walked around the entire room. I couldn't figure out what the beasts who brought offerings received in return. All I could determine was that this bastard was ready to accept all these "somethings."

Take a risk and sacrifice some of my essences? Why not — I had so many krona essences that I had no place to put them. And was I going to offer them to the Temple of Skron? The question was — how much? The graven images showed a toothy little creature dragging a whole mountain of orbs as an offering. Should I be petty, greedy, only give away two or three items? What would be the point? At that point it would be better to just not give anything at all and avoid a confrontation. No, if I did sacrifice, it would have to be a decent amount to immediately demonstrate the seriousness of my intentions. Fifty essences, I think, would be enough. Anyway, after I'd gotten the infected essences and the entire collection was divided into levels, working with low-level essences had become boring. It was a pity to throw them away, and I knew that armor cannot be made from such disgusting materials.

It was decided! I approached the white seraphim and winced. Standing too near this being was still difficult, despite the Abyssal gem. The creature exuded an aura that pressed on my brain worse than the one in the rifts. Stopping three meters away, I opened the inventory and began to manifest essence after essence, stacking them into a pretty little pyramid. Despite being perfect spheres, the essences did not roll or slide, which allowed me to work with them on any surface.

The pressure decreased with each new essence. At some point, even the muttering stopped. The white seraph lowered his hands, stopped shaking and bowed his monstrous, scary head, watching me work. I continued to form the pyramid and at some point I realized that I wouldn't be able to get away with just fifty pieces. I had made too big a base. I didn't think about it. However, I didn't want to go back now. I liked the creature's reaction and the way it began to shift on its four spider legs, as if barely able to contain its impatience. Setting down the final essence, I rose to my feet, assessing my creation. I had to spend almost a hundred balls, but it was stupid to regret it now. I needed to check.

The white seraphim could barely contain its excitement, but something held it back. Or someone. I was also standing near the pyramid. Deciding to move a little further, I backed away, and as soon as there were a few meters of distance between me and the essences, the white seraph scurried forward. All four paws began to grab the essences and stuff them into its toothy mouth. A disgusting chomping sound was heard — the seemingly solid essences were ground up like boiled eggs. All hundred disappeared into its belly in a matter of seconds. Making sure that there was nothing left, the white seraphim took a few steps back, returning to his place. For some time, nothing happened. I even began to suspect that my actions had no result, when suddenly a completely comprehensible human voice rang out. The voice was eerie, resonant, low. It seemed that space itself was speaking.

"Human, you were able to pique the Abyss' interest. The Abyss is pleased and ready to talk to you. You are given the right to two questions, then you will be returned to the main world. The Abyss adores those who bring it gifts."

Chapter 12

"ALRIGHT, I UNDERSTAND. Before I voice my demand, I want to show you what the Abyss will be losing out on. And yes, I know places where you can collect enough of these essences to satiate even you. But this is no longer important. Here you go!"

I pulled out one of my most valuable and important essences — an infected level Thirty warden. I got it in the rift, when I almost died. Of course, this wasn't entirely true — obtaining items like this posed huge problems, but I needed to keep the being interested. My inner Kimal Sarento had woken up. Two questions. There was no doubt — if I had asked: "Can you answer any question?" it would have immediately been counted as my first question. So no indignant screams, no verbal constructions ending in a question. Only affirmative sentences. Only clear confidence in what I was saying.

The essence rolled across the floor like some kind of bauble, but the way the white seraphim took off after it spoke volumes. The chomping sound was heard again, and this time it sounded much more satisfied. I had managed to please the Abyss being.

"Now that the Abyss understands what it can get from me if we establish cooperation, send me back. I will not ask questions of a being I do not understand. It could easily turn out that each question I ask will impose certain restrictions or other limitations on me. When I return to the ordinary world, I will become an enemy of all living things. Perhaps each question will suck the life force out of me. I don't know for sure, but I'm not going to risk it — until I have a clear understanding of what you are, there will be no questions from my side. Now I will return home and never come here again. Find another source of essences. Send me back."

"Do you know whose essence you just gave to the Abyss?" asked the room.

"Naturally. I got it myself. A warden from the thirtieth level of the infected rift. It wasn't easy, but I managed."

"Do you have the essence of a Master?"

"Here, no. At home in my treasury, yes." I didn't deny it, but I wasn't going to risk being locked up in this place either. In a couple of weeks, I'd be ready to give everything I have just to get out of here. I needed to bargain. To do what I hated most in my life.

"What level are these essences?" the white seraph began to shift impatiently from foot to foot again. Apparently, it was the source of the voice after all. Even though its mouth didn't move.

"I don't have a list. I don't even remember the exact number. I know for sure that there are fifteenth level ones, twenty-first, but this is not a complete list. There are more. I am concerned about the fact that I am still in the Abyss. Send me back to the big world."

"You didn't ask questions. You won't leave the Abyss until you exercise your right."

"That's exactly what I was worried about. Apparently, for good reason — you've started making demands. I repeat — I will not ask questions until I understand what you are. I have no desire to burden myself with additional problems associated with communicating with the Abyss. You see that I am part of the Light. I am afraid that I will lose my predisposition. Which I would not be very happy about."

"You won't lose anything. Communication with the Abyss doesn't leave any marks on a person. Especially on those who have already given themselves to one side."

"These are nothing more than words. No specifics. But fine, let's have it your way. You know what essences I can get. I see that you liked my gift. If you say that there will be no consequences for me, I will have to believe you. I don't think I will ever have the desire to visit the Abyss again. It is too expensive and completely unprofitable. My questions are the following: what is two plus two and what is two times two? Answer, send me back, and we will end our conversation here. Any questions of substance I may have are easier posed in the Fog Stalker Arena."

"You must get there first." Was it just me, or was there mockery in its voice?

"That's not a problem at all." I was glad that I had recently embodied one of the passes. Showing it to the white seraphim I just shrugged: "Passing thirty waves is not a problem. It's too early for me to do more, but even after thirty, the Fog Stalker will answer any question that concerns me. When I visited last time, the first thing it did was explain who it was, what it was and why it existed. The terms and conditions were perfectly clear there, but not here. That's why I asked questions, the answers to which I already knew, so that the knowledge received from the Abyss would not lie on me as a heavy burden. At the same time, I will check the completeness of the answer. But this point is moot now. The questions have been asked, answer and send me back. Or does the Abyss go back on its words?"

"What is your limit, human?"

"The thirty-first level of an infected rift," I answered, having understood the question correctly. "The thirty-fifth to fortieth in a normal one. I've never reached invert levels. But I plan to."

"The Abyss will not answer questions you know the answers to. The Abyss does not need to be tested. The Abyss is ready to cooperate. The Abyss liked the gifts, it wants more. We are ready to tell you what we are and why we appeared in this world, after which you will be granted the right to repeat your questions. Does this suit you, human?"

"It does," I agreed. "Go on."

"The Abyss is one of the many entities that came to this world a thousand years ago. Skron, Light and Chaos, entities of the highest level, seized power over the planet. Entities of the first order, such as the Abyss and Pharapho, took over the areas that were of no interest to the higher ones. Entities of the second and lower levels, such as offworlders, mechanoids, phantoms, undergrounders and others, were content with what we left them. Over a thousand years, the system has stabilized, but there is always someone trying to upset the balance of power."

"That doesn't quite fit with the story I know thus far," I intervened, again trying not to ask questions. "Skron and Light appeared a thousand years ago. I've never heard of Chaos. Pharapho is only four hundred years old. As are the offworlders. The rest are just names from fairy tales."

"All entities appeared a thousand years ago, when a hole tore open in space. The people who inhabited the planet before conducted reckless experiments. They opened a way to their world to those who did not share their diplomacy. In fact, your world was destroyed, and new people came in their place. Those who no longer remembered anything about the past. Skron and Light began to fight for supremacy. Now Skron is winning, Light has only a few territories left, although five hundred years ago the situation was the opposite. Chaos maintains neutrality, occasionally helping one party or another when called. But the fight is not only on the upper levels. Pharapho and I are locked in a constant battle to destroy each other. His fog against my rifts."

"Stop!" I suddenly realized. "The Rifts belong to Skron. Every child knows that."

"Rifts are the essence of the Abyss. This is my creation, recognized for destroying the Fog of Pharapho in all of its manifestations. Skron took notice of my creation about seven hundred years ago. He took over the rifts, filled them with his creatures, but was never able to fully understand what had been created. His minions still cannot enter the rift. Nor can the converts, nor the dark ones. This requires additional help, and Pharapho, my opponent, provided it by giving the creatures of Skron the development crystals. *Adaptation* became the stat that allowed the minions of darkness to enter the rifts. But the essence of this does not change — the rifts are created by the Abyss or its closest henchmen in the human world."

"The churchmen at the Fortress," I nodded knowingly. "And they're followers of the Light."

"That is why anyone who walks in the Light may travel openly through my rifts. I do not block them out. But not Skron. His dark aura gets stronger with each level, up to the hundredth. At that moment, the influence on a human is comparable to being in the presence of Skron himself."

Rifts could only reach a hundred levels? Good information — the infected level seventy-one rift would not destroy the planet if it started to uncontrollably absorb other rifts. It also had a limit.

"But there are infected rifts. Where your creation has malfunctioned, gone out of control. Both yours and Skron's."

"And came under the control of the offworlders. The magic stones with which the rifts are infected are their creation. The offworlders know how to work with physics of a different order, they know how to subjugate current processes and adapt them to their needs. They are dangerous creatures. The only reason they haven't captured this world yet is their inability to adapt to the darkness. Skron holds them in one place, but doesn't destroy them. The Dark One doesn't like to kill at all. He wants everyone to obey him. But let's return to the fact that the Abyss is the essence of the rifts. Their fiefdom. Their home world. The Riftmaster is the only creature that remains from my original plan, but Skron changed even those, forcing them to print the monsters he needed. The way you made it to the Abyss says a lot — you managed to reach the source of the rift's power. If it weren't for the gloves made of Pharapho's flesh, you would be dead. Thanks to them, you were able to get all the way to me. But they won't help you defeat me. Here, in the place of my power, mithril is useless."

"I didn't know that mithril was Pharapho's flesh," I chuckled thoughtfully.

"That is why they can penetrate and destroy matter of the ordinary world, as well as any creatures belonging to entities of all orders that have appeared in the world. Except, as you now know, Pharapho himself and high-level manifestations of each entity."

"Mithril is great at penetrating Pharapho soldiers and sergeants," I disagreed.

"The ones born in the fog? These are not real creatures. Copies. Echoes of this world, woven from the fog. You could have met the real creatures of Pharapho in the Fog Stalker Arena. If you really went through it, you should have seen the difference."

"Mithril didn't work in the arena," I nodded. "Vyrma doesn't work in the Abyss."

"That which is the essence of my creation cannot affect me or my servants. But only my real servants. The dark beasts that roam both normal and infected rifts alike no longer have anything to do with me. Except for the Master."

"Mithril was able to destroy an incarnation of Skron," I remembered. "It was a fairly high-level Skron beast, but Pharapho's flesh still managed to take it down."

"The incarnation of Skron is a normal

monster that the dark ones use to form Waves. High-level dark ones are the servants of the Temple of Skron, starting with Nine. Mithril will not work on them. Did that answer your question, human?"

"I didn't ask any questions," I replied.

"Let me rephrase: do you understand what the Abyss is and why cooperation with it can be profitable?"

"No. You told me about the first thing — about who you are. But you didn't say a word about our collaboration."

"I need essences from the rifts. Pharapho's flesh is able to rip essences from almost any creature that has them. That's how you got the Abyss gem, by killing one of the white seraphim. By absorbing essences, the Abyss regains the ability to influence the rifts. Gradually takes them away from Skron. And for this, the Abyss is ready to share information."

"There's just one problem: you hardly have any information about the current state of our world."

"No. Information reaches me with a big delay. About fifty to sixty years. However, I know everything that concerns practically the entire period starting from our appearance in the world. The good thing about the Abyss is that everyone comes here. Even Chaos."

I scowled. This entity wouldn't be able to give me Alia's location. Or the name of whoever kidnapped her. Fifty years behind...that was a pretty big lag. While the Fog Stalker could deal in current affairs, the Abyss, driven deep underground, proved too inert.

"Yes, you explained what the Abyss is. But I haven't figured out how we'll be able to communicate. I don't really want to have to spend hours tunneling to you every time."

"You will be granted the right to open a portal to the Abyss. This right will require payment — ten essences. Either this, or you can go through the rift and the absorption of its source of power. There are no other ways to get into the Abyss."

"Now the only thing left is figuring out why collaborating with you is useful to me. Because right now I don't see any real use for knowledge about events that happened more than half a century ago. But alright, I'll test you. I have a question — right now I'm heading off to some ancient swamp, in the middle of which stands a ruined palace. The Temple of Skron believes that this palace is the birthplace of the offworlders and seeks to destroy it. To destroy all the creatures that interfere with the dark ones' relationship with the mechanoids. The question is — do the offworlders of different levels have any special fighting features? Starting from simple soldiers and ending with the highest in rank.

"A good question that demands a long story," the white seraphim answered after a pause. "The Abyss is uninterested in the offworlders. They were the ones to bring symbol magic into this world. Runes, pictograms, seals. Everything that disrupts the normal mechanics of the world, including the formation of infected rifts. Skron absorbed some of these forces, adapting them to his needs, but the foundational knowledge remained with the offworlders. If they are destroyed, the world will breathe a sigh of relief. However, the limitations of higher beings have not gone away. The flesh of Pharapho cannot destroy the Twins. That is the name of the two entities that control the offworlders on this planet. They are indeed located in the palace you are heading toward, twenty levels deep. The battle against ordinary creatures will not cause you any trouble. I see a piece of Skron in you, sealed in a box made of vyrma. The influence of this creature will be lethal for all offworlders. But this trick will not work with the Twins. Neither the flesh of Pharapho, nor Skron's creatures, nor the fire of Light, not even the blades of tsellar will help you. And there is no tsellar on this planet yet — not a single one of my rifts has reached level ninety."

"That's why the master runescribe is coming with me."

"Useless. Runes cannot harm the offworlders, as they were the ones who created them. Just as no weapon made from the resources in my rifts can harm me."

"How can the Twins be destroyed?"

"Is that your second question?"

"Yes."

"There are only two options. To summon Skron, as the dominant entity of this world, or to use a weapon that has not undergone modernization. A weapon that was created before all entities appeared in this world. A weapon of the ancients."

"You said that the ancients were destroyed. That nothing was left of them and we live in another world."

"The humans came and went, the knowledge was lost. The world did not disappear. Pharapho captured the ruins, flooding them with his spawn and altars. But he did not absorb all the ancient buildings. The real ones, where the ancient secrets are kept, remained untouched. Because even now, a thousand years after we came to this world, no entity can break through the protective forces keeping them closed. But the story is different for humans. In the history of this world, there was a man, a simple peasant who managed to penetrate the closed territory and gained knowledge there that allowed him to become great. He made a deal with the Light and practically destroyed Skron. Only the intervention of Chaos, a third force, prevented the Light from destroying Skron eight hundred years ago. If you want to find a weapon against the Twins without resorting to the power of Skron, you need to find a descendant of that man. Because he has the key to the closed location."

"Yes, I know him. The eldest son of the first emperor of the light empires."

"He's dead. You need the grandson. The one to whom the first emperor of the bright lands passed on all his knowledge. The one he trained as his closest and most trusted disciple. The one who killed the first emperor."

"That's impossible! The first emperor died of old age!"

"He was immortal, like any higher being of the ancients. Having gained power and strength, the first emperor lost his name, lost his nature. He ceased to be human. However, some part of him retained his mind. It was this part that ordered his pupil, grandson and closest companion to kill him. The grandson had to make a great effort to erase from the memory of humanity all mentions of what happened in the time of his grandfather. About how he destroyed entire nations, driven by his thirst for the supremacy of Light. You have received full answers to your questions, human. The Abyss cannot hold you for too long, in ten minutes the sun will rise. You know how to get here. Here is your key. Combine it with the flesh of Pharapho, so no one will ever know of its existence."

A small triangle materialized in my hands.

"Place ten essences around the key, and it will activate the passage. See you soon, human. The Abyss is interested in our continuing collaboration. We will be waiting for you."

I put the triangle to my belt and it immediately disappeared, dissolving into the mithril. The space around me suddenly darkened, and when the light returned, I found myself standing next to the entrance to the rift. Or rather, to the place where the entrance to the twenty-seven-level rift used to be. All my things that I had removed and set aside on level Twenty-Five were nearby. A pile of stones, clothes, the bracelet to identify invisible people. I couldn't hide the latter under the mithril glove — the katars and crossbow got in the way. I had to wear it on top and protect it from any rot. The notebook blinked madly, inviting me to look at new information. Quickly assessing the new section titled "Abyss," I tried to contact Alia again. Nothing. I had to call my city manager to find out the latest news.

"Eleanore, what do you have?"

"Nothing. We've turned Hearth inside out — Alia isn't here. We sent the best trackers we could find. The Citadel agreed to involve the dark ones, and under the supervision of two commanders, the servants of the Temple of Skron set out into the depths of the Zarak Empire. We are digging as deep as we can, but so far we have no leads. Whoever kidnapped her knew the resources you would devote to getting her back, and acted too prudently. Far too prudently. What have you decided? Are you coming back, or will you finish what you went for?"

"First the offworlders, then I'll return to Hearth," I decided, realizing that my presence would in no way accelerate the search for Alia.

"The right decision. Finish your business. Whoever kidnapped Alia must understand that you will not throw yourself into reckless behavior for her sake. It could throw him off track, and he will make a mistake. We need at least the slightest clue now. The Temple of Skron has come forward with a proposal to involve the Interrogator, the Citadel is silent for now. The issue, as I understand it, is of payment — who will front the bill."

"This is an outstanding circumstance," I answered after thinking. "First, I need to talk to Magister Meram. Surely, there is some way to trace a person through their communication symbol. I need to consult with him, but I won't be able to for another hour."

"Okay, keep me posted. If I have any information, I'll let you know."

Quickly getting dressed, I ran back to the camp. The sun had already risen, so I was in for a punishment from my mentor. I was sure that even the information that we couldn't defeat the offworlders wouldn't save me from that. So I didn't try to kill myself sprinting the fifteen-kilometer distance in thirty minutes. I did it in an hour.

"You know what's going to happen now, Valevsky?" the nasty old man drawled contentedly, sipping tea from a beautiful cup. I didn't even know he was carrying something like that around with him.

"I know, I don't care. Alia has been kidnapped."

The old man's eyebrows rose — the news seemed to surprise him. He clarified:

"We're talking about your pregnant woman, right? The one with the full suit of *Thunderer* armor? That's intriguing enough to capture even my interest."

"That's right. Now the Citadel, the Temple of Skron and my people are doing everything to find her. To no avail. She has a communication symbol. Can we use it to determine where she is?"

"So you can't get in touch with her?"

"She's not answering. The call goes through, but there's no response."

"Have you considered the fact that maybe she just ran away from you and doesn't want to talk to you anymore? Girls do that sometimes."

"She was kidnapped. My manager found the house where the battle between her and her unknown assailant took place. Alia has level twenty stones and a *Thunderer* set. Nevertheless, she lost."

"That's more interesting. Okay, let's say she wants to contact you, but can't. Either she's unconscious, or her hands are tied and she simply can't place her palm on the symbol."

"She has a status bar and a notebook artifact integrated with mine. If she were conscious, she would have written at least a few words there by now."

"In that case, Valevsky, I can't help you. You can't identify a person when they're unconscious. One of the few limitations of symbolic magic. It requires consciousness. But that doesn't save you from punishment. You're late, and some ridiculous excuses won't save you. Fardi, come out! You're being punished!"

"I hope you die, Valevsky!" Karina hissed with hatred. Judging by her condition, she had been busy forming symbols all night, and, as usual, she had failed. I suppressed my first impulse to heal the girl and coiled like a spring, ready for the punishment. There was no way to avoid it — Magister Meram was reveling in his power. Symbols flew at my back, and the world ceased to exist for some time. The last thought that went through my head before pain filled my mind was that I needed to tell Eleanore that I was ready to involve the Interrogator. Screw it all! The price, the punishment, the Citadel's opinion. If Magister Meram couldn't help me, I would turn to Chaos. It couldn't be for nothing that he was considered the third-most powerful entity in this world.

Chapter 13

"THE CITADEL REFUSES TO EMPLOY the Interrogator. We cannot sacrifice people, even despite Alia's missing person status. All potential kidnappers have already been spoken to, no one is supposedly aware of what happened. It is impossible to check whether they are telling the truth. The Interrogator's services are required, but we can't utilize this force. The Inquisitor cannot determine whether the light ones are telling the truth."

"Understood. I'll be back soon and we'll sort out the Interrogator's fee. I just can't up and leave right now. We're almost there."

I wasn't too happy about Eleanore's report, but there was nothing I could do about it right now. Four days had passed since my visit to the Abyss, but Alia had still not been found. She was not in Hearth. The kidnapper had not shown himself, and all attempts to contact the girl had ended with the same result — complete silence. After the last punishment involving my tardiness, the runescribe had calmed down a bit and began to behave more reasonably. He had not even snapped at me or Fardi. Moreover, the closer we got to the goal of our journey, the more collected the old man became. Eventually, he even stopped throwing snide remarks our way. Even though I was unable to cast three-symbol combinations, as usual. And Fardi couldn't handle her two.

"Everyone out!" ordered Magister Meram as he stepped out of the carriage. Jumping down, I frowned. About a hundred meters ahead was the edge of a strange terrain that had a dark red hue. The color was everywhere, but I was not the only one ill at ease. Everything as far as the eye could see was twisted and distorted — trees, stones, even the ground itself. It was difficult to describe what I saw. Even the notebook where lines of data began to appear used the word "distortion." For example, not a single tree had a straight line — the trunk and branches were twisted, screwed, bent, and throughout their entire length. And the trunk itself looked rather strange, eaten away, in some places all the way through. Some parts were wide then grew thin as a knitting needle. Complete madness, multiplied by horror.

"We arrived undetected?" Fardi asked, surprised.

"Who said that?" Magister Meram nodded behind us. In the distance there was a whole detachment of dark beasts, among which were several kronas. The legion of dark creatures in the service of the barrier squads. They didn't touch us — the seal of the Temple of Skron gave us permission to move freely through all of Kerux. Now I knew that it was huge, but not endless — Kerux was bordered by two other enormous dark empires. Although their names were not marked on the map. Just "Empire 1" and "Empire 2." But what caught my eye was the fact that there were also rifts here. The Abyssal spawn had infiltrated this world fully and entirely.

"Alright! There really aren't that many options," Magister Meram said, performing a few brief stretches. "We leave the supreme converts and the carriage here and go on foot. The swamp is not far from the border; we should be there by morning. Valevsky, you handle the offworlders. Fardi, you handle the bags."

"Yes, mentor." Karina shot me a hateful look, but didn't ask questions as she hoisted a huge bag with provisions and a tent onto her shoulders. The overall journey would take more than a day and Magister Meram adored his creature comforts. I was also given a backpack, but a smaller one. Because I had a different task — eliminating all offworlders. Our mentor traveled light, carrying only the flower he had picked along the way. He examined the petals closely, which had also begun to distort due to the proximity of the offworlder's territory to our own.

The boundary between the two worlds was

distinct. No smooth transitions — the space instantly acquired a dark red hue, when literally a centimeter away, green grass grew.

"Turn off your shield," Magister Meram demanded. "Do not use magic stones in there. Only after you test how they behave. Valevsky, why are you standing there? Do you need a special invitation? Forward march. As soon as you enter, the creatures will start crawling all over you. Even though it looks empty now. The entire area is like a huge fog of Pharapho. The offworlders approach from all sides."

Begrudgingly deactivating *Golden Dome of Protection* and rendering myself essentially naked, I raised my leg to take the fateful first step. Just six months ago, I could have never dreamed of traveling to worlds so unfamiliar to my own. Now it was becoming a common occurrence — the Fog Stalker Arena, the Abyss, its rifts, and now the land of the offworlders.

"Would you go already?" Even Fardi couldn't help but chime in, annoyed by my hesitation. Deciding that I couldn't let her chide me again, I lowered my foot onto the red earth and transferred the weight of my body to it, plunging into the dark red zone. Things immediately became...unusual. A feeling of unreal freedom overcame me. I wanted to fly, and for some reason I had a clear confidence that if I wanted to, I could. Not right away, it would require some preparation, but I could fly! My head was spinning, and I had to make a great effort to keep from losing it completely. Everything was different here — the air, the sensations, even my thoughts somehow ran through my head differently. It was as if it wasn't my brain that was making decisions, but the small of my back, just below my waist. Bending down, I picked up a heavy-looking stone. It seemed to be woven from thin air — it weighed nothing at all. I let go of the stone and it hung in the air for a while before reluctantly beginning its descent to the ground. However, I caught the boulder in midair and spun it around, staring at the symbol inscribed on its surface, vaguely reminiscent of the dark pentagrams from Kerux textbook. Picking up another stone, I found a similar symbol on it. As well as on the next. My notebook immediately made a bunch of notes on the location, but the magical seal from the stone was not copied over. This seemed strange to me — I had stared at the symbol for quite some time. I'd even run *Analyze* on it, but didn't notice anything strange about it. For *Analyze,* this symbol didn't exist.

"What are you dawdling for?" Magister Meram's voice spurred me on. "Why are you messing with those rocks? Keep going!"

"I need time, Magister." I continued to scrutinize the intricate seal. I even ran my finger along each line, trying to remember the path. It didn't work — nothing appeared in the notebook.

"What do you have there? Fardi, stay there." An irritated Magister Meram threw caution to the wind and walked calmly over to me, crossing the line. From the way the old man gasped convulsively, it was clear that this was his first time visiting the territory. Because when I came back here again, I'd know exactly what to expect.

"Well? What did you see?" The old man almost snatched the stone from my hands and turned it around, examining it from different sides. "A simple boulder. Fardi, come here! What do you see?"

"That Valevsky's too much of a coward to move further," snorted Karina, but she picked up the rock and also examined it from all sides. "There's a symbol here, Magister."

"A symbol? Where?" The runescribe snatched the stone back. But he turned it around again, to no avail. "There's nothing here!"

"There is, Magister," I said. It would be silly to try and hide what Fardi had already given away. "It's complicated, I can't copy it. But I see it."

"I see it too. It's right there." Karina pointed.

"Draw it." Magister Meram pulled a crumpled piece of paper out of his pocket and handed it to Karina.

"I don't have any writing utensils, Magister." She was taken aback by such a demand.

"Valevsky!" His desiccated hand held out a piece of paper to me.

"I'm afraid another punishment awaits us, Magister. I have nothing to write with either. But perhaps there is an option — I could write it in the dirt."

"Are you out of your mind, Valevsky?" The old man somehow managed to slap me on the back of the head, although he was standing at a distance from me. "Drawing an unknown symbol on unknown territory? Do you know what will happen? If you make a mistake in even one stroke, it will be a different seal! Applied to active land! Symbolic magic is only inert on paper! Morons...Almighty Skron, why do I have to teach such incompetent morons?"

"Mentor, why do we see the magic seal on the stone, but you don't?"

"Because both you and Valevsky have fragments of the higher powers in your eyes! Skron and the Light. If I remove my development crystal, I'll also start seeing these damned invisible symbols, but of course I will not do that."

The old man didn't give any reasons why, but it was clear that without *Dark Indifference*, as soon as Skron realized the warrior he suddenly had at his disposal, he would immediately do everything he could to ensure that Magister Meram would never insert another development crystal into his field again. Nevertheless, this interaction revealed one important detail for me: rune magic, for some reason, did not work on paper. The question arose: why not? Because it was finely ground wood? Or because of some special property that wood pulp acquires during processing? Maybe, for instance, that paper was made from straight trees. Here, in this maroon wasteland, there was not a single straight plant. Even the grass curled like rams' wool. But none of this mattered now. When the old man sent his symbols at me, I'd be able to channel them through the mithril and order it to turn them to paper. I wondered if it would work. Was I ready to suffer the punishment again if it didn't and the old senile man found a way to break through my defenses?

"Skron's balls," I muttered when I failed to repeat the symbol again. Something kept slipping and throwing me off. My finger seemed to move along the line without any problems, but as soon as I repeated these movements on a piece of paper, something got in the way. It turned out completely different from what I had intended.

"Okay, Valevsky, calm down." Magister Meram assumed a mentorly tone. Even though he couldn't see the symbols, he could teach us how to use them. "You're seeing the magical seal as a combination of lines and shapes. You can't do that. It's a cohesive whole. You can't draw it with your finger. You need to form it in its entirety."

"Then how do they print seals on paper, Mentor?" Fardi was clearly not distinguished by her patience or subservience.

"Line by line, you dolt," Magister Meram dismissed. "How else can you draw a magic seal if not line by line? What are you even talking about?"

"You were just talking about taking it as a whole!"

"Because Valevsky can hold an entire seal, while you, blockhead, can't even combine two symbols to make a word! Any magical seal, especially large ones, is formed line by line. But there are instances when you can embody it entirely, without resorting to crutches in the form of drawing. Your mentor, for example, Magister Elor, is as talentless as you are. Despite his amazing success in constructing pentagrams, he was never able to get away from drawing. Just think about it — spending weeks forming the seal to open the Wave portal. Mine eyes had never seen such a thing! No, Valevsky, if you go down that path — I'll kill you! I'll kill you for certain! Because that's the path of blockheads and talentless people like Fardi and Elor! You reached single symbols on your own, I didn't even have to push you, you handled two, you're on your way to three, and all this after six months of work. Cast aside all limitations! Think only about the symbol. About how it is a single whole. Remember the details, but don't concentrate on them! Nothing should prevail. Every little thing is important, not one specific piece! Fardi, get out of here!"

The mentor's voice was hypnotizing, forcing me to truly cast aside all thoughts and concentrate only on the stone. No, on the magical seal that was etched into it. Not on each line, but on the whole picture. To hold it entirely. To make it obey. To force it to submit and admit defeat...

The world spun, and I felt my head hit the rocks hard. Stars danced before my eyes, a salty taste appeared in my mouth, and an unpleasant feeling of burst capillaries appeared in my nose, but these were all small things. What was important was that before my eyes hung a glowing golden...symbol? No. It was definitely not a symbol. It was the same magic seal, the pentagram, that I saw on the rock. And the longer it hung before my eyes, the worse I felt, as if I had to give my life to support this creation."

"Alright, at ease." I heard Magister Meram's command, and the seal vanished, as if it had been awaiting his word. My head cleared up, but it didn't get any easier. I felt as if I had tried to form a three-syllable word two or three times in a row.

"I did it!" I found the strength to smile and only now realized that I was being dragged somewhere. Turning my head, I saw that Magister Meram was dragging me away by the scruff of the neck. Fardi was walking nearby, but he didn't trust her with my body.

"Yes, it worked," the old man said thoughtfully. Seating me next to the carriage, he gestured to the supreme converts to take care of me. They immediately rushed to do their usual work — open my mouth, stuff food in, close my mouth. My body did the rest, swallowing without even chewing. The area filled with the churning sounds of my digestion. An unpleasant serenade, but one that no one had heeded for a long time. For both me and Fardi, they were constant companions in the educational process. Continuing to swallow, I opened the notebook and grinned — a new symbol had appeared. An exact copy of what was once on the stone. Now the stone was still in my hands, but the magical seal was no longer on it. It disappeared as soon as we left offworlder territory.

"Mentor, is something wrong?" Fardi noticed the old man's unusual state.

"Much has happened," the runescribe muttered, irritated at the distraction from his thoughts. "First of all, everything I know about offworlders is no longer worth its salt. Their physics is different from ours, it breaks the very foundations of the world...Nonsense! Maybe their physics is different, but the reason why objects become different is not in the miraculous fairy-tale auras of an alien world, but in banal magical seals. On every object, the Light would tear them apart! How much patience and energy is needed to create something like that? That's why magic stones don't work there — conditions that break standard magic were stuffed into the pictograms. Valevsky, embody the symbol again!"

"It will kill me, mentor," I replied as I gulped down my next bite.

"Talentless...Weren't you told that you needed to keep progressing? You were. Weren't you warned that symbolic magic absorbs life force? You were. What did you do to neutralize it? Nothing! Absolutely nothing!"

"Firstly, Mentor, unlike Fardi, I didn't have a whole team of people preparing me to study with you. Secondly, you showed up unexpectedly and prevented me from using the altar. The fact that your pupil was not ready for simple constructions is entirely your fault. What would it have cost us to wait a couple of days until the altar became active again?"

"I'd like to punish you now for such impudence, but I'm afraid you'll die," the old man said, growing irate. "So what should we do with you? How can we keep progressing if you fall unconscious at every symbol?"

"Work without symbols?" I suggested, to which the runescribe only snorted.

"After what you demonstrated? No, Valevsky, now you have to work for the good of society. That is, for me."

"Mentor, what has this amateur demonstrated?" Fardi couldn't help but ask.

"Amateur?" Magister Meram turned to the girl, measuring her with a contemptuous look. "This amateur was able to do what even your favorite teacher could not. He managed to hold a magic seal. A simple one, but still a full-fledged seal. This is what my pupils usually only manage to do in the second year of study. And even then, not all of them can. The second level of mastery, when you can move on from runes to seals. They are more effective. They are more powerful. They are more complex. But the rollback for them is an order of magnitude stronger. Look, it drained Valevsky just as much as drawing a three-syllable word in one fell swoop. Although the seal, I repeat, is simple. For a significant reduction in weight. Tied to the energy emitted by this red location. It will not be possible to use it directly, but as further experiments, to isolate unnecessary elements and replace them with something more digestible, it is just right. It would not hurt you, Fardi, to be the same level of amateur as Valevsky. You're still at level zero, even though you've been studying with me for longer than your partner."

"He is only my partner for the duration of my studies," Fardi couldn't help but say. "In two years, as soon as we finish learning the runic science, I will kill him. No matter what power level he has reached by then."

"You'll kill him?" Magister Meram's eyebrows shot up. "In two years? Someone who has already mastered magic seals? I won't even punish you for such nonsense. Kill him, then. If you succeed, you will receive a reward from me. Such a reward that even Magister Elor will envy you. What's more, if that's the case, I'll even arrange a competition. I'll organize it all myself! And it will be when I decide that you have completed your training, and not in two years. It could be tomorrow, or in ten years, if you slack off. As soon as your training is over, we'll arrange a duel. Fardi versus Valevsky. Skron versus Light. The winner will live, the loser will die without the right to revive. No restrictions! Is that good enough motivation for you to study harder, Fardi?"

"Yes, mentor." The girl's voice was so full of venom it could kill. "That's more than enough for me. When I finish my training, Valevsky will die."

"Have you had enough?" the old man instantly forgot about Karina and turned towards me. "Next time you decide to embody the symbol you just learned, you won't get any food. Enter it into your skills table right away. Then pass it on to me. Come on, Valevsky, get to work! Magic seals won't find themselves. In order to deal with the offworlders, we need to understand everything they've constructed here. If that means we have to stand here for a few years, we'll do so. Stones are lighter here. That's clear. What else? I need answers. And you'll get them for me. There's no hope for Fardi. Wake her up and send her to work preparing dinner. We're definitely not going anywhere today. Are you still here? Go, I said! The red zone awaits!"

My body digested food at the same rate that it digested thought. By the time I reached the red zone, staggering from side to side, I was hungry again. My stomach was growling angrily, dissatisfied with this turn of events, so I was glad when one of the supreme converts thrust a piece of dried meat into my hand. I bit off a whole piece and stepped onto the red earth. The bubbling immediately stopped — my stomach seemed to understand that we had entered the danger zone. I had no companions around me to worry about, so I could pull out the level fifteen ousel cube and unlatch it. Now no random nasty thing would be able to come up and attack me from behind. Especially considering that I had no protection.

But the piece of meat almost got stuck in my throat when the surrounding space started to twist. The radius of my aura was only thirteen meters, and in a matter of seconds any mention of offworlders disappeared from it. With an unpleasant hiss, the magic seals began to evaporate from the stones and a howl sounded that almost made all my teeth fall out. I clenched to see if they were still there and it sent electric shocks through my jaw. But the funniest part was that I finally saw the offworlders. They were crawling out of all the cracks, shelters, and large boulders. They were trying to get out of the zone of my aura, but not everyone succeeded. Those who escaped immediately dissolved in the atmosphere. Those who did not find the strength froze like broken dolls, allowing me to examine them closer. I shuddered involuntarily — the offworlders looked like creatures from my nightmares. A dark red, smooth humanoid body with exceedingly long arms and legs. The head was just one huge mouth filled with several dozen sharp fangs. No eyes, no nostrils, no ears. No hair either. Or any distinguishing sexual characteristics. On the hands and feet there were fingers with impressive claws, and from the way the bodies lay, it seemed that there were no bones inside them at all. I could not resist, bent over one body and winced — the dead offworlders exuded a monstrous stench. The vyrma came free and made an incision — there really were no bones. The organs told me little — there were, in fact, organs, but I was not going to stoop to anatomical details. The only solid parts of the offworlder's body were teeth and claws. How the creature moved remained a mystery. But I saw with my own eyes that it could move.

I moved further into the maroon territory. The space hissed, ran and died. The number of opponents was astounding — it seemed that there were several dozen of them for every meter. Making a large circle around there, I returned to the initial point from which I started and assessed my path. It stood out like scorched earth in the middle of the red forest. Even the few trees I approached tried to straighten up, freed from the oppression of the magic of an alien world. Unlike the creatures of Phrapho, the offworlders were in no hurry to fill the territory. This required something more than fog. It was necessary to re-draw the magic seals. Which the dark creatures clearly were not going to do now.

"If you're a blockhead, then be a blockhead!" I heard Magister Meram shout. "Turn off your aura, Valevsky! Why did I send you there? For symbols! And what did you do? Why did you bring this to me?"

Leaving the red zone, I decided to examine the offworlders in more detail, so I took one of the stinking bodies with me.

"For study. How many dark ones have studied these creatures?"

"Enough to understand that you shouldn't mess with them. Those claws can cut through steel with ease. Next time, Valevsky, if you don't follow a clear order, I'll punish you. And just one! What are you standing there for? Bring the body here! Let's try to lift it. We need to find out if these creatures can speak. No one has ever conducted such experiments. There's something in you that makes you turn a blind eye to the rules. A thirst for knowledge. I love people like you. I can't stand you as well, but I do. Fardi, you train. You're not old enough for these experiments yet."

The virtuosity with which Master Meram operated the four symbols inspired respect. When you didn't understand what was behind the movements, it didn't look so difficult. But when you knew that each time you cast a four-component word, it sapped a huge amount of your life force, you began to look at runescribes in a different light. My mentor didn't even notice the loss. His eyes were burning with anticipation. The alien's body twitched and spread out across the surface, hiding in the smallest crevices of the earth. None of us had expected this. Even the mentor was taken aback. However, he quickly pulled himself together and demanded:

"Stand up and speak. Who and what are you?"

Amazingly, the creature obeyed. It stopped sinking into the ground and rose to its feet. A chattering sound was heard — the alien speech was hardly resembling anything that the human ear could perceive.

"Be quiet," Magister Meram interrupted the chatter. "Answer the questions either 'yes' or 'no.' If 'yes,' raise your right hand. If 'no,' raise your left. Is the order clear?"

The offworlder's right hand rose, but immediately fell back down, hanging like a whip.

"Do you have a name?"

Right hand. They had some kind of identity.

They weren't ants or bees controlled by a single mind. They were separate individuals.

"Where is…Valevsky, what did you bring me?! Couldn't you have found a normal body?!"

Magister Meram's indignation was in response to the fact that the offworlder did not wait for a second question. He collapsed to the ground in a shapeless, lifeless heap.

"Should I bring some more?" I asked. I liked the idea of interrogation.

"I'm too old to do two interrogations," the old runescribe winced. "Their lifespan is short… Too short. Only ten seconds. It's hard. No, I need to think. You'll bring back a body tomorrow morning."

"Magister, why did he understand you?"

"Valevsky, don't tell me you're a complete moron! No, that you're a talentless Fardi! Look at the symbols that make up a word, think, think. Sometimes it's useful. It develops your brain. That's it, go. In the morning, tell me why the offworlder understood me. I'm going to think about how to extend the lifespan of corpses. Ten seconds is not enough for me…Fardi, work! The sun is still high! Give me two symbols, otherwise I won't know what to do with you!

Chapter 14

"MENTOR, ARE YOU SURE this is necessary?"

"Of course it is, how else? Such a fat alien can't die as quickly, I've already remade the seal. Get me one of them! That's it, Valevsky, get to work! The offworlders won't kill themselves. Fardi, may the Light rip you apart, when will you stop slacking off?"

I nodded and walked into the red zone without turning on the dark aura. Fighting offworlders using only *Dark Spike* had its own long-forgotten flavor. It harkened back to a time when everything depended only on me and my skills, and not on an ousel in a vyrma cage. Practice had shown that when I switched my dark aura on, the creatures died in droves, but it was impossible to get new symbols this way. Because they evaporated. So I had to infiltrate the offworlder lands as an ordinary human being. And that's when, to put it eloquently, the complete shitshow began. Offworlders crawled out of all the cracks and crevasses, and I, after using *Dark Thorn* once to good effect, began to destroy the creatures no less efficiently than with my aura. Their magic affected both light and dark stones, but it couldn't even imagine a light-dark gem like mine. My *Golden Dome of Protection*, which was a purely dark stone, didn't work. More precisely, it did form a dome, but one filled with toxic vapors. I was glad that I tested this stone on the border with our normal terrain. When my lungs nearly jumped out of my body from the sharp pain, I leapt out of the maroon land and used *Heal,* returning me to consciousness. Incidentally, *Heal* also behaved rather strangely in the alien zone — it did not heal. It did not work at all, at least at first glance. I didn't care to do more tests and see how it actually functioned. I had neither protection nor any sensible amount of healing magic for my foray into the alien zone. Although I did have one option. *Healing Aura,* which I had integrated through fire, was also considered a light-dark stone. Everything else had to be switched off or not used. Except that *Praxis* was not damaged in any way — it acted exclusively on me, without extending outside my body, so it did not fall under the influence of the strange alien magic.

So it turned out that my life depended on my attack and reaction times. A feeling I had forgotten from a time when everything depended only on me and my abilities. Even in the Fog Stalker Arena and the Abyss, I hadn't faced that — I had protection there. Nevertheless, I enjoyed it, rejoicing, like a small child when everything goes their way. I even pulled out a spear at one point! My erstwhile weapon, which I became well acquainted with in my first eighteen years, but which I had abandoned as soon as I acquired katars and magic. The dance of death was magnificent — entering into a state of combat meditation, I destroyed aliens by the dozens without any fear for my own safety.

Until *he* arrived. Wasn't that always the case — whenever everything's going well, "he" always arrives. A beast of a different class. One that stands head and shoulders above the rest. Huge, broad, and what I disliked the most, possessing magic. If you discounted its size, the creature differed little from its relatives in appearance — a bald, dark red body, a toothy mouth, no eyes. Everything was the same, just sized up and a little beefier. *Analyze* identified my opponent as "gamma." Who or what that meant was unclear. Another important detail: the monster had strength, speed and magic. And it almost finished me off when it switched on its terrible aura. My blood felt like it was boiling in my veins! Strange sensations, even the rift guards didn't have such an aura. My body almost failed, my speed slowed to nearly null, the small creatures known as "deltas" rushed at me with redoubled force, I even fell to my knees, unable to cope with the overwhelming sensations. My body simply refused to work! Something red and unpleasant flew into my chest, but the mithril chest plate handled it. This sobered me up quite a bit and, not allowing my opponents to build on their success, I turned on my dark aura. That was it, I'd had enough of playing with spears!

What a show! The small creatures died immediately, without even a twitch. The mithril belt had materialized the level Twenty-Five ousel into my hands. For the offworlders, this was too much. The gamma was also in trouble — the creature fell on its back and squealed like a small pig. Blood began to flow from my ears, but now that the space around was cleared of the offworlder's magic, I could calmly use *Heal.* gamma didn't die, however, demonstrating that he was a fairly strong opponent. Surviving the aura of a dark beast from the twenty-fifth level of the rift was an impressive feat. Few creatures were capable of this. I had to finish off the creature by hand, tearing out a strange stone.

1 of 100 Offworlder Vault Key Fragments obtained. Total: 1

I wanted to rejoice in the new and intriguing loot drop, but my condition wouldn't allow it. Despite *Heal,* my blood continued to boil. My body was still unable to process the new aura, even though it had ceased to proliferate around the area. Even after using *Heal* a dozen times, it didn't get any easier. It would ease up for literally a moment, but then it would well over me again, forcing me to collapse to the ground and writhe in agony. This was almost the first moment during my entire encounter with the aliens when I openly panicked. I didn't understand what was happening to me or how to deal with it. And I was about to run, or rather crawl, back to the camp to ask Magister Meram for help, when everything suddenly stopped. The boiling in my blood stopped, my body stopped shaking, and several *Heal*s returned me to normal. My notebook began to blink actively. Moreover, as if sensing my confusion, the artifact highlighted the necessary entry, comparing what it understood about gamma with what I had experienced.

Tainted Blood. *Description: An aura that deals significant damage over time for 60 seconds (?, requires confirmation). Unblockable by defensive mechanics. Damage type undefined.*

Tainted Blood proved to be an extremely unpleasant aura, which I absolutely did not want to encounter again. Looking at my chest, I bared my teeth — a huge scorched spot had formed in the place where gamma's ability had struck. My clothes could not withstand the attack and had dissolved, as if they had been burned by acid. If not for the mithril plate, I would have been toast. I could never view the offworlders as a simple or easy opponent. Beasts of the gamma's caliber were capable of dealing a lot of damage.

Grabbing the stocky body, I trudged back to the camp with it, where Magister Meram happily accepted my loot. A few moments later, the fat carcass rose to its feet and the interrogation began, which resulted in me being sent for a new gamma. The creature could not speak, but it understood the speech of the one who had resurrected it perfectly well. As I now knew, this was one of the conditions of the *Live* symbol. The fat creature turned out to be the third most powerful or dominant creature among the offworlders. The dark, bald, spineless creatures were the fourth. The old runescribe managed to hold gamma for a whole minute before it collapsed as an ugly, stinking mass to the ground. Having figured out why the smaller beasts had only been able to hold on for such a short period after being revived, the old man sent me for a new body, without a thought for how I'd have to obtain it. He was only interested in knowledge and the opportunity to experiment.

In fact, I had no objections — I was interested in the questions that Magister Meram asked. After all, the offworlders turned out to be an intriguing society. Take *Tainted Blood,* for example. How did they do it? What kind of aura was it? How did it work and how could you avoid its effects? Or — and this was also vital — how could I get my hands on it? I wouldn't turn down such a weapon of mass destruction. Even if my opponent could acclimate to the dark influence, the blood aura would definitely take them out. And it wasn't curable, you just had to wait for the effect time to pass. A compelling solution. It would surely come in handy.

Another hunt began. deltas were climbing on

me like crazy. Yes, they had some kind of intelligence, but it clearly had nothing to do with the instinct of self-preservation. The creatures died not even in dozens, but in hundreds, but they continued their march forward, crawling out of all the holes. I no longer used the spear, relying solely on *Dark Spike*. As practice showed, in a state of combat meditation, I began to behave too recklessly, rejoicing at new opponents. For half an hour I cut down the poor deltas, delving deeper and deeper into offworlder territory, until finally another gamma appeared. The fat creature jumped out of the ground so suddenly that I didn't even have time to react to the attack. A red gob flew into my chest. Damn it — I'd just changed my clothes! How much longer could this go on?! The mithril absorbed the shot again and I dragged the body to the mentor. A living, screaming body!

Unfortunately, no good came of it — the gamma still had to be killed. The creature screamed too loudly; it was dangerous. Magister Meram revived the monster again, and this time the old man began to stagger — using four symbols of this level twice in a row was difficult even for him. The gamma straightened up, preparing to answer questions, but suddenly the mentor looked at me:

"Valevsky, ask your questions. You have a minute."

"Is there a way to avoid *Tainted Blood*?" I didn't have to ask twice. The right hand shot up. The answer was yes.

"Is there a way for humans to wield *Tainted Blood*?"

Another right hand.

"Is some sort of tool required for this?"

Left hand. Negative.

"It's an ability?"

Right.

"Can it be gained through a stone?"

Left.

"So you could teach me to use it?"

Right at first, then the left shot up.

"You can't in your current state?"

Now only the right one. Only a living gamma can teach a human to use *Tainted Blood*. Interesting knowledge. I needed more.

"In order for me to be trained, do I need to offer something in return?"

A positive response.

"Essences of living beings? Objects? Human lives? Resources?"

The answer was always negative. It was possible to trade with the offworlders, but no resource I could think of would do. The minute had passed and the gamma collapsed to the ground, unable to communicate what was so valuable to these creatures from another world.

"Now, Valevsky, tell me," Magister Meram demanded. "What is *Tainted Blood*, and why is this the first time I've heard of it?"

Fardi also pricked up her ears, so I had to limit myself to using general terms.

"Undefined damage that bypasses your

defenses?" Magister Meram frowned. "Something at the symbol level? They don't give a damn about defense either."

"Something like that." I did not go into detail, admitting that I had already come up with a defense against the symbols. However, Magister Meram was able to draw his own conclusions.

"If there's a way to combat *Tainted Blood,* despite its properties, then there's a way to fight the symbols too. This news doesn't make me happy at all, Valevsky. All you do is upset your mentor. Should I punish you?"

I didn't react — in most cases, Magister Meram's grumbling ended in nothing. The old man had lived on this planet for so long that, it seemed to me, he had already begun to lose his bearings. After all, he himself said that his symbols did not work on paper. Couldn't he imagine that someone might wrap all the important parts of their body in paper before putting up their defenses? And that no runescribe would be able to do anything against such a sly fox? Not to mention mithril. Runic magic was strong, yes, but it had an unfortunate drawback that cunning people could take advantage of. I, for example, planned to do just that.

"Alright, it's all hopeless. Let's stop the experiments, they only cause confusion and bring no benefit. Valevsky, you go first, paving the way. Fardi, one of the converts and I will follow. Let's go without stopping or taking a break. We've already been delayed here because of your sluggishness.

Instead of working, all you do is fill my head with nonsense."

No, Magister Meram was definitely in his own world. His inconsistency was infuriating. And very much so. However, his strength was now so great that only an immortal could argue with him. For he would kill a mortal, resurrect him, and kill him again. I shouldered my small backpack and, checking the map, moved forward, burning through the lands of the offworlders. In the two days that we had been hanging around at the border, I managed to find and comprehend only three symbols, including the one that made the stones lighter. Nevertheless, I liked the result — I did not understand the meaning of the new symbols, but I managed to "perceive" them without embodiment. Immediately into the notebook and the runescribe functionality. Magister Meram copied all the symbols himself, after which he gave me something completely unprecedented: praise. The mentor rarely praised anyone — this was the first time in my memory. I didn't even know that he knew such words.

Our venture into alien territory became a routine. I walked ahead, a little behind me, outside the range of my dark aura, walked Meram, and Fardi and the supreme convert followed behind. And Fardi tried to stay as far away from me as possible — the aura acted on her like pure poison. I even had to heal the dark one several times, who had never considered integrating such a trifle as the *Adaptation* parameter. Apparently, those who had prepared Fardi didn't consider that she would be dealing with rift magic. In any case, even though she had two development crystals, none of them contained anything to block the Abyss' effects. Which only worked to my advantage. On the day when I'd have to fight Fardi, she would be met with a twenty-fifth level ousel. Without rings like I had, it was impossible to prepare for this.

The deltas were dying, the gammas were screaming, the number of fragments was increasing, we were moving along. That's all I could say about our journey. Several times, the creatures tried to ambush me from the sides when the gammas' spit gob exceeded the range of my aura. I dodged the first attack, the second never came — Magister Meram, who was following behind, destroyed the bastards with amazing ease. The creatures of the other world turned out to be susceptible to their own magic, and even a single-component curse turned them into slabs of meat.

We did not stop at night — four light crystals illuminated the space more brightly than the sun. Soon the air began to smell of dampness, mustiness and the disgusting stench I had come to associate with dead aliens. By morning, exhausted, we nevertheless reached the first key point of our journey. The swamp. Although it was a stretch to call what appeared before our eyes a swamp. In the middle of the reddish vegetation, patches of dark bubbling water were visible. Air bubbles rose from the depths and burst with a loud pop, spreading a monstrous stench throughout the area. It got to the point that even the seasoned Magister Meram had to put a handkerchief to his nose to shield himself from this smell. As for me and Fardi, we had already emptied our stomachs several times, covered ourselves with sleeves, rags, anything we could to block the stench, but it was of little help. The smell seemed to seep right into the skin. There was a feeling of filthiness and I desperately wanted to dip into a hot bath to wash it all off like a bad dream.

"We have to go straight through this water," Magister Meram said thoughtfully, checking the map. "Judging by the reports of the dark ones who were here last time, any deviation from the path will lead to death. Ready to swim?"

"Mentor!" Fardi cried piteously. All her arrogance had dissolved in this hostile environment. Frankly, I wasn't too keen on the prospect of plunging into this muck either.

"'Mentor' what? Get in the boat."

"Boat?" We were so surprised that we even stopped wincing.

"Don't tell me that you haven't gone through my things during all this time. I'll never believe it." Magister Meram looked first at me, then at Fardi, and his eyebrows shot up: "What, you really haven't gone through my things? Have you completely lost your mind? Great Skron, what fate these students have given you! Okay, Fardi, you're talentless by definition, but you, Valevsky, should have been interested in what I hid among my possessions! You are a scholar at heart! Why the hell didn't you go through my bag? Why did I place the protective seals over it in the first place?"

"Next time, mentor, I'll definitely get into your bag to please you," I assured him, barely holding back a grin. The senile old man also turned out to be a kleptomaniac and couldn't even imagine that someone else wouldn't do the same thing he would.

Fardi placed the huge backpack on the ground. Magister Meram dug into it, only to pull out a bunched up mass. Unrolling it, the mentor looked at us triumphantly. From a distance, it really did look like a boat — one that a giant had stepped on and turned into a pancake.

"The legacy of the ancients," a shadow of displeasure flashed across his face when Fardi and I failed to grasp the epic nature of the moment. "This boat is over a thousand years old!"

"Mentor, I'm afraid to seem ignorant, but time has not been kind to it," Fardi said cautiously, looking anxiously at what the mentor had called a boat. "It's impossible to sail in something like that."

"Talentless then, talentless now. Valevsky?"

"'Valevsky' what? This thing clearly won't float in this form. So, something needs to be done with it. Right now it looks like a wrinkled, thousand-year-old human. It needs to be smoothed out somehow."

"Or inflate it," Karina chimed in. "You can't smooth it out from the outside. You have to do it from the inside."

"My pupils have finally begun to see reason. Fardi, you are first. Do you see this tube? Remove the cap, plug the hole with your tongue, take a full lungful of air and then blow it through the hole. Don't forget to plug the hole after each breath, otherwise all the air will come out. Repeat this process until the boat is whole. Valevsky will trade places with you when you get tired. Then you will trade with him, and so on in a circle until the boat is fully inflated. Let's go."

We did it in half an hour, turning the flat cloth into a four-seater boat. The technology it was made with was amazing. It wasn't an artifact, there was no sense of magic here. It was just some kind of flexible material that became dense under the influence of air. Fardi did most of the work. With her strength, there were no problems in inflating the boat. I only had to help her twice, each time carefully wiping the tube after her. It would be just like her to cover the cap in poison. Magister Meram pulled a pair of folding oars from his backpack, then sat down in the boat and gestured forward. He was ready for the journey. The old runescribe had made the most of his position — his pupils did all the dirty work for him. What was the point of putting excess strain on the supreme convert?

The dark, seething water was viscous, murky, and repulsive. I had no desire to touch this substance. With each stroke, the oars were covered with an additional layer of muck, and after a few minutes, even Fardi had a hard time rowing. We had to constantly scrape them against the boat. We slowed down, and at some point we felt like we were standing still. The boat had come to a standstill.

Everyone looked questioningly at Magister Meram, but he only fidgeted in his seat. finding a comfortable position. Judging by the mentor's face, he had thought up another nasty thing and was glad that the time had come to make it a reality. We sat like that for several minutes — even Fardi didn't want to ask the cantankerous old man a question. She understood that this path led to punishment. He saw a way out of the situation, and we amateurs did not. So we needed to be brainwashed through symbols.

Symbols.

I opened the runescribe functionality — among the many letters of the alphabet were the three magical seals of the aliens. What two of them did was unclear, but I knew for sure that the third one worked, significantly reducing the weight of objects. Because of the stuck goo, the boat had become so heavy that it could not move further. If we reduced the weight of each of us, plus the weight of the boat itself, then purely theoretically, we would move further, despite the extra weight. We would slide along the surface, without going deep into the goo. Was it a solution? It was. There was just one downside: my limitations. I could probably cast one seal, but lacked the physical strength to cast a second. It would kill me.

But hadn't I passed the symbols along to Magister Meram for a reason? He'd be able to finish what I started without any problems. The main thing now was to show him that I had a solution, albeit bound by the limitations of my body. Concentrating, I left this world for a few moments. All that remained was the offworlder seal and me as I tried to recreate it. For a long time, nothing happened — until now, I had only remembered the magic pentagrams, without trying to repeat them. Now it was time to implement everything that I learned earlier. My head was spinning, an unpleasant taste appeared in my mouth, even the stench became less sharp, but the result was achieved: the magic seal sparkled in front of me. Realizing that I was starting to lose consciousness, I lowered it onto the boat and closed my eyes. Literally for a moment, as it seemed to me. When I opened them again, the sun had already shifted several inches to one side. I had been unconscious for several hours. Fardi and the convert rowed diligently, the boat moved slowly, but was moving. Opening the map, I chuckled — we had covered almost half the distance to the central island. Raising my head, I saw stone buildings in the distance. The purpose of our visit beckoned and suggested going straight ahead, but this wasn't the right path. Of course, I had certain doubts about the knowledge of the ancient dark ones who had traveled here, but they had somehow managed to get to the island. That meant they knew something.

"The welcome party's here," Magister Meram said. Following his gaze, I saw a huge crowd of offworlders on the shore. They were following our movements, clearly hinting at evil intentions. Several times the creatures tried to send red lightning at us, but they did not reach us — the distance was still too great. I was planning on returning to the boat to continue suffering from my ever-draining life force and the lack of food, when my attention was drawn by some strange creatures. There were only a few of them, very few, but they were strikingly different from the deltas and gammas that made up the overwhelming majority of the crowd. The new monsters were much larger than the rest and towered over their fellow tribesmen, like the towers of the magic academy over the capital. From afar, it was impossible to make out the details, but I could not shake the feeling that these creatures could use magic. The shimmer around their bodies was too strange, similar to a protective aura. Where there was an aura, there was also an attack. So simply approaching the shore was out of the question.

Magister Meram also knew how to draw conclusions. But, unlike me, he also made decisions.

"Valevsky, stand up and turn your back to me," the old man ordered. A symbol appeared in front of him, reducing weight. I didn't like the idea, but arguing with the old man in a cramped boat was dangerous. After I carried out the order, I felt a slight burning sensation in my lower back, after which my body acquired an unprecedented lightness.

"Fardi, you've wanted to throw your partner out of the boat for a long time, haven't you? Here's your chance. Throw Valevsky out. Stop! Listen to me first, you flighty fool! Do you see the shore? Your task is to throw Valevsky there."

"Mentor, what if I don't make it?" I was categorically against the old man's idea.

"Then you'll learn to swim. But if I were you, I wouldn't worry about not flying far enough, but about overflying. Keep in mind — when you use the dark aura, the offworlder symbol will disappear. Use it to return to earth. Fardi, keep in mind, if you don't throw him far enough, I'll be upset. Is everyone ready? No? That's great. You'll find your footing in midair. Fardi, throw him!"

Chapter 15

IF ANYONE THINKS THAT FLYING IS FUN, I invite them to join my group. To join forces with this crazy old man and his equally batty dark pupil. Flying wasn't just no fun, Skron damn it, it was frankly scary! Terrifying! I never knew I could scream so loudly. I even lost my voice, cursing my mentor, Fardi, the offworlders, and the entire world in which it is permissible to toss an archduke! Flying over the dark sludge and crimson thickets, I once again swore to myself never to leave Hearth again. Once I found Alia and brought her home, that would be it. No one would ever catch me outside the autonomous city again! Even if the whole rest of the world collapsed!

The distance between the inflatable boat and the central island was several hundred meters. An ordinary person would hardly be able to throw even a small object, but Fardi was not an ordinary person. Combined with the fact that my weight was approaching zero, I was not going to come back down. Quite the opposite — I was gradually gaining altitude, threatening to fly over the towering structure situated at the very front of the island. Flipping around midair, which proved quite a challenge, I began to look for a place to land. The flat platform at the top of this tower was the best option. It seemed to be made for flying Valevskys, and it was located exactly along my line of trajectory. I stopped shrieking like a pig being slaughtered and waited for the right moment to switch on my aura.

The offworlders noticed me long before I stopped making wild sounds. They even shot a few red lightning bolts, but to no avail. And then those tall creatures joined in. They started shooting at me! But not with magic — with something that looked like crossbows! My shoulder burned terribly — a hole had appeared in my clothing. Similar sensations passed through my calves as they were also pierced through. But my body and upper legs suffered the most. It seemed like hail was pounding me, that's how precise and concentrated the volley was. My mithril armor coped with this disaster, and when my cheek started burning, I had to cover my head with my palms, leaving a small slit to peek out of. Most unfortunate of all was that each hit carried me even further from the ground, and at some point I began to suspect that I might miss the platform.

I had to start taking risks. The sharp bites

continued, but now that I had reached the island, the offworlders were concentrating all their shots on my chest and head. Apparently, they considered them to be the most vulnerable spots. Another hit to my arm caused the unpleasant sensations to arise again as my blood began to boil. I realized that *Tainted Blood* could work not only as an aura, but also be applied remotely through shots. My condition began to deteriorate sharply, and then I activated the dark aura. My body suddenly gained mass. I was still flying forward, but all upward momentum was rendered null. In fact, I began to make a rapid descent. All I could do was pour *Heal* into myself over and over again, preparing for the blow, and turn on *Golden Dome of Protection* so that it would take the brunt of the blow. I couldn't pull myself together enough to fall gracefully — I was in such a dreadful condition that it was impossible to concentrate. It was hard to do anything when your blood was boiling and seething. It was hard to even describe.

My impact against the stone almost knocked the wind out of me, despite all my protection. The only thing that saved me was that my body already had several enhancements going for it, as well as my constant healing. Even when I fell and everything went dark before my eyes, I continued to cast *Healing* on myself, keeping myself just on the edge of consciousness. From the pain I felt, it seemed that I had broken every bone in my body, but I'd accomplished my main task: to stay conscious, even after crashing into what was essentially a brick wall at full speed.

However, the stun took its toll — I couldn't immediately spring into action. I didn't have to worry about these things when I had my second development crystal installed. The key skill *Indestructibility* saved me from such issues. Now, after I was compelled to remove the stone and replace it with the Abyss gem, stuns worked on me as well as on any living creature. The only good thing was that it didn't prevent me from using *Heal* or holding my mirror. Even in a semi-conscious state, I could defend myself.

The deafening screech of a gamma brought me to my senses and I shook my head to clear it. The offworlders were already here! Despite the proximity of the swamp with its incessant stench, the smell of dead deltas reached my nostrils. Opening my eyes, I nearly flinched. I was lying on the very edge of the tall tower. I was lucky to land on a flat surface and, picking up speed, crashed into the back wall, obliterating it. My head and part of my body hung over the abyss, while the rest of my body, pinned down by stones, held me in place. Carefully, afraid to make an unnecessary move, I freed myself from this unexpected trap and even pulled myself to my feet. My body ached terribly, the effect of the constant onslaught of the offworlders. Moreover, in the places where their strange shells hit, there were scars. *Heal* was unable to treat the damage. Dark fire? My chest and shoulders were already disfigured by terrible scars — Magister Meram's symbols would be with me for a long time, until I visited the Bartolomeo Clan and they put me through their purification system. By the time I showed up on the doorstep of my would-be wife and her family, I would need to make sure that they were fully dependent on my services.

If I even made it out of here alive!

"Alia?" I habitually put my hand to my thigh, as I had done every hour before this, attempting to contact my other erstwhile bride. I didn't count on a response. I was already used to the girl not responding, but this time was different.

"Max?" her weak voice responded. "Where am I? Why is everything dark?"

"Alia!" I cried, barely containing my emotion. "Are you okay?! How do you feel?"

"I feel strange. Dreadfully weak. Hard to speak. Darkness like I've never known. Max, they attacked me!"

"Who? Give me the bastard's name and we won't leave any Skron-damned stone unturned."

"I...I don't know. At first I thought it was Kimal Sarento in disguise. Very similar in behavior and speech, but then I saw the face. It's not the chancellor. I don't know who it is, Max. I've never seen this man before. When I realized that something was wrong, I attacked, but he had no problems against the *Thunderer* set. It was as if I wasn't wearing it, although I know I was. Then he was nearby and did something. I don't know what, but after that I don't remember anything. I only just woke up. How many days have I been gone?"

"You were gone for almost three weeks," I said.

"But...I see. So, the map. Max, I'm in some uncharted area. This is definitely not Hearth or the Zarak Empire. This is...much further north. Have I been kidnapped by the dark ones?"

"The Temple of Skron has already stated that they gave no such order and are actively involved in looking for you. The entire world is looking for you. Everyone who can has joined the search party. The Citadel, the Temple of Skron, Hearth, the Zarak Empire. I was planning to call the Interrogator or Inquisitor as soon as I got back."

"You're not in Hearth?"

"No, I'm also far north. In the lands of the offworlders."

"There are no landmarks," Alia answered after a pause. "Nothing to latch onto. Just a dot in empty space. Wait. Look, if I zoom out really far, I see the border where Turb and Hearth lie! So, to scale, I'll count now. I'm about forty times farther north than the distance between Hearth and the capital. Wow, that's far!"

"I'm much further east," I used the same unit of measurement, secretly hoping that Alia was not far. Repeating what the girl had told me, I stared at the barren land. According to Master Meram's map, these lands did not belong to any of the clans. Neutral territory, overrun with monsters, rifts, and dark creatures of various levels.

"I'll give Eleanore the information, you'll be back soon," I promised. "Now that we know the direction, everything will be fine."

"Max, I'm worried. Three weeks without food. I'm not worried for myself, but what if something happens to the baby?"

"The baby will be fine. You weren't kidnapped to be killed. The kidnappers will demand something from me, we're just not sure what yet. Just focus on recovering. Are your hands free?"

"They're bound. I can't move them."

"How are you communicating with me?" I frowned.

"They're bound in a strange way. One is along my body, the other…The palm of my other hand is on the communication symbol. Whoever tied me up wanted you to talk to me. Max, I — aah!"

"Alia? Alia?!" I screamed, but there was no answer. The seal had not changed, but the girl did not respond to me anymore, no matter how many times I called her. Apparently, the kidnapper had knocked her unconscious again. In fact, I was starting to worry too — three weeks without food and water had seriously exhausted Alia. The bastard who had kidnapped her did not care about feeding his victim. He allowed us to talk and, as soon as she realized that her location was being revealed, knocked Alia unconscious. Fighting back hysterics, I put my hand to my other thigh.

"Eleanore, new info. I contacted Alia. She's alive, but she's not doing well. Do you have a map? I'll tell you the direction where they took her."

"Give me a minute, Max. I'm talking to a Temple servant right now. We've got no leads in the investigation whatsoever. Nothing! Alright, we got a map, tell us."

I repeated what Alia had told me and after a few minutes received a disappointing answer.

"That's the land of the Orthodox, the Temple of Skron has no control over them. They have completely rejected them and their way of life, deciding that they know Skron's desires better."

"The Orthodox? What do they want with me?"

"The Temple of Skron does not have an answer. Seven has just been sent out to investigate. It will take time to get an answer."

"Alright, keep me posted," I said and took my hand off my thigh. The Orthodox. Those who wanted to destroy Light, Chaos and entities of lower orders. But what did they need Alia for? She was barely even a member of the church anymore. And the Orthodox had no qualms with Hearth. We hadn't ever even crossed paths...

Or it could be a setup. It just so happened that Alia woke up in their lands, used the map, and her hand was on the communication seal. And when my personal attendant reported all the necessary information, she was put to sleep again. It all pointed to the idea that they deliberately allowed us to talk in order to set up the Orthodox, while the real kidnapper would go in the other direction. But how did Alia end up so far from home? The Minotaurs swore that she didn't use the portals. Had they really been traveling all these past three weeks? That's why she was exhausted. Damn it, I needed information! Now!

A bright sheaf of sparks brought me back to reality. The tall monsters were crawling onto the platform. Despite the fact that the ousel was actively emitting its aura, the creatures were moving without any particular difficulties. I couldn't see any gammas or deltas — evidently, they could not overcome the dark aura. But these ones could. They were now close enough that I could see what I was working with. *Analyze* did its part as well. The new monsters were called "betas." They did not possess magic — the aura that I had taken for a magic shield was formed by some device that the monsters wore on their belts. Visually, the betas were significantly different from the gammas and deltas. While the others had a smooth, crimson body, closer in proportion to a human from a distance, then here we had a light gray body with monstrously disproportionate paws. They significantly exceeded two meters in height. I'm not sure that I would have reached their heads, even if I stood up as tall as I could. And its long, thin arms reached all the way to its feet! The small head, similar to an egg, held nothing except a mouth, but I had no doubt that the three betas could see me perfectly well. These creatures did not have clothes, in the usual sense, however, they were not naked. On the belt of each beta was visible a device from which a shimmering field emanated, enveloping the body entirely. And on each long arm there was something similar to a clerical crossbow, only more intricate. And now all six crossbows were pointed in my direction, periodically releasing projectiles. *Golden Dome of Protection* easily dealt with these shots, but the speed with which my mana began to leave me was frightening. Just sitting and waiting would not work, I needed to act.

Since my dark aura had burned away any trace of anything from another world ever being on the roof of this tower, the magic stones worked perfectly. *Dash* took me to the first beta, and his energy armor couldn't stop my mithril gauntlet.

10 of 100 Offworlder Vault Key Fragments obtained. Total: 22

One beta gave better loot drops than ten gammas. I still didn't understand what the vault key was and where it led, but I wasn't going to ask the Temple of Skron anymore. They would pin me to the wall and demand the key for themselves. Despite the death of the wearer, the belt continued to work. It generated a protective field, behind which I managed to hide, like a shield. The other betas continued to shoot at me with all four hands, but they could not penetrate their own defenses. An interesting solution; I'd definitely have to take it for myself. And these were man-made objects — *Devour* ignored both the weapon and the belt.

"Can we talk?" I shouted, hoping that the higher-level aliens would be much more intelligent than their fellows. I was wrong. The most I could achieve was a chirping sound similar to that of the gammas and deltas. It was quite possible that this was intelligent speech imbued with semantic meaning, but this meaning eluded me. Moreover, they did not stop firing for a second as they tried to break through the shield. Throwing the now useless body of the beta aside, I *Dashe*d to the next opponent. Another ten fragments of the vault key fell into my inventory, and again I hid behind the energy shield, trying to appeal to the beta's reason. Moreover, I did so in both the light and dark tongues.

To no avail. The tall creature continued shooting at me, sparing not a thought for escaping and saving itself. The aliens had no instinct for self-preservation. I had to kill the third one, and then pause and deal with their weapons and belts. Even though my mentor was waiting in a boat somewhere off in the swamp, I didn't want to miss this opportunity.

First of all, the weapon — I was extremely interested in obtaining *Tainted Blood*. Slicing off the creature's arm at the elbow, I came closer to the passage to block the appearance of gammas and deltas with a dark aura, after which I began to figure out how this device was attached to the beta's body. It seemed that it was an integral part of the arm and a direct extension of it. I could not see any fasteners or clasps. But this did not stop me — my mithril gloves, for example, also had no fasteners, and I'd like to see anyone try to take them from me!

I pulled the weapon in one direction and the white flesh in the other. It took some effort, but the result was achieved. The creature's three-fingered paw, equipped with the same long claws as the gammas, fell out of the device with an unpleasant squelching sound. Judging by the traces left in the flesh, there had been some expanders and fasteners inside that had penetrated into the body. This was how the device was held in place. Perhaps even how it was powered. I suddenly lost the desire to experiment — sticking my hand into an unknown device with unknown conditions seemed like madness. Of course, *Heal* would be able to restore my lost limb and even pull me back from the other world if it poisoned me, but...

No. I needed a volunteer. I wasn't about to create a new crisis for myself, trying to pry this alien tech from my arm. Instead, I had a smart idea — steal the second weapon and throw both items in my backpack. I'd deal with them in Hearth. A similar problem arose with the belt — it also did not have a single fastener or clasp, so I needed to cut the beta's body to remove the device creating the protective field. Incidentally, this field easily blocked vyrma, but as soon as I activated the katars inside, there was no resistance. As a result, when the belt slid off the alien's body, it turned off his defense, which allowed me to study the object in more detail. On the inside, where the surface laid flat against the body, there were several long, sharp pins. What kind of sadomasochistic belt was this? If you wanted protection, be prepared to pay with pain and dark crimson blood? *Analyze* was no help. For the gem, both the weapon and the belt were unidentified objects that required further study. The belt went into my backpack and I descended the tower. No matter how I looked at it, I needed to rid the shore of a bunch of aliens so that my team could dock.

"You certainly were in no hurry!" Magister Meram was still dissatisfied. Although there wasn't a single living offworlder left on the shore, and that I had to walk around the tower and the buildings nearby, the old man still found something to complain about. My speed! As if I could have gone faster.

"Next time, I'll definitely keep up the pace," I answered with the usual sass. I just kept subtle enough that the runescribe didn't suffer another attack of aggression.

"Can I communicate with them?" Master Meram pointed to the body of a beta lying on the shore. I'd already finished off five of the long-armed beings, so I only needed to finish off two more gammas before I got the vault key. Or one beta. No fragments fell from the deltas. In any case, I'd have the key soon, and I'd need to answer the question of how to study it.

"No. I tried to talk to them in both light and dark. Nothing. The weapon and belt are part of their body. Fully integrated. Inside the objects there are pins that go into the body."

"Yes, the ancient dark ones wrote of something similar — the weapon and belt feed on the life force of the wearer. These creatures have no mana, so they give what they have. These tall freaks, by the way, were the reason why the ancient dark ones had to return. They live only on this island. The dark ones managed to destroy only a few creatures, while the creatures themselves finished off almost half of the dark army."

"But the wise mentor sent me here without even a briefing?" I said, trying to control my anger. He had set me up again, that bastard!

"Valevsky, one more outburst like that and I will punish you! My pupils must prove every day that they are worthy of being in my presence. They must work their asses off to show that they deserve the next level. Yes, there was a certain danger. But you managed fine, right? You handled it. What else do you need? Consider yourself one step closer to the next level."

I kept silent, although I really wanted to ask about Fardi. What kind of tests does the old senile man arrange for her, the one who he kept close?

"Can these be used?" Fardi nodded towards the alien weapons.

"For about five minutes. Although you could last maybe fifteen minutes, you are still developing correctly, unlike your talentless partner. If you believe the archives of the Temple of Skron, the dark ones lost several dozen people before they realized the stupidity of this idea. The weapon and belt absorb too much life force, which, by the way, cannot even be fully quantified. If you want to die, you can put it on. You will feel strong and protected for a short while."

"But Valevsky managed to defeat them. Because of his idiotic dark aura?"

"That's why he's on the team," confirmed

Magister Meram. "Alright, I'm tired of talking. Valevsky — we're operating on the plan we already established. To get rid of the aliens, we need to completely clear this city. We only have three days to do that. Then I need to go back."

"Mentor, there is no point in clearing the city," I said, deciding to reveal some information about what would await us on this island. "There are twenty underground levels below us. On the twentieth live creatures called the Twins. To guarantee the complete destruction of the offworlders, we must destroy the Twins."

"Where did you get this information from, and why didn't you disclose it before?" His tone did not bode well.

"I received this information in the Fog Stalker Arena, and I didn't tell you earlier because I only learned it recently."

"You were in the Fog Stalker Arena?" Magister Meram jumped up and tried to rush towards me, but *Golden Dome of Protection* flared up, throwing the old man to the side. "Valevsky!"

The painfully familiar three-syllable word flew towards me, but this time I was not going to back down. *"Adapt,"* I ordered the mithril plate. The word crashed into my stomach area, the only place free of runes or scars. I cringed, ready for pain and suffering, but none came. The mithril armor, momentarily paper, took the brunt of the symbols and dealt with them calmly. Symbols were ineffective on paper.

"I don't understand," Magister Meram rose to

his feet. There was no trace of his former irritation. "That definitely connected, I know that for sure. Valevsky, what did you do?"

"I found protection against rune magic," I answered, holding the runescribe's gaze. "I didn't just ask the Fog Stalker how to resist the offworlders. I also asked how to resist my mentor."

"A mutiny?" Magister Meram grinned. His expression had begun to acquire a mad gleam. A four-syllable word appeared before him. I knew what was about to happen, but I was not going to retreat. What difference did it make when to test my strength? Now or later, in a few years?

"A mutiny," I confirmed, preparing to catch the symbols on my gloves. "I am ready to be a pupil, but not ready to be a whipping boy. And for this I am ready to fight."

The word rushed towards me, but evaporated a few meters from me. Magister Meram straightened up and laughed maliciously:

"Welcome to the basic level of training, pupil Maximilian. I will call you Max, it is more convenient. You have proven your right to my knowledge. Fardi, stop frowning, you still do not have enough brains to understand what just happened. From now on, you are not one. When we return to the lands of the dark, you will leave me. From now on, you are no longer my pupil, do not even think of calling me a mentor. I will punish you. Despite all your enhancements, you are talentless and stupid. You do not want to work. You do not see the obvious. Let them study you in the Temple of Skron, I am no longer interested in you. Now, my only pupil, I want to know how you got to the Fog Stalker Area and what you found out there about the Twins. And the first issue is much more pressing."

Chapter 16

"YOU CAN'T REFUSE ME!" Fardi cried, not giving me a chance to say a word.

"What do you mean, I can't?" Magister Meram grinned. "I've already done it. But it won't go into effect now — when we return to the Temple of Skron. For now, you are still counted among my students. No, a course auditor, more precisely. But don't you dare call me a mentor anymore. You haven't earned that right."

"The Temple of Skron and Magister Elor will not allow you to abandon me!" Karina looked ridiculous. She was angry, but she understood perfectly well that all her anger was useless against this opponent.

"As if I'm going to ask them," Fardi's emotions clearly amused the mentor. He even turned away from me, as if he'd forgotten that he wanted to interrogate me thoroughly about the Fog Stalker.

"The only person whose opinion I'm willing to listen to told me not to make any concessions to you. If one of you two is unable to continue training, I must kick them out. Max was able to become a full-fledged pupil, but you weren't. You're not ready. Maybe later, in twenty years, when your arrogance has worn off, when you've gotten used to your strength, your abilities. Mastery is not a parameter in a development model. Not a boost. It's the ability to use what you have. You were given a lot, but you weren't taught how to use it all. Which really saddens me. You seem promising, persistent, stubborn. But no, you're ready to reject everything for the sake of your emotions."

"Are you talking about Kimal Sarento?" I asked when there was a pause.

"Who else? Unfortunately, that young man did not become my student. Runes were not his path. But he was an extremely promising mage. It has been interesting to watch him grow, gain strength, mature, and finally turn into who he is now. An influential figure not only in the Zarak Empire, but in the Light lands as a whole. Even the Citadel heeds his opinion."

"What about your mentor?" I couldn't help but ask. "Wouldn't you heed his opinion?"

"If I knew where the Light had taken him, maybe I would. But I haven't heard from him for a hundred years. I know he's alive, but that's all. Considering how cleverly he can change guises, I wouldn't be surprised if you, Pupil Max suddenly

turned out to be him. Just to test me. So no —
Kimal Sarento's opinion is the only one I might
heed, and even then, not always. Only when his
advice coincides with my desires. Right now, even
he can't make me keep Fardi as an apprentice. I
don't like talentless people."

"I'm not talentless, you senile old man!"
Karina's emotions overtook her. "The fact that I
can't cast two symbols doesn't mean I can't do
anything! I can easily crush this little creep into
dust! You promised us a duel when we finish our
studies. Will you keep to your word, or will you
hide behind your excuses?"

"I promised you a duel, Fardi, after you both
finished your studies. The fact that your studies
have ended early doesn't mean that Max has
completed his. Enough, I tire of this conversation.
Until we reach the Temple of Skron, you are still
an auditor of my courses, so enjoy the last drops
of wisdom that you can glean from me. Pupil Max,
tell me about the Twins."

"I think they are the ones behind the betas,
those long, tall creatures. They live on the
twentieth underground level. They won't be killed
by any simple means. They are immune to almost
any magic, including symbolic. The twins are the
source of runic magic. It won't work on them."

"Nonsense! You have a weapon made of
vyrma, which slices clean through rift beasts. The
Fog Stalker has fooled you, pupil. That is its
function — to confuse. That is why you must not
ask questions of it — the answers it gives do not

reflect the true state of affairs. The Fog Stalker is only good for the valuable resources it bestows. How many waves did you pass?"

"Twenty. I didn't want to go any further. After all, it was my first visit."

"Twenty waves? Fascinating, fascinating. Later, when we have the time, you'll have to tell me how you did it. I stopped at the seventeenth — the beasts overwhelmed me before I had time to cast symbols. I had to retreat. Next time you are going to the arena — or get there by accident, everything happens by accident for you — choose items. Make a list and give it to me for approval. It would be stupid to get into such a place and demand some trinket."

I didn't explain that he was wrong. If he sincerely believed that he could defeat the Twins, let him dream. I wouldn't dissuade him. If the offworlders devoured both him and Fardi, I wouldn't shed a tear. And the old man wasn't even fazed by the fact that his symbols didn't work on me anymore! Sometimes excessive wisdom only did harm.

"Alright, we've been sitting here too long. Fardi, bring the body of the new creature here. We need to find the entrance to the underground levels."

Karina only fulfilled Magister Meram's order on the second try. At first she refused, but after writhing on the ground for a few minutes, all her arrogance passed. The old runescribe did not stand on ceremony — as soon as someone did something he did not like, he immediately cast his pain symbols. All of Karina's vaunted resistance to pain gave out. She submitted. Having lifted the tall creature, Master Meram began the interrogation. This time it lasted much longer than usual — the body stood for almost five minutes. We learned not only the entry point, but even the approximate number of creatures in the depths. It turns out that the Twins and the last, fourth, type of offworlders were not the same. The strongest representatives of the alien world were in the dungeon, starting from the tenth level. Ordinary creatures did not have access there. Betas also knew who the Twins were. The only time the right hand flew up was when the runescribe said the word "god." For the aliens, the Twins were a god. The source of their strength.

"We're moving out. Max first, Fardi brings up the rear."

The island turned out to be quite large — about ten kilometers across. The entrance to the underground was located in the very center of the city, as per usual in these situations. At one point, I even considered trying to increase the radius of my aura. The skill probably existed somewhere in the development model. The reason was simple: even though I easily cut down everything within a radius of thirteen meters, the creatures would not give up. In the city, even deltas ignored the bubble of cleared land around me. They died in droves, but continued leaping into my aura to get to us. As for the gammas and deltas, they diligently continued their constant attack, sending either red gobs or projectiles from their sadomasochistic crossbows. One thing I was glad of was that at least I was their only target. They did not touch the group trailing behind me. As if they did not perceive them as a serious threat. Or — and I knew the mentor could do such a thing — they had simply become invisible to the offworlders. Were we huddling so close for no reason?

I didn't ask, keeping myself entertained by *Dash*ing from one beta to the next, sometimes even stooping to kill off a gamma. I'd already collected enough fragments to make my first offworlder vault key and I was on my way to the second. Even if there was a whole heap of trouble awaiting me on the other side, it was still worth visiting. Just to record it in my notes. For posterity's sake.

Alia didn't respond anymore. The kidnapper was keeping the girl unconscious again, although I persistently tried to contact her about once every thirty minutes. After some time, a huge building appeared ahead. It was located on a wide square and was strikingly different from the other buildings. Like an imperial palace among peasant huts. Time had not touched the city — there was no dust, no dirt, no desolation. The humans had simply disappeared, replaced by huge crowds of offworlders. I ran across the square, thoroughly clearing it. As a result, the entire ground was covered with the bodies of the creatures that had no desire to run. Moreover, with each passing minute, there were more and more rushing headlong into the cleared space. The rest of my group remained untouched, but my defenses began sending off alarm bells to tell me that a few betas were giving me a little too much attention. My mana dropped, and I even had to pull out a few elixirs to restore it. Something I hadn't done for a long time.

"This way!" I waved to the group, having found a passage. It was located in the main hall of the central palace and was a huge black hole. I had to put on a light crystal to light the way. Unlike the rifts, the lair of the offworlders lacked any air of hospitality. Dark narrow passages branched and looped around, worse than the labyrinth in the Pharapho dungeon. The walls were made of some incomprehensible red material, similar to the flesh of a monster. Unable to resist, I cut into the wall, but there were no consequences. Even when I managed to tear out a huge piece of this material. No trembling, no blood, nothing. As if the soft material was not a living substance. There were fewer monsters on the first level than above, but due to the narrow corridors and the desire to quickly get to us, the creatures blocked the passages and I had to pile the fetid bodies that filled the corridors almost to the ceiling. Life had not prepared me for this. Our progress through the underground was slowed because due to my dark aura, no one could come to my aid. And the monsters didn't stop their attack for a moment. Gammas and even betas climbed after us, trying to stop our advance. Magister Meram had to show all his skill to hold the opponents at a distance. Two- and three-syllable words formed in the air almost every second. Personally, this approach upset me — too much loot was lost. But I could not be in two places at the same time. Whenever they found Alia and pulled her out, I'd definitely give her the mithril armor. Together, we would conquer this crazy world.

"Halt!" Magister Meram's cry was heard when we reached the descent. It was a spiral slope, crafted in the same way as the ones in the rifts. I went down lower, but felt no negative effects as I had in the rifts. The new level was just a new level, and not a zone with its own aura. The offworlders had sealed all the passages again, trying to get to the uninvited guests who had invaded their home, so we didn't even have to put up protection. I removed the aura, allowing the group to approach. Judging by the dark bags on Magister Meram's face, he had been working hard to cover the rear.

"Food," the runescribe ordered. The supreme convert pulled out several pieces of dried meat and a bottle of wine and handed them to the old man. There was a chomping sound, followed by the sounds of vomiting. The surrounding stench was so foul that Fardi, despite all her hardened exterior, could not quell her body's reaction when it realized that someone could consume food in this environment.

"Twenty levels, you say?" Judging by his tone, Magister Meram had begun to doubt the success of the current undertaking.

"Twenty," I said. "But I have an idea about how to take a shortcut. Climbing through these narrow tunnels and looking for a passage down is too long and tedious. We must dig down directly."

"We have tried before, but it won't work," the mentor replied. "Even steel can't cut through the walls."

"That's why we need vyrma. What else is Fardi doing here other than freeloading? If she has vyrma armor, she probably has vyrma weapons as well."

"Fardi?" Magister Meram looked to the girl.

"I do," she said, seeing no point in hiding it. "A knife."

"Try it," the mentor ordered. Fardi, who had turned green, cast an unpleasant glance at us, but she could not disobey. She knew what would follow for disobedience, even if she was no longer listed on the class roster. The knife easily entered the floor, and soon Karina had dug a huge hole, throwing pieces of strange matter aside. There turned out to be quite an impressive amount of material between levels — about a meter. The girl finished cutting out the last piece, and it fell through the hole. The unpleasant chirping of offworlders was heard as the creatures realized that something bad was happening.

"Max." Meram gestured to the hole, to which I sincerely frowned and pointed to the spiral descent. Karina had cut a hole next to the passage to the second level. Of course, this was necessary in terms of testing her abilities, but not in terms of efficient use of resources.

"Couldn't you tell me earlier?" Karina almost choked on her anger.

"Don't you have a brain and eyes?" I couldn't help myself. "Or are you ready to always do what your elders say, even if they say something blatantly stupid?"

"Someone will have to be punished now," Magister Meram said, but I paid him no mind. The punishment symbol was a three-parter. In his current state, the old man was not capable of such a feat. Sure, he might still do it, but he would suffer no less than me. And he understood this perfectly well, but because of his mischievous character, he could not help but say it.

"I'll go first, you two follow behind. I won't switch off my aura. We'll need to cut another hole down."

With these words, I jumped through the hole, landing easily on my feet. *Dark Spike* immediately came into play — a crowd of deltas rushed out of the passage. Some of them were lying motionless below, as my aura easily pierced the partitions between the floors. The offworlders' lair in no way resembled a standard rift.

Soon the others appeared from the spiral passageway. Judging by Fardi's face, she was ready to kill me here and now. I could see her regripping her knife to figure out how to throw it more conveniently.

"I have a proposal," I said, interrupting this train of thought. "You go back, Karina gives me the knife, I make a hole, jump down, kill all the aliens, then shout up to you, and you go down to the level below. There will always be one level between us so my aura will not reach you."

"Fardi," Magister Meram pointed at the weapon the girl was still holding. I had a strong feeling that the blade would end up in my body, so I turned on *Golden Dome of Protection* just in case. This part of the level had already been cleared so I faced no issues using the magic stone. However, Karina managed to rein in her emotions. Sticking her knife into the floor up to the hilt, she picked up her backpack and silently went back up the slope.

"To make things easier," Magister Meram warned and a connection symbol appeared before his face. Remarkably, he didn't send it at me immediately without asking. He had warned me first, and even explained, which was never his habit. Could there really be a kernel of good in this nasty old man? I doubted it. Most likely, he was already on his last legs, and if I had dared to protest, the runescribe's life force would have been wasted.

"I agree, it will be easier." I allowed the symbol to be imprinted on my stomach. Judging by the fact that Magister Meram had stuck his symbol on his ankle, he had no more places on his body for a long time. Everything was occupied by either scars or symbols. The old man and the supreme convert returned to the floor above, and I began to form a passage. I did not need Fardi's knife, but leaving the weapon with her would only cause more issues. After all, the Temple of Skron had prepared the girl a little too well.

I used the katars to get down to level three. They were much more convenient than Fardi's small knife. I hung it on my belt, and the mithril armor formed a small holster. I didn't hide it, letting it hang on my belt with my coin purse. Which, by the way, was still with me. There was even some gold in it. The hole was wide, but not big enough for the gammas to get through. I finished the final touches inside the pit, making several circular cuts along the entire length of the blades and jumping up several times. The partition gave way, and I fell through.

Directly onto the heads of three betas!

No matter how combat-ready the offworlders were, they clearly couldn't prepare for a human to fall on their heads on the third level of their home. The creatures were taken aback, which allowed me to turn on the dark aura, getting rid of the gammas and a couple of deltas, turn on *Golden Dome of Protection* to protect myself from shots, and also stick the glove into the creature closest to me, increasing my fragments by ten. In total, I already had more than two hundred, which was enough to form two vault keys.

I had to work hard to seal the passages. I had no problems with the aliens — they continued to crawl in from both sides. But it wasn't easy to block off both passages with the bodies. I wasn't worried about not being able to get through to the lower levels. Each floor of the aliens' lair was a huge empty space with numerous passages. The only possible surprise I might encounter was if I hit a wall. In this case, I would have to dig slightly to one side. I'd gotten lucky with the first home, so I hoped that my luck would continue in the future.

Making sure the passages were tightly blocked off, I began to cut the next hole. If I understood the situation correctly, there would be no problems up to level ten.

My assumption turned out to be prophetic — I easily cut through the partitions, fell, killed everyone on the new level, and began to install barriers. Starting from the sixth level, the deltas disappeared. From the eighth, there were gammas. Only the betas remained, which I couldn't help but rejoice in. Each tall creature dropped ten key fragments.

By the time I began to break through to the tenth level, I already had four full keys. The other two constantly stayed two levels above and tried not to make noise. Surely, Magister Meram used the symbols that made everyone invisible, so they had no problems with the offworlders.

My lucky streak lasted all the way down to level ten. In all that time, I only had to redo a hole once when I hit a wall directly. Falling to the floor, I turned around sharply, assessing the situation, and reflexively raised my hands, accepting an intricate magic seal on them. I didn't even have to order the gloves to adapt — Pharapho's flesh understood what needed to be done. Out of the corner of my eye, I noticed movement and immediately used *Dash* to bring myself to the next enemy. I missed! The nimble creature managed to jump back, and again the offworlder's symbol rushed towards me. I retreated to the wall, accepting this blow on my gloves as well, after which I finally managed to get a good view of the enemy.

It was a small creature that barely reached my stomach in height. It had six short legs attached to a flat body that looked similar to a large discus. I'd thrown something like it back in the magic academy's arena. The only difference was that this disc bulged more in the center. The four thin paws were attached, and there was a protrusion on top that played the role of a toothy head. Also eyeless, since there was never any light in the alien territory. Eyes were of no use here. *Analyze* identified this creature as an alpha. It had magic, extreme speed and strength.

And another unpleasant surprise — it didn't react to the dark aura. Apparently, the twenty-fifth level ousel was small fry to these beasts. Or they were not susceptible to Abyssal magic at all.

The alpha was constantly moving his limbs to form, as I understood it, another magical seal. I had finally met the creators of this dark red land. Until now, I had no idea why the offworlders had used anything but rune magic. It turned out that it had been given over to the alphas.

Another symbol flew at me again, but the mithril quickly transformed into paper and easily dealt with the attack this time too. In response, I fired a vyrma crossbow bolt, but the nimble monster easily stepped aside, letting the projectile pass by.

And it went immediately into forming the next seal! The situation was starting to get out of control. I tried using *Dash, Dark Spike,* even *Heal* — everything flew by, and the creature didn't react to *Heal* at all. This magic did it no harm. When I turned off the dark aura to call Magister Meram, the space began to fill with the dark red substance. And at a monstrous speed, as if there were a dozen of such invisible alphas somewhere applying symbols to stones. I had to put my aura back up and think about what to do. The alpha did not stop trying to get me with magical seals, I used my entire attack arsenal to get to him, but we remained at a standstill. Neither one of us could reach the other.

There was a noise from the corridors. Other alphas were probably rushing to help. If I didn't come up with something urgently, I'd be in trouble.

When I caught another seal that dissolved on my mithril, I realized what I had to do. Magister Meram, if he were here, would have called me a good-for-nothing and a slacker long ago.

I extended my hand and began to form the two-syllable curse symbol *Shackles of Time.* It slowed down the opponents significantly, which I needed like air right now.

The alpha's movements slowed down. It

clearly hadn't expected to go up against an opponent with a similar weapon. I wasn't my mentor, of course — in order to form a curse in an instant, I had to spend several seconds and move my hands as quickly as possible. This was something that the mentor did on an instinctive level.

Burning symbols appeared in front of me, and I sent them forward. The alpha dissolved into the air, moving from one point to another with the speed of lightning, but the advantage of rune magic was that it followed its target. The creature even rushed further down the passage, taking the symbol with it, when I felt it make contact. *Shackles of Time* had caught up with the enemy and imprinted themselves on its body.

Realizing that I was taking a risk, I rushed further down the passage, preparing to catch the magical seals flying at me.

The alpha was found ten meters around the corner. It moved so slowly and unnaturally that I could use *Dash* to get next to it.

The blow from the mithril gloves was impossible to block, and when I pulled my hand out of the alpha's body, something small, dark and sparkling appeared in my palm.

Twenty fragments of the offworlder vault key fell into my inventory, but none of that mattered. *Analyze*, which I immediately used on my prey, took a long time to digest the information it had received. I even began to think that it wouldn't tell me anything, when finally an answer appeared:

Dark Fluid. Used as a substitute for vitality when forming magical seals and symbols. (? Needs verification) uses remaining.

A substitute for vitality? I even felt a fire of anticipation flare up in my chest. Where were the alphas? I had an unpleasant surprise for them! Today I would learn to form three-symbol words!

Chapter 17

"HOW DID YOU DO THAT?" Magister Meram stared at the three-part word that was floating in front of me and frowned. The mentor did not understand why it was hanging in the air, and why I was smiling instead of lying on the floor unconscious.

"I'm a genius?" I suggested and dispelled the symbol.

"Don't make me angry, pupil." The mentor was clearly not pleased with the situation. "Have you found the altar or a substitute?"

"No altars," I glanced sideways at Fardi, who stood behind Magister Meram and looked darker than a thundercloud. "The answer is actually simple, Magister. By killing the creatures called alphas, I have become stronger."

"So much so that you managed to make the jump to casting three symbols at once?"

"You'd learn to do much more if your survival

depended on it." I wasn't going to tell him about the dark fluid. As with practically all my loot, it had fallen safely into my inventory, forming a new section titled *Offworld,* and the symbols I formed automatically took power from the dark sparkling stones, without forcing me to do such a stupid thing as embodying them. The charge of one dark fluid was enough for ten three-symbol words, twenty weight-reducing magic seals, or thirty two-symbol words. More than sufficient to completely wipe the alphas on this level from the face of this earth. I hunted them up and down. Eventually, they even started avoiding me. On the tenth, ninth and eighth levels, the alphas had sought me out, but on the seventh and up, I had to run around and find them. This slowed my progress significantly. I stopped cutting passages between the floors. Considering that below the tenth level there were only alphas and no betas, gammas or deltas, there was no longer any point in the dark aura. My main weapon in the hunt was *Shackles of Time*, which was permanently hanging in front of me. Magister Meram, who joined me, was initially sarcastic, grinning, even calling me a mediocrity, but when I formed a three-syllable word and remained completely upright, he was taken aback.

"This doesn't happen." He didn't give up, trying to get to the truth. "How did you kill them?"

"Fardi's knife," I demonstrated the weapon I had received. "*Shackles of Time* slows them down, allowing you to get closer. They have no defenses against vyrma."

"Why not just kill them?" He formed two curse symbols and, when we met another alpha, sent the word forward. The construction formed by Magister Meram flew an order of magnitude faster than mine, and the result looked much more frightening — a shapeless pile of flesh fell to the floor. I stuck my hand inside, letting *Devour* do its thing, but there was nothing there. I couldn't obtain any dark fluid.

"You can do it that way too," I answered reluctantly, trying not to show my displeasure. "*Shackles of Time* is much easier for me to cast, plus I like killing creatures in hand-to-hand combat. The similarities to the rifts are having their effect on me."

"Alright, let's say I have no more questions about the alphas. Still, how did you manage to cast a three-symbol word and remain upright? Where did you get the life force?"

"I don't have an answer to that question, mentor. Maybe when I kill creatures in close combat, I get some kind of invisible aura from them, which allows me to work with runes without punishment, or increases my skill? There are many possibilities, actually. I decided that it was silly to stop now and figure out why everything is working for me. There's only one level left before we meet the gods of the offworlders. Business first, then we can deal with the details."

"No, pupil, when we return, I'll deal with you myself. I will figure out what in Light's name has made you so powerful. Miracles like this do not happen. Fardi, can you keep going?"

"I'll try," the flushed girl croaked. Starting from level fifteen, Karina's condition had been getting worse and worse. I even had to hold *Healing Aura* permanently to somehow lessen her burden. Because I had promised that we would take care of each other before the duel. However, it didn't help. Or rather, it helped, but not much. The lower we went, the worse Fardi became. I even had to go up a couple of levels to give her a chance to catch her breath. The supreme convert, strangely enough, seemed to feel fine. The house of the aliens didn't present any problems for him.

"Where else would you go?" Magister Meram said to himself. "If you survive, I'll give you a second chance. In three years, I'll be ready to see you again. If Max hasn't killed you by then. Where's the descent?"

"Around the corner." I stopped near the final spiral staircase. We were on the nineteenth level. Below, according to the betas and one alpha Meram resurrected, lay God. And everyone was talking about the Twins in the singular. As if there were not two creatures, but one. We specifically clarified this point. It peeved me that I didn't have the opportunity to talk to the alpha. Of all the four types of offworlders, these seemed more intelligent and capable of complex dialogues, but the presence of spectators interfered with this. I needed to learn the word that raised corpses for further dialogue. True, these are four symbols that

I couldn't handle even now, with dark fluid. I needed training.

"You take Fardi," Magister Meram ordered the convert, after which he determinedly stepped down. Now that the runescribe had realized that no magical alpha seals could suddenly fly at him, he felt confident. Which was strange — if the alphas knew how to throw runes, then their god should have this ability by default. Nevertheless, Magister Meram was not afraid, descending with large strides to the twentieth level.

A few moments later, his displeased voice sounded in my head:

"And? Why are you hesitating, student? Why don't I see you next to me? What's with your sluggishness? Tell the convert to drag Fardi down. This is no place to rest."

Having passed his order along, I walked over to the spiral staircase. Unlike all the previous descents, this one had five full turns. That meant that the floor separating the nineteenth and twentieth levels was almost ten meters thick! I would have had to dig for ages! Below, I found a spacious cave. In terms of height, it could easily accommodate a beta. The ceiling was at least three meters high. Magister Meram was gazing intently at some structure in the center of the cave. It looked like a pedestal on which the busts of prominent figures or emperors were usually displayed, but now it was empty.

There came a wheeze from behind us. Fardi had passed out from the pain as she was dragged down to the next level. Magister Meram waved her off, ordering me to come closer, but I handed the convert a few recovery elixirs nevertheless. I wanted to kill Karina personally; I didn't want some mysterious aura to do it for me.

"Do you know what that is?" asked Meram when I approached the pedestal. Up close it became clear that it was not empty — it held a small goblet.

"A sacrificial altar?" I asked, already knowing the answer. *Analyze* had encountered such a thing before. Magister Meram scowled — I had clearly ruined some good prank or joke he was planning. Nevertheless, he continued:

"Not just a sacrificial altar! This is an altar of summoning! This entire room is the dwelling place of the Twins. But they will not just appear. They must be summoned."

"Where did you obtain this information, mentor?"

"Did you think I started planning this expedition yesterday? I've been nurturing the idea of taking care of the offworlders for at least fifty years. During that time, I've managed to do a lot, including visiting the Fog Stalker Arena. Yes, many of his answers were confusing and imprecise, but in regards to this place, his answers were clear."

"So you knew about the Twins?" I asked, surprised.

"No. I asked about how to get to the place where I could destroy the offworlders, and, most importantly, how to destroy them. The answer to the first question is before your eyes. The sacrificial altar."

"I didn't really like the word 'sacrificial.' Someone needs to be sacrificed?"

"Of course, that's why you're here," Master Meram stared at me so bloodthirstily that I jumped aside and prepared to catch his symbols. The old man burst into laughter, pleased with the effect he had achieved.

"No, pupil, there is no need to kill anyone. Not even you."

"What about the second question? How to kill them?"

"Exactly as I planned — with symbols. For this purpose, I have long been developing my own runic magic, different from that taught in the dark academy of Kerux. There they focus more on pentagrams, and the more complex they are, the better the result. In my opinion, this is the wrong approach. An error in just one line will result in a completely different seal."

"Is the alphabet your invention?" I was surprised.

"No, the invention of my mentor," Magister Meram reluctantly admitted. "He was the one who laid the foundation."

"Okay, but where did he get it from? Did he pull it from his own mind?"

"I believe from his direct relative. The first emperor."

"Your mentor is the grandson of the first

emperor?" My eyebrows shot up.

"Hmm…and why not his eldest son?" he asked slyly.

"Because his eldest son is dead. The grandson was a student of the first emperor, having adopted all his wisdom. I have also been collecting information about this man for a long time. In the Citadel, in the Temple of Skron, and with Kimal Sarento."

"Yes, the chancellor adores the first emperor. For Sarento, he is an idol, the likes of which you can hardly find. But you understand, Pupil Max, that neither the Temple of Skron, nor the Citadel, nor, especially, Kimal Sarento, have any information that the eldest son is dead. Do you have anything to tell me?"

"No." I smiled, inviting trouble. "You don't think I'm going to reveal my sources of information, do you? They exist, and they are quite reliable. And they're not the Fog Stalker or its arena. I've only been there once."

"You know how to upset me, pupil. You have upset me before, and you upset me now. Maybe I shouldn't have kicked Fardi out. At least she could have been guided. You're completely uncontrollable. You're annoying."

"That's why you keep me close. To remember what emotions are." I didn't mince my words. Now that the mentor had become essentially harmless to me, I could show off a little. "So what should I do with this cup?"

"Fill it. You could use blood, of course, but

pure water will work as well. Any liquid at all. This is somehow vital for the creature that rules this place."

"So that's why Fardi was dragging that bottle around!"

"Naturally. Pay no attention to the apparent size of the cup — you need at least ten liters to fill it. That's it, pupil, step aside. Now's when the show starts. Try to make sure neither you nor Fardi get hurt. I still have to hand her over to the Temple of Skron. They have certain plans for you, after all."

"Destroying the light ones?"

"Why not? Have they ever been anything but a pain in the neck to you? I'm not talking about all light ones. Just the Church of the Light. No one plans on touching normal citizens. They don't really care who they worship. Light, Skron. Ninety percent of people in light empires don't even consider the fact that the Light is out there somewhere or that it may punish them. People are so used to relying only on themselves that they won't notice anything if their patron god changes. Just as they didn't respect the Light, they won't respect Skron either. As for the churchmen...I repeat — what good have they done you? Shove the Light into your eyes? I was there when it happened. As far as I remember, you weren't particularly eager to become part of the Church of the Light. Has something changed?"

"The Light gives me immunity to curses," I replied. "That's useful to me now, and I don't really want to give up that kind of protection. So I will be against what Fardi is going to do."

"It's all in your hands, young one! You have a duel scheduled, and as I understand it, it will take place immediately after our return to the Temple of Skron. Finish her off, and that's the end of it. Just make it so that she can't be revived. Think of a way to do that. Keep in mind that Fardi already probably has a slew of fascinating symbols all over her body. Why lie — I gave her *Az* again. And not only that. Plus amulets. Your battle will be fun. Alright, enough, I grow weary of this conversation. These are all just details to sort out upon our return. First, we need to finish up here. Water!"

The convert placed Fardi on the floor and pulled a large, flat flask from her backpack.

"Pour it," Meram ordered and stepped aside, stretching his shoulders as if preparing for battle. This was enough of a warning for me, and a few moments later I was at the spiral staircase, ready to sprint the entire way back up. I had no desire to face this god, as the Twins were known. The supreme convert poured out the water and, taking Fardi, joined me. The imperturbable dark one treated everything with such indifference that I even began to doubt that he was human at all. No, not human — that was exactly what the converts weren't. A living being. Judging by the way the convert reacted to what was happening, he was more reminiscent of the offworlders — zero emotions, zero instinct for self-preservation, a total desire to fulfill the order of his master. Meram had prepared himself the perfect slave.

The flask was almost entirely gone — the cup really was not what it appeared. For a while nothing happened, but then the space shook noticeably and Fardi groaned. Even unconscious, she felt terrible. Something like a portal, formed without the use of arches, flashed, its surface whirled around, and the one called the Twins entered the cave.

"Great Light!" I whispered. The Twins deserved their name — there really were two of them. But they also were one being, somehow monstrously divided into two independent parts. It seemed as if in the distant past the body had been severed in twain by a giant sword, but not completely. At the very bottom, where four powerful elephant paws were, the body was whole. Instead of sewing the halves together, this unknown force had given each of them its own consciousness. At the same time, the creature's appearance was distorted into an ugly piece of flesh. If there had once been a head, arms, or torso, now all of this was gone, leaving only two pieces of dirty clay stuck to a platform with legs. The hideous mass had two toothy mouths, several constantly moving appendages that acted as paws, and, for the first time ever, eyes. The Twins had two eyes. One for each half. The god of the offworlders stood not far from Magister Meram, so it was easy to compare their heights. The Twins were almost twice as tall as a standard human.

If the Twins' appearance had any effect on Magister Meram, he did not show it. A four-symbol word materialized before him and moved towards the beast. It almost reached the body, but then exploded with a very loud bang. And this, finally, made an impression. The way he stood straight up showed that the old runescribe was taken aback. He clearly had not expected this — the Fog Stalker Arena had told him something completely different.

The Twins went on the offensive. The appendages began to flash with astonishing speed, forming something unlike we had ever seen before. It was not a sentence — it was a full publication! Like the pentagram used to summon the Wave, and it took up even more space! The Twins' creation was so large that it completely covered the huge creature's body. Magister Meram reacted instantly, despite some bewilderment — before the seal had time to fully form, another word of four symbols flew into it. The old man noticeably swayed from the loss of vitality, but it was all for naught. The word flew unhindered through the forming symbol and again disappeared with a loud clap.

"Cover her and prepare to open a portal," I ordered the supreme convert. I didn't know if I was allowed to give orders, but it didn't matter anymore — I was acting according to the situation. I couldn't use *Dash* — my dark aura was turned off, and it didn't work on high-level offworlders. So I had to get to the mentor on foot. And just as I ran up to Magister Meram, who was looking dejectedly at his hands, as if he couldn't believe that all the strength had left them, the Twins struck. The huge three-meter seal flew in our direction. Wherever it touched the floor, the floor simply vanished. Without a sound, without flashes, without fumes. It simply disappeared. No fancy flourishes — they only wanted to destroy us as quickly as possible. Realizing that I couldn't avoid a fight, I stood in front of the mentor and stretched my palms forward to take the brunt of the blow. Magister Meram couldn't handle such an attack. I could. Probably.

Adapt!

The gloves heeded my order! Literally an instant before impact, they lost their density, turning into paper. The seal cut into the mithril gloves and, instead of destroying my armor, slowed down significantly. But not completely, continuing to press on me. My feet slipped, and there was nothing I could do — I did not have boots that could adapt and grow claws for me.

Master Meram's hands pressed against my back, trying to stop me. It didn't help. The offworlder magic proved too powerful. He understood that his actions were futile and ran off to one side, fleeing the Twins' magic seal. The seal didn't follow suit, instead continuing its straight path.

"Get out of the way!" Meram played the voice of reason. Once I was sure I had gained enough distance, I tore one hand away from the seal and lowered it to my belt. The pressure accelerated significantly — it was as if the magic was alive and felt that my defense was beginning to crack at the seams. I was almost pressed against the wall, but at the last moment I managed to turn on the dark aura and return my other hand to its place. There was only half a meter left to the wall! My idea was simple — use *Dash* and move to the side, but completely unexpectedly, I felt the pressure let up. The seal stopped in its tracks. It still pressed against my hands, but the ousel box had drained much of its power.

An unpleasant cackle filled the cave — the Twins were angry. Or trying to express that they were impressed. The seal disappeared, which allowed me to find myself near the creature with two *Dash*es. The Abyss warned that Pharapho's flesh would not be able to do anything to a high-level monster, but I wanted to see for myself. Trust, but verify. Besides, the weight reduction seal was already hanging in front of me. I wanted to see how the Twins reacted to their own magic. Maybe they could block any runes except their own!

I stretched my hand towards the creature's body to check its density, but it was a huge mistake. It shook me as if a hundred lightning bolts had struck me at once! There was an unpleasant smell of burnt meat, and then a monstrous pain followed. My right arm was simply dissolved all the way to the shoulder. If it weren't for the body plate that took the brunt of the blow, this stupidity would probably have been my last action in this life, but before screaming from the monstrous pain, I managed to use *Dash* again and *Heal* at the same time. Then, of course, I had to scream. Why hide the truth? Even though *Heal* took away the most acute pain and even started to grow my arm back, the attack still rocked me to the very core of my soul. Maybe even deeper.

Only after five *Heal*s was I able to perceive the world around me normally. My arm had been regrown, but it no longer had either the katar, the crossbow, or, what saddened me most of all, the mithril glove. Pharapho's flesh was powerless here. Moreover, the second glove had lost its function, transforming into a huge shapeless piece of iron that was attached to the katar from above. And again, damn these Twins to Skron — my *Phantom* detecting hoop had disappeared! It must have been my fate to lose it!

However, there were no subsequent attacks, which befuddled me. The Twins were standing with their backs to me, as if they did not perceive me as a dangerous opponent. Or that its main opponent was where the convert stood. Magister Meram was lying a little to the side. The old man looked...grim. It was as if he had been pushed through a meat grinder — his clothes were all torn, his flesh was cut. I was too far away to see any details, but I knew for certain that he was still alive. He was trying to crawl toward the passage. I did not see him — it so happened that the body of the monstrous monster was standing directly between me and the exit, blocking my view. But what I did know for sure was that Fardi's wheezing had stopped! Instead, there was the muttering of the supreme converts, calling the portal to save her, as well as a new, incomprehensible sound. Buzzing. Like lightning harnessed by a skilled mage that obediently jumped back and forth between his hands. I'd seen Kimal Sarento pull off this trick once, very impressive. Was the chancellor really here? I pulled off the now-useless glove and threw it on the floor. They wouldn't work unless they were a pair.

Magister Meram was crawling, despite his condition, and I wondered what he was going for. Suddenly, another huge seal formed in front of the Twins' face, which flew to where Fardi and the converts were standing. I swallowed, imagining what was about to happen, but to my surprise, the seal stopped a few meters from the Twins, began to blink actively and disappeared in a bright flash.

I circled around, trying to get as far from the Twins as possible. The Abyss had been right — humans could not stand up against the offworlder deity. We were too weak against a being from the highest orders of entities in our world. Humanity still had a long way to grow before we reached that level. Although...what I had seen when I ducked to the side had planted doubt. Fardi ceased her bellowing and got to her feet. She stretched out her arm toward the Twins and a dark, misty thread flew from her hand, hitting the side of its shield. Dark waves thrummed rhythmically from Fardi, like an expanding sphere, and, as I understood, Magister Meram was crawling to escape this aura.

Because the supreme convert, who was not far from the creature that was once Karina Fardi, also looked like he had been through a meat grinder. Not a single piece of healthy, living flesh, not even clothes remained. Everything had rotted away.

Another magical seal appeared in front of the Twins, but once again exploded with a bright flash. Karina took a step forward, forcing the Twins to take a small step back. And another step forward, and again a step back. With each passing moment, the pulsating sphere that beat like a heartbeat increased in size. It was already extending a good five or six meters from Fardi, preventing Meram from crawling away.

Fardi's head turned towards me, and something inside me began to break, twist, and contort. A nimble, dark, misty snake flew out of Fardi's hand and struck me in the chest. I could neither dodge nor avoid this blow. My body arched from the horrendous pain, but it quickly passed. When I was able to perceive reality normally again, Fardi's attention was again focused on the Twins. She'd forgotten me again. But this brief encounter was enough to tell me who we were dealing with. There was no trace of Fardi left in that body. Skron had taken his puppet under his control. And it wasn't just an echo of Skron like the one that overtook the converts. Some significant part of one of the beings that controlled this world was inside her. It perceived me as a representative of the Light and burned the Inquisitor's gift out of me. In theory, I should have died, but it was not to be —

the dark mirror, which I never let down, showed Fardi-Skron that I was on the same side as him. He decided not to finish me off and returned to the main enemy.

The pulsating aura was growing, so I had to run around the two beings in a wide arc. It helped that Fardi was advancing on the Twins, and they retreated to the wall farthest from the forming portal. I reached Magister Meram. The old man was already relying solely on his own sheer power of will to keep moving. The proximity to the true Skron had a strong effect on the mentor, transforming him into a defenseless slab of flesh. All his protective measures had been swept away as something trivial and insignificant. My first thought was to pierce his rotten heart through with a vyrma blade, but instead I cast *Heal* several times. Why? Because I realized that I needed the knowledge that was stored in his head. I needed to understand how to build structures from four symbols, how to speed up the formation of words, how to design my own words. Many questions remained, and there was only one place to find the answers — this nasty old man who had lingered too long in this life.

"Max?" Magister Meram's gaze gained consciousness. Seeing Fardi continuing to advance on the Twins, the old man's eyes widened in horror. Sincere. Deep. Soul-consuming.

"We need to get out," I grabbed the frightened man and, in the same wide arc, began to approach the supreme convert. By this time, he had pulled out a knife and began to cut his body, forming a portal. The humming stopped for a moment. Fardi-Skron realized that something unusual was happening and turned around. Seeing the portal, the dark creature began to drag one of its hands towards it in order to send a misty snake that would destroy the shimmering veil. The minotaur appeared, but immediately froze, staring at Fardi. Judging by the beastman's face, he was as frightened and shocked as Magister Meram. The misty snake struck the minotaur, turning it into ash, but it took a moment. And that was enough for me to dive into the portal with a powerful jump. The space around us swam and lost its integrity. I no longer heard the explosion that scattered the remains of the portal and the spiral staircase along with it.

We had outrun Skron!

Chapter 18

"HEARTH?" I LOOKED AROUND in surprise, assessing where we had landed. It was, in fact, my city. A shrill siren rang in my ears, and a tall pillar of light suddenly appeared above me. Or rather, two pillars — the second came from Magister Meram. He was unconscious — the dark aura that I had used to heal him had a negative effect on the old man's condition. It was good that I had guessed to use the fifteenth-level aura. I think that if it were the twenty-fifth, his body simply would have disintegrated and I would have had to sort out rune magic myself. The idea was certainly tempting, but not now. I had already lost the Light from my eyes. Fardi-Skron had burned it out. I needed protection. So I still needed this bastard who saw humans as nothing more than a power source.

"Don't move!" The order sounded and an

impressive group of guards with crossbows surrounded us. "If none of you have vyrma, I will punish everyone!"

"Mandatory inspection, Your Radiance!" The platoon leader stepped forward. "By order of Lady Eleanore. All who receive the pillar of light, regardless of their appearance, are required to undergo inspection. Messengers have already been sent for Lady Eleanore. Please, do not make any sudden movements, otherwise we will be forced to shoot. We have vyrma bolts. We are simply doing our duty."

The security system that had been installed in Hearth during my absence pleased me. At least at first glance. I turned off the dark aura so that the guards would not accidentally fall under its influence, mentally giving myself the task of setting some boundaries that the guards should not cross under any circumstances. For example, the thirteen-meter diameter that my aura covered. Because who knows who or what would emerge from the portal.

Soon Eleanore appeared. Pregnancy clearly suited her. The body that had survived eight years in the rifts was still perfect, but it had developed curves that made the woman even more desirable. In some ways, it was a shame that Eleanore had decided to go her own way. As far as I knew, she already had a suitor, and one from a good family, with feelings which she herself reciprocated. When the child was born, Eleanore would have to be given a baronial title. She deserved it.

"Max, if that's you, raise your right hand," her voice said in my mind. The distance between us was large, so there was no way I could have heard her words out loud. Fulfilling her order, I waited for her to approach before asking:

"Why such complicated measures?"

"You will be given the maximum level of access, I had to make sure that you were yourself and not another Faceless One."

"Are there any precedents for this?"

"Two. They rule the city as if it were their own. They have received the status of guests and interfere with the construction. We almost caught them twice, but each time they managed to escape. We can successfully block the new ones, while the dark ones' device allows us to determine the true essence of a person, but these two managed to undergo initiation before the hole in the functionality was discovered, as they said in the Temple of Skron. However, we are working to narrow the circle of suspects. Each time the Faceless change their appearance, a pillar of light appears, which cannot be eliminated even underground. What access should we give Meram?"

"Guest. Heard anything from Alia?"

"The Temple of Skron is continuing its search," someone replied, and a Temple servant stepped out from behind Eleanore. "The territory in which she was located during your last communication belongs to a new group of Orthodox led by Magister Elor."

"Fardi's mentor." An involuntary grimace of hatred distorted my face.

"The Temple of Skron wants to know the result of your expedition to the lands of the offworlders. Why is Magister Meram unconscious? Where is Karina Fardi? Where did your katar and exclusive rings go?"

My chest suddenly stabbed as I realized that along with the right glove, I had lost the three exclusive rings that were on my hand. I had gotten so used to the mithril glove and the fact that it followed the contours of my body that I had completely forgotten what was underneath. After checking the remaining rings, I sighed with relief — the main ones were on my left hand, including protection from mental control and blocking the influence of rot. Otherwise, it would have been a colossal loss!

"The information about our expedition is confidential," I answered. The pillar of light above me and the mentor disappeared — we were on the list of welcome guests in Hearth. At the same time, the siren fell silent, and only after that did the guards stop aiming their crossbows at us. Viscount Kurpatsky had trained my people well; I'd have to give him a special thank you.

"The Temple of Skron understands and invites Archduke Valevsky to visit." He indicated the shimmering portal. The gloomy minotaurs that stood around the archway cast me an accusing glance. They still hadn't forgiven me for killing one of their own. There were now very few Minotaurs left, as I now knew. They reproduced extremely reluctantly, grew slowly, and gained strength slowly. So the death of any one of them was a critical hit to the entire tribe.

"Archduke Valevsky of Hearth is no longer going anywhere," I announced. "If you'd like to speak to me, I will graciously accept you in my office. By the way, I need another bracelet that identifies *Phantom*s. I assume the Temple of Skron would not begrudge me such a small trinket?"

"The third in not yet a month?" Apparently he was surprised.

"These things happen. I await another bracelet, and then I will tell you what happened in the lair of the offworlders."

"The Temple of Skron would like to know right now — where is Karina Fardi?"

"That is precisely the detail that remains confidential. And which we will only discuss after you present me with another bracelet. I need to ensure there are no invisible eyes or ears in my office."

"The security system installed in the city works on everyone."

"So you missed two Faceless', but certainly not any *Phantom*s who might also have registered as workers?"

Judging by the silence, they hadn't thought of that. And Eleanore frowned.

"Can we clear all the lists and start from scratch? This time, with me here," I asked. "Only when I stare into the eyes of everyone in the city, no matter how many there are, will I be sure that there is no one among them who can hide in the shadows or take on someone else's appearance."

"That will take a lot of time," said Eleanore. "We have deadlines."

"How much time could it take? A day? Two? A week? I think that security is much more important than any sort of arbitrary deadlines. Eleanore, arrange for all the workers to come through the palace. Let's start today. I'm not putting it off for later. Alia is not the only mother of my child, and I don't want to lose you because of some deadline."

The look she gave me spoke volumes. I opened the security settings and found the functionality I needed pretty quickly. I had to confirm my actions several times, as if the mechanoid device couldn't even imagine in its worst nightmare that someone would decide to reset the lists. Finally, the last immaterial buttons were pressed and Hearth exploded with the sounds of sirens. A tall pillar of light appeared above each person. Even above the minotaur that stood near the portal, although he was dark. No, he was a beastman. Not dark. Despite the gradation of the dark, from Skron's incarnations to ordinary converted ones, the minotaurs still feared Skron. And he, in turn, destroyed their portals. This was a point I definitely needed to clarify. Because now, I wondered if the portals even had anything to do with Skron. They, like the rifts, were the brainchild of another force, and the dark god simply appropriated them for himself. And, as with the Abyssal rifts, not completely. I needed the Fog Stalker or the Abyss. I needed answers.

After fiddling with the settings a bit, I turned off the strident alarm sound while new lists were being created and ran *Analyze* first on Eleanore, then on everyone standing next to us, adding them to the lists only after a personal check. I had no trust in anyone's word. Imagine my surprise when one of the guards, who was so confidently pointing a crossbow in my direction, turned out to be gray! Not Faceless, not invisible. Gray! Dark with a special development crystal! Quite rare, in fact. At least until I started producing the crystals on an industrial level.

"Okay," I muttered, unpleasantly surprised. In any case, I didn't show it. Instead, I dug into the mechanoid device settings again, trying to figure out how to close this loophole. The situation was as follows: if a person was not on the list, a pillar of light appeared above their head. But as soon as a person was placed on the list, the pillar disappeared. The dark ones, for example, the servants of the Temple of Skron, were not taken into account by this system. It didn't even see them, so it didn't form any pillars above their heads. The gray one pretending to be one of the guards had passed all the various security measures and joined the service as a spy. But how many ordinary dark humans were running around Hearth without a pillar of light? Now I'd start verifying people myself, and then that would be it — these dark ones could calmly walk among us, continuing whatever they came to Hearth to do. And it wouldn't be possible to check whether or not someone had passed through my verification system. As long as there was no pillar of light and the siren wasn't blaring, everyone would be satisfied. The Temple of Skron saw me as a convenient tool, but an extremely limited one. One that wasn't suitable in all situations.

I looked at Eleanore — the light pillar above her had already disappeared. She had been given the highest level of access, but she was not going to add people to the lists anymore. She understood how important it was to go through everyone with *Analyze*. But how could I tell that this particular person had already passed my test, and the others had not yet?

It dawned on me when I opened the group settings and clicked on the one called "Senior Management." At the very bottom of the list of all the capabilities and access levels, there was an interesting feature. It formed a special symbol from an approved list above the heads of all group members. I selected the golden crown, and immediately a small translucent projection appeared above my head and above Eleanore. There it was! There were few groups in the Hearth section: senior management, trusted persons, guards, residents, guests. Everyone could be distributed into these categories and, depending on the location, a pillar of light and an alarm could be formed, indicating that a person had entered where they should not. For example, the palace, which was also my home, was closed to everyone except senior management and trusted persons. Servants, mentors, loved ones. All those whom I trusted. I suppose there was no need to complicate things right now — if I needed to add a new category later, I would. But that didn't change the key point: I could adjust the settings for each group, and from now on, everyone who had passed through the verification would have a sign hanging above their heads.

"What's that for?" Eleanore frowned, looking at the crown hovering above me.

"From now on, anyone who doesn't have a light pillar or a special icon above their head, as well as your or my personal permission to visit Hearth, special emphasis on the word "personal," are enemies subject to immediate elimination. The security system doesn't work for dark ones. It can't identify them. That's why the respected servant of the Temple of Skron stands without identification marks. How many others are running around Hearth? Or how many of those are like this brave warrior, who is a gray spy?"

I pointed at the guard who had passed all the other verifications. But not mine. *Analyze* was hard to fool, especially when buffed as much as mine was.

"Stand down!" I commanded as the other guards surrounded the gray man. "Today, we will indulge the spies. Hand over your weapons and armor and leave Hearth. Through the portal or the front gate — the choice is yours. If you are seen in the city tomorrow, without bearing the status of "guest," you will be eliminated. Eleanore, make sure that all of Hearth comes through my palace. Guards and servants are a priority. There are likely Faceless or invisible ones among them. Temple servants, you need some kind of identification mark so that my people do not finish you off."

"Our outward appearance is not enough?" a surprised voice was heard.

"No. They would be easy for the Faceless to replicate. You need some object that will clearly identify you as servants of the Temple of Skron. Since you won't have any identifying symbols, you'll need something else.

"The Temple of Skron will consider your request," the dark one replied. Translated into human language, this meant that they were giving me the runaround, but I wasn't going to leave it at that. The Fog Stalker or the Abyss will help me. Plus, I must not forget that I also have a pass to the offworlder vault. I could probably find the information I needed there.

"The Temple of Skron wishes to know why Magister Meram is unconscious. Is this also confidential?"

"Magister Meram fell under the influence of my aura and decided he needed to rest for a while," I answered, although I myself was already beginning to worry about the runescribe. He was breathing, but raggedly. Moreover, he periodically twitched, as if he was being contorted and twisted from the inside. This was alarming — I needed the old man alive and well. We still had training to do.

"The Temple of Skron is ready to speak with you in a private setting," the Temple servant said, to which I merely shook my head.

"Without the bracelet that can detect invisible people, there will be no conversation. I must make sure that there is not a single person in possession of the *Phantom* stone within the walls of my city. I expect you in a few hours. Eleanore, start letting people in. I think everyone must already be concerned about what the pillars of light above their heads signify."

The Temple of Skron did not insist. And they weren't given the chance — I was not in the mood to argue with anyone. Not after Skron had almost finished me off! Having picked up the mentor, I went to the main hall. The servants who wanted to take Magister Meram came running, but I refused. Instead, I ordered a couch to be brought, where I laid the limp body. The old man began to groan and did not react at all to *Heal.* Ten casts did nothing, as the problem lay not in the physical, but in the mental plane. Which was nonreactive to my treatments. Alright, I'd have to figure this out. But first — the townsfolk.

The first to pass through were the former residents of the Valevsky estate, as well as the guards, including Viscount Kurpatsky. When the head of Hearth's security service learned that among his guards there was a gray one who had escaped from the city through the portal, he wanted to resign. According to him, he was inadequate to handle the task. I even had to raise my voice and explain that from now on, Kurpatsky would have to evaluate people more carefully. When I went through twenty trusted guards and did not find a single spy among them, an interesting thought suddenly popped into my head. The magic stone *Analyze.* I was given it in the Fortress, moreover, I knew for sure that someone in the Citadel had the same one, as well as the head of the Bartolomeo Clan and the Evil Engineer, a completely ordinary dark human who was digging a mine under the magic academy and considered this his life purpose. That is, the stone was not unique. However, in half a year of my ordeals in the rifts, destroying hundreds of exclusive and elite creatures, I had never come across such a stone! Not once! I'd seen all the rest — *Phantom* and *Golden Dome of Protection*, and a whole scattering of red stones that formed auras. But not a single *Analyze*! Which gave rise to the natural question — where did they get it from? It cannot be that in so many rifts, I would never come across a single *Analyze.* So this stone was not mined from the rifts. Then from where?

As always, two people could give me the answer. Father Urg and Kimal Sarento. But I didn't want to turn to either of them, lest I face the consequences. I didn't want to bargain now. I'd get Alia back, ensure that the city was secure, then maybe...Speaking of security!

"Eleanore, come see me," I said. She showed up with another crowd demanding an inspection. Judging by the hastily compiled lists, there were only Hearth residents here. Workers, builders, craftsmen. Eleanore approached the process with the utmost care — she personally interviewed everyone, who they were, and compiled lists for me. Such a simple double-check.

"What did you want?"

"Find a smith who will make vyrma armor for our guards. Running around with just crossbows is no good. Some dark bastard may also get their hands on a vyrma weapon. I do not intend to trade the lives of my people. I hope that I can keep it that way for a while."

With these words, I embodied four hundred kilograms of the metal. My inventory currently maxed out at four hundred and fifty units. To increase it to six hundred kilograms, I needed an *Amplify, Augment* and *Mentor*, all second-level, and there was no way I could get them for now. Without gloves, I felt naked, but I also did not want to demand that my people risk their health and urgently form mithril for me. Judging by the dark circles under Eleanore's eyes, she hadn't known rest in days. My other loved ones fared no better, so I would probably do without gloves for a couple of days. Nothing critical.

Eleanore's eyebrows shot up as she realized what I had just carelessly thrown to the floor.

"You know how to keep me on my toes, Max,"

she said. It was obvious that her gears were turning. "There must be only one smith. He needs protection and control. Otherwise, half of the material could go missing. Is it critical for you to make the armor right now or after we add the entire city to the lists?"

"Now is even better. If someone is not on the list, there will be a pillar of light above their head. If there is neither him nor the group's identification mark, then this is an enemy who can be safely destroyed."

"If they are dark, what right do they have to be in Hearth?"

"They must have some sort of confirmation that they are here with our permission. Think about how that might work. These kinds of verifications can only be issued in two places — near the portal and at the central gates of the city. Any other dark humans are illegals who can be killed. Information about this must be posted on every street corner."

"Got it. I've got an idea of how to do it. Okay, we'll make the armor. Speaking of which, Kimal Sarento sent a letter, saying he needs a Thunderer set."

"Invite him to Hearth. Tell him to try it on. No matter how you look at it, old debts need to be paid off. I owe a lot to the chancellor. I want to close this chapter and forget about it. From now on, we must only communicate as partners. What about Count Vyazemsky?"

"All our projects have been shut down. There

is news that a schism is forming within the high society of the Zarak Empire. Our relationships with Counts Shub and Kuzmin trouble many. Everyone sees how profitable it is, so they do not understand why they should carry out the will of Count Vyazemsky. Four counts, so far from remote regions, have already contacted us directly, bypassing the council. They offer cooperation and trade at favorable rates. This issue is currently being examined. Vyazemsky himself is not doing anything, as if he is waiting for something. This is dangerous."

"Let him wait. I gave you the task of determining the source of his financial stability."

"It's done, but I haven't generated a report for you yet. The information about what will be there is highly confidential. Considering that we have several Faceless, I couldn't risk it."

"You did the right thing. One more thing — prepare a similar report on Duke Odoevsky."

"I knew you would give that order." A smile appeared on Eleanore's tired face. "Everything is ready. Everything is much simpler with him than with Count Vyazemsky. True, we will have to act carefully. Count Fardi is one of the closest confidants of the Emperor. We are not yet ready to enter into open conflict with the Zarak Empire."

"I have no plans to destroy Fardi in the next two days. I've waited for six months, I can wait a few more. Alright — bring the craftsmen here and organize the armor creation process. I need a protected guard. Ready for any troubles from either the light or the dark."

The steady stream of townsfolk did not subside. The residents of Hearth flowed into the palace like a full-fledged river, all scrambling to get a universal pass. At first, many were frightened by the picture above their heads, but people quickly got used to it and looked down on those who had not yet received such an adornment. Those people, they said, were guaranteed to become part of something bigger than just a city. They were now family. They were on the lists, and Archduke Valevsky, together with his manager Eleanore, had personally added them. I even had to send people to the treasury for several mana elixirs. I didn't have the time to recover it, and I wasn't going to trust just my eyes, even when an ordinary child appeared in front of me. Everyone who became part of Hearth today would go through Analyze. Those who did not wish to do this would be destroyed or expelled. For the first two days, as already announced, I would pardon all spies in Hearth. Then the purges would begin. Viscount Kurpatsky had already been informed.

Three hours later, I began to realize that I was gradually running out of steam. The constant use of magic, especially at such a high level, was having a detrimental effect on my overall well-being. At one point, my nose even started bleeding! What came as an unpleasant surprise was that I needed to urgently strengthen my body. I had to go to the treasury, to the altar of development, but I simply did not have enough time even for such a small detour. The city must be safe! Mithril and personal enhancements could wait.

"Take a break! Be back in an hour!" I commanded after another group and tiredly collapsed on the throne. Yes, I now had a throne. Useless, of course, but I had to receive guests in it. Status, you couldn't escape it. Closing my eyes, I almost instantly fell asleep, but suddenly I heard a drawn-out groan from Magister Meram, who had been lying on the couch all this time. There was so much pain and suffering in this groan that my fatigue disappeared as if by magic. Incomprehensively, the old runescribe had begun to change — it was as if he began to age at an accelerated pace right before my eyes. It took a lot of effort to block this process. Thirty Heals, no less! Only after that did the rapid aging stop and, unexpectedly, the mentor opened his eyes. He abruptly jumped to his feet, almost tripping. Our eyes met, and I saw...shock? Helplessness? What I read in the eyes of Magister Meram seemed impossible. In anyone else, just not this man who had once nearly counted himself among the gods.

"What..." I wanted to ask the runescribe why he had risen to his feet, but it soon became a moot point:

Runescribe skill removed.
Rune Magic removed.
Offworlder Vault Shards removed.
Log removed.
All your symbols will be removed in 30 days.

The offworlders have left this world.

It took me a moment to comprehend what I had read, after which I cursed sincerely and obscenely, as Gustav had taught me. Skron and Light damn it all! Another unprecedented event! We had played around too much! Instead of gaining new knowledge in runic magic, learning to form a word from four symbols, and also understanding the pentagrams of offworlders, we had destroyed it all! And the entire reason behind this continued to stare slack-jawed at me as he realized that he was no longer the center of the universe. And that all those enemies that he managed to make over the long time of his existence were now able to grab hold of his two-hundred-year-old body.

One of the guards ran into the hall. He already boasted a symbol above his head.

"Your Radiance, the servants of the Temple of Skron have come to see you! They say they have an urgent matter."

Of course it was urgent. I knew very well how urgent this matter was. In thirty days, all forty-two sealed infected rifts would gain freedom and rush to fill this world. But the Temple of Skron did not know that along with the offworlders, the resource that made the rifts infected had also disappeared. There was no more log, which meant that the infected beasts would disappear along with the seals. But no one would disclose this to the Temple. Finally, a situation had arisen when this world urgently needed a high-level rift conqueror.

And would have to negotiate with him. Otherwise, most of the world would vanish.

"Call them in. We have much to discuss."

Chapter 19

"ARCHDUKE, THE TEMPLE OF SKRON wishes to know what just occurred." I had, apparently, learned to identify the Temple servants by their voices. Seven had paid me a visit.

"What are you talking about?" I made an innocent face. "Has the Temple of Skron brought me a bracelet to identify *Phantom* wielders?"

"Why has rune magic disappeared?" He clarified.

"This is the essence of our confidential conversation, but off the top of my head, I can say that all your qualms are with Karina Fardi and this venerable elder." I indicated Magister Meram, who still could not quite come to his senses. "As paradoxical as it may sound, I had nothing to do with the expulsion of offworlders from our world. It was all done by these two. It's offensive to even be grouped in with them."

"The Temple of Skron demands details!"

"With pleasure. As soon as I receive the bracelet, I will immediately pass on to the Temple of Skron all the information I have about the campaign. Starting from what types of offworlders exist, ending with their features, appearance and details of the battle. I hope you arrived in Hearth with the bracelet in tow?"

Indeed, they had. I checked the item with *Analyze* — you couldn't trust anyone. The offworlders had weapons with spikes. Life had not prepared me for this, but having once seen an example, I did not want to accidentally fall into a trap by misplacing my trust. What if the Temple of Skron brought me something similar that would make me suffer and give over everything to them, just to make the pain stop? Did I really need that?

"Magister Meram, come closer," I ordered the old man. He looked at me with crazed eyes and obeyed, taking a few steps forward. Turning my gaze to the servant of the Temple of Skron, I asked:

"Will you set up a canopy? Or maybe communicate in such a way so that those around you will not bear witness to our meeting?"

"You could have installed a canopy near the portal." Seven moved his hand, and a protective field appeared around us, protecting us from the encroachments of invisible spies. Of course, there were none in the hall, but habit demanded that we observe the secrecy regime even in such a small matter.

"I could have. But in that case, I wouldn't

have received the bracelet. So, what happened with the offworlders and why did rune magic disappear? In order to explain, I'll have to go way back. From the moment our preparations began..."

My story went on for a long time. Seven periodically interrupted me, demanding details. I was not angry — I wanted to figure out what happened myself, and also to convey my version of what happened to the Temple servants. Before they heard it from Karina Fardi. I had no doubt that she had survived. Skron would not destroy such a valuable asset. A person who can withstand hosting a piece of the dark god without crumbling into dust like the minotaurs.

"...That't it, actually. I grabbed Magister Meram and jumped into the portal. Skron, who captured Fardi, wanted to destroy the portal, but he was literally a moment too late. In fact, the minotaur saved us by taking the blow."

The only thing I kept silent about was the dark fluid. This particular resource had not disappeared. And that was quite telling. Everything else, including the vault fragments, had been sent away from our world, while the resource that was mined exclusively from the creatures of another world remained on the planet. Except that the "Offworld" section had disappeared from my inventory, and the dark liquid was included in the list of standard resources. What did this mean? That the source of this dark liquid has been preserved in our world.

The resource that replaced itself in the process of spending life force. Quite an interesting observation with far-reaching conclusions. What were they? I dug into the status bar, and my heart often beat when I found one inconspicuous section. The "Rune Writer" skill had disappeared — I could no longer use runes. But there was more to this world than just runes! So I needed to keep this information for now. The Temple of Skron certainly didn't need to know.

"We only have thirty days left?" Judging by his voice, Seven was dissatisfied. Extremely dissatisfied. But not with me — his gaze was not visible through the fog, but the servant of the Temple of Skron had turned toward Magister Meram. Quite suddenly, the old man, who only yesterday was an extremely important figure in this world, had turned into a useless person. Who a good half of this world would like to sink their teeth into.

"Yes," I said. "Once Magister Meram recovers from the shock, he will confirm my words. Or, alternatively, when Karina Fardi is reborn in your secret lair. Isn't that where she reappeared last time? If Skron left her a memory of the event, she will confirm my words."

"The Temple of Skron needs to think on this information and figure out what to do with it," Seventh said, but I wasn't going to let the dark one off that easily.

"Why did Skron attack the minotaur and destroy the portal? Why was the minotaur terrified when it saw Skron?"

"That is not information the Temple of Skron is willing to discuss with outside parties," said Seven. Nevertheless, even this answer was informative. The dark ones knew something about the reasons for the strange behavior of the god who had possessed Fardi. The portals were not his invention! It turned out that the only domain that actually belonged to Skron was magic stones! And even that wasn't entirely true — most stones were neutral, which allowed both followers of the Light and Skron to use them. There were only a few truly dark stones. Only a few that I knew of, at least. The *Golden Dome of Protection* was one of them. What if gems were not Skron's brainchild either? Maybe they had belonged to the mechanoids, but the dark entity took them for itself? Skron was a parasite of planetary scale who stuck his greedy paws everywhere they could reach, but, as in the case of the Abyss rifts, it did not always work out as originally intended.

Seven stood there for a moment, clearly communicating with his colleagues, and then said:

"The Temple of Skron believes that you must use your skills as a Riftmaster to destroy the infected rifts under seals. If you do not do this within thirty days, the world will perish."

"What gave you that idea?" I grinned. I was ready for this conversation. "The world will not perish. According to certain intel, which I have confirmed, all rifts, including infected ones, are limited to level one hundred. This is the maximum limit, above which they cannot grow. Even if each infected rift takes two hundred kilometers of land and turns them into lifeless deserts, it still will not destroy the light empires. And they won't come close to touching Hearth. There are no infected rifts near my city, and you will no longer be able to create them. I do not care what happens in Kerux."

"Create? Are you trying to say that the infected rifts were created artificially?"

Either Seven was a great actor, or he really didn't know anything about the log. Figuring that divulging this information wouldn't do me any harm, I replied:

"I'm not just trying to say it — I am saying it. I received information that along with the offworlders, a resource called log has left this world. I have information, unfortunately unconfirmed, that with the help of this resource it was possible to form infected rifts. The material belonged to the offworlders — it was their creation. Nothing has happened by chance in this world. All infected rifts were the product of living beings. Either from our world or from someone else's. Infected rifts never spontaneously appeared."

"Where did you obtain this information?" Seven practically loomed over me.

"From the Fog Stalker." It was so nice to be able to back up any source of information with unquestionable authority. Even if the Fog Stalker wasn't the one who had said it.

"How did the infection occur?" He was clearly

moved by my words and wanted to know the details.

"I don't have any details. I wasn't particularly interested in this topic. Let's get back to the original question. I think the dark ones have enough rift conquerors to deal with the infected rifts themselves, without my involvement. Besides, the Temple of Skron got itself into this situation. So you'll have to figure it out yourself."

"The Temple of Skron does not understand this last point."

"It isn't a point, it's a direct accusation. You knew where we were going. You prepared Karina Fardi for the expedition, crafting her into the perfect vessel for Skron. You provided Magister Meram with all the resources he needed without even bothering to figure out what he was going to do. It was so easy to connect the pieces that I'm amazed at your shortsightedness. Since rune magic comes from offworlders and their seals, then surely destroying the source of their power would have some effect on the magic system on the whole. For some reason, the Temple of Skron did not see what I saw as soon as I realized what the mentor had planned. But I could not sway the course of events when we were already deep in the offworlder lair. If I had been given complete intel about the aliens, none of this would have happened. But I was not given this. Did you consider me unworthy? The same goes for the offworlders themselves — what did it cost you to give me information about what types of monsters are found within the territory and how to fight them? I lacked this intel as well, and it almost killed me. The Temple of Skron prepared everyone for the campaign except me. And now, when all those who you prepared so well started doing things that made you tear your hair out, you come to me. So suddenly I'm worthy of your attention? No, Seven, things are not done this way and you will have to answer for your actions. You have the Gourfan Clan, which specializes in rifts. They have thirty days to close all or the vast majority of the infected rifts. If they fail, then in thirty days you might have some problems. And they won't be global, but in fact very localized. And you must solve these problems yourself. Based on the decisions you made previously. As you can see, I have no part in this plan."

"The Temple of Skron has heard you," said Seven after a pause. "Is that your final word, or are you willing to negotiate?"

"Kostrish is always open to dialogue, Seven. If a worthy offer comes in, why not discuss it? But if my memory serves me right, during our cooperation I have repeatedly indicated where my interests lie. The Temple of Skron has provided some of the items I am looking for, but most of my requests have remained unfulfilled. Which makes me wary about further fruitful cooperation. Okay, I'm getting carried away. Such emotional monologues. If the Temple of Skron wants to involve me in closing the rifts, they will have to pay well for it. I'm not going to just run around your lands, saving your asses for free."

"The Temple of Skron will make its offer in the near future. Do not forget, Archduke Valevsky, that we are taking the most active part in the search for the mother of your child, despite the fact that she is a Bishop of the Fortress. We are violating all our principles by cooperating with you, and would like to see the same attitude from you. We have one more issue that needs to be resolved — the Temple of Skron wants to take this man for further proceedings."

Seven pointed at Magister Meram. During my conversation, the old man seemed to have come to his senses. Now he looked like a cornered rat, ready to bite and scratch anyone who came near. Only the rat was old, toothless, and its claws were already worn out.

"That will be impossible. Magister Meram will remain in Hearth. At least, until I figure out what to do with him."

"This man must answer to the court of the Temple of Skron," Seven insisted.

"Karina Fardi must answer to me. She tried to kill me. She destroyed rune magic. Shall we trade? You give me Fardi and I give you Magister Meram? No? Then what question can there be about my former mentor?"

"The idea of destroying the offworlders came from Meram. Fardi only acted as a tool of Skron. Any responsibility for her actions lies with him. He is the one to blame. Including the current situation in Kerus, as well as other dark territories. The magic academy instantly lost everything that had given it meaning and purpose for many centuries. What is the point of studying runes and pentagrams if they cannot be used? All the previously existing seals disappeared. Hordes of hungry and angry monsters rushed to the lands of the dark ones. Even now, just an hour after rune magic left our world, the greater Kerux area is suffering unprecedented disasters. We ended up having to involve Two! Which has not happened for an entire century! Someone must answer for all this. Meram is the perfect candidate. His obsessive desire to destroy the offworlders caused a massive mess that the dark territories will be cleaning up for a long time to come. And it's still unclear whether we will succeed in this."

"Magister Meram remains in Hearth." I stood my ground. "I need him now. I suggest we put off any conversations about handing him over to the Temple for a few months. You won't hear any other answer from me now."

"We can take him by force."

"Is Seven speaking for the Temple of Skron or for himself?" I asked. I did not like his tone at all. For that alone, I wanted to keep Meram.

"It was just a suggestion. My own. The Temple of Skron needs an official scapegoat. Meram has done enough in his long life to deserve to be brought to justice. In three days, the Temple of Skron will make you an offer on the infected rifts and provide additional arguments as to why this man should be handed over to us for a fair trial.

We know how you feel about other people's lives. We will provide the exact number of people from the light empires this man has killed for his runes. The Temple of Skron can collect such information."

The dark ones knew what nerve to hit. The way my former mentor had viewed ordinary people made me extremely uncomfortable. That was why I was going to finish off the old man myself. But my thoughts and desires did not influence the decision not to hand Meram over to the dark ones. I still needed the old man.

The Temple servant lifted the canopy of silence and left the main hall. Eleanore began to let people in again to be added to the lists, but I gestured for them to wait. Judging by the fact that Magister Meram's gaze had cleared up during this conversation, I could finally have a talk with him. Which was precisely what I planned to do.

"Leave us," I ordered the guards. After ensuring that they all had gone, I turned to the silent man, who was looking at me sullenly from under his brows. "Whose idea was it to destroy the offworlders?"

"I don't understand the question," he said after a beat.

"You said you spent fifty years trying to destroy these creatures. Why? Why did you suddenly become obsessed with destroying creatures that never did anything to you?"

The old man continued to look at me sullenly.

"You don't have to answer. In that case, I'll

have to hand you over to the dark ones. I pulled you out of Skron's clutches, which repaid any debt I may have to you. We're even. And now, if you want to live, you need to prove your usefulness. So I'll ask again: why did you decide to destroy the offworlders? Was it your decision? Or did it come from another source?"

"What are you hinting at?" he all but hissed at me. "That I have been dancing to someone else's tune for the past fifty years?"

"What do you mean, 'someone?'" We both know it's a very specific person. Your mentor. The one who taught you symbol magic. Magister Meram, have you even looked at your status bar since the offworlders disappeared?"

The old man was taken aback and his gaze turned toward infinity. He was delving into his status bar. I was in no hurry — I needed rest anyway. Dark fluid was directly connected to the Runescribe skill, so when actively forming symbols, it was spent even from the inventory. Now, when I actively used high-level magic *Analyze*, I had to pay with my own life force. Everything in this life had a cost.

"And what am I supposed to be looking at here?" Meram asked irritably. "Do you think that..."

He fell silent. His pupils widened in amazement, as if he had seen a miracle. The former runescribe moved his hand, as if he wanted to form a symbol, but nothing happened. The mentor sank to the floor with a groan, it felt like a rod had been pulled from his spine, and that was my cue. I pulled out one unit of dark liquid and began moving my hands, forming the simplest of my symbols: *Yat*. Despite the fact that the movements were familiar, for some reason there was resistance. The last strokes required incredible effort. The dark fluid, which was enough for a dozen three-syllable words, was completely exhausted. Just enough for one simple symbol! Sweat began to cloud my eyes, several waves of unpleasant spasms passed through my body, but I managed. Before my eyes appeared the strengthening symbol. With the small difference: now it did not burn with fire, but appeared cold and lifeless, like a piece of ice. The blue symbol hung in the air for a few moments, and I sent it to my shoulder. To the spot where there was a terrible scar from the dark flame.

Missing skill *Author*.

You cannot establish words or symbols.

The symbol dissipated with a loud bang before it reached my body. But I had accomplished my main task: I had figured out why I still had the alphabet tab. Not even all of it — just a limited selection. Only those symbols that I had already managed to use in my life. And no two-syllable words, like *Shackles of Time*.

"But how?" Magister Meram's flabbergasted expression delighted me. "Why?"

"Because symbol magic doesn't have anything to do with the offworlders," I explained the obvious. "You were taught by your mentor, he learned it from his grandfather, and he, in turn, learned it from somewhere in the closed vaults of the ancients. Where even Pharapho does not have access. The offworlders left, taking with them the runic magic, and since it was closely connected with the symbolic that we all used, one was superimposed on the other. At the same time, the seals that were installed with the help of symbols did not disappear immediately. Because they contain a particle of another force. More ancient than Skron himself. So what if the old symbols were based on runic magic that will evaporate in a month? If they are redone with the help of a new skill, everything will run smoothly again. Runic magic will be replaced by symbolic.

"What skill?" Magister Meram looked at me with the gaze of a man who suddenly saw a glimpse of salvation from a hopeless situation.

"We will discuss this, former mentor, after you contact your mentor. You still have a communication symbol connected to him, right? It's time to use it. I want to know why he sent you on a campaign against the offworlders."

"He didn't!" Meram man exclaimed hotly, and even surprised himself with his own words. Having calmed down, Meram explained: "We only discussed it a few times, that it would be nice to get rid of the offworlders, and that was long before I started working with them! I came to this idea myself! No one pushed me to it! So don't anger me, pupil! What skill are you talking about?"

"Place your hand on the seal, make the

connection, and speak. When you lost rune magic, Magister Meram, you ceased to become my mentor. How can you be my mentor if you can't do it yourself? Any attempt to form a symbol will end in your death. You don't have enough life force. I do. If you have any objections, you can leave Hearth now. The Temple of Skron will happily take you. I'm sure you'll have plenty to talk about with them."

"You wouldn't dare give me up to the dark ones!"

"Do you want to test that?" I was determined. "I'll give you a minute to make a decision. If you continue to resist, we have nothing more to discuss. You'll leave Hearth, I will inform the dark ones about this. I'll give you a head start of 24 hours. I wonder how long you can last without the ability to create symbols? I haven't forgotten your punishments, Magister Meram, which you inflicted upon me every day. I haven't forgotten the pain I had to endure. I haven't forgotten the people you killed to prolong your own life or to install symbols on someone else. The Temple even plans to tell me the exact number soon. How many will there be? Tens of thousands? Hundreds? If you think that all this has made me feel grateful, then I have some unpleasant news for you. You're wrong. I only need you now for the simple reason that you have a connection with your mentor. I need him. No connection — no Magister Meram. Time is up. Your answer?"

"I raised and trained my own demise,"

Magister Meram muttered discontentedly. Putting his hand to his heart, he said: "Mentor, we need to talk. I don't know who you are now or where you are, but the matter cannot wait. Yes, I know that you promised to kill me if I contacted you again. Yes, I'm in Hearth. Yes, he is here too. It is he who wishes to speak with you."

With these words, a portal suddenly appeared in the center of my hall. Exactly the same technology that the Twins used to form it — without a stationary arch, without converts. Just a portal hanging in thin air. The shimmering veil began to swirl, and a man came out of it. I barely managed to keep my jaw in place when I realized who it was. I was tired of the surprises.

"Well, pupil, you won't be killed today. Although, I must admit, my hands are itching. Greetings, Maximilian of the Valevsky line. Here we finally meet, as I promised you almost fifteen years ago. Why are you frozen like a statue? Don't you want to give your grandad a hug?"

Chapter 20

"GRANDPA?" I TOOK A FEW STEPS BACK. The last time I saw this man... actually, I never really did. I was three years old when he left the family. Even if he had interacted with me before that time, I don't remember anything about it. And even more so, I don't remember any promises he made to me. The only thing I remembered of grandfather was his portrait, which, for some reason, hung in my bedroom. My father never liked him, but he didn't want to throw the portrait out or burn it. I, as the youngest, had inherited this "family heirloom." At first, the painting hung in my older brother's house, then in the middle one's, and eventually, it came to me.

"Did you expect someone else?" Valdemar Valevsky chuckled. He hadn't changed at all in fifteen years. He looked very much like my father, but while the latter looked his age, Valdemar looked forty at the oldest. Even compared to Kimal Sarento, the emperor's grandson looked younger. Turning to the runescribe, my guest said:

"Leave us, Meram."

"Let him stay a while. I want him to know. Why did you order him to destroy the offworlders?"

"What do you mean 'why?' Maximilian, I'm starting to doubt your sanity. Was I too hasty in coming to visit you? I sent Meram to destroy the offworlders, to destroy the ungodly rune magic. It had been too much of a hindrance to me all this time. It extended life, brought people back from the dead, protected them from deadly attacks. How could one not be against rune magic existing on our planet? Especially since it was taking control of symbolic magic, infecting it with its influence. The same magic, by the way, that existed on the planet before all these ungodly forces came here. So I had to plant the desire in the head of one crazy runescribe, who imagined himself a god, to deal with the aliens. Using the very source of his own power."

"But you can't act on your own. If you have such teleportation capabilities, you could have appeared in the Twins' lair in a matter of seconds. You decided to destroy the offworlders through your pupil because you yourself are bound by restrictions," I muttered, processing the incoming information at lightning speed.

"Ah, you do have a brain after all! That's right, grandson, I have practically no ability to do anything on my own in this world."

"Why?"

Valdemar Valevsky looked pointedly at Magister Meram, who was standing with his mouth wide open. The old man looked ridiculous. His world had once again turned upside down. He had been used after all!

"Okay, before we let Meram go, I want to give him a carrot to chase. Can you give us the Author skill?"

"You, yes. Some of my blood runs through you, so I can affect my influence on you without arousing the suspicions of these ungodly forces. What you do next, who you give this skill to, who you take it from — that is another question. In any case, it is of no interest to me."

"Meram, leave us," I ordered my former mentor and, as it seemed to me, future pupil. Why would I need him, considering everything he had done in his life? It was hard to say, but the answer was too mundane: resources. During his life, this old curmudgeon had amassed a good fortune, acquired a bunch of important connections. As Maximilian Valevsky, a simple man, I would like to finish off the bastard to avenge all the lives he had ruined. As Archduke Valevsky, who had an entire city behind him, I had no such right. My city needed resources, and I planned to squeeze Meram to the last silver coin. Hearth must become strong.

While Meram was leaving the hall, my grandfather disappeared into the portal, only to emerge from it with an intricate chair. Sitting down opposite, Valdemar asked:

"Okay, you've intrigued me. Tell me, why do you need this old man? He's already lived his life."

"This is not a topic I'd like to discuss with a man I only know from the portrait hanging in my room."

"So you don't remember me at all?" Valdemar sighed.

"I was three years old when you disappeared."

"I didn't disappear, I was banished," my grandfather corrected me. "Choose your words correctly. And by whom? By my own son!"

"My father kicked you out of the house?" I was taken aback. "For what?"

"Judging by the sincerity in your eyes, you haven't been told this story. I see. Okay, let's go back to the not-so-distant past. Apparently, it is part of our family's fate that the eldest children always go against their father. My father went against my grandfather, and my son against me. He didn't like what I was preparing him for. That's why he went far away. Locked himself in his estate, like some kind of hermit. He even refused enhancements for his children! Although, you know, he had more than enough of them himself. I made my boy strong enough for him to continue my work. But he couldn't. Couldn't handle the pressure. Couldn't adapt. It's sad, but this is probably my mistake. I pushed him too hard."

"Eldest son. So, you have other children somewhere?"

"What a stupid question. Of course I do! Six

official ones, and as for the number of random, illegitimate children, I don't even want to think about it. I've never been particularly worried about my bastard children. So they're out there somewhere. Who cares?"

"So it was because of you that our family had such a vast estate? I used to take it for granted, but now that I have my own city, I understand how wrong I was. Our territories were simply enormous. Especially for backwater barons."

"I always liked those lands. Lots of forests, greenery, the cleanest air, even in the hot summer it was always cool there. If your father hadn't kicked up a fuss and refused the count's title at the time, the Valevsky lands could have become the center of trade not only for the Zarak Empire, but for all the light lands. They could have become a great city. But instead, you went downhill. You became a useless village. I lost all interest in you and switched to another family. There are always other families. Nevertheless, I didn't leave my grandchildren without a parting gift. Moreover, fifteen years ago I made a promise that we would meet someday and I would appreciate your potential. Well, here we are."

"You made such a promise to your grandchildren?" I darkened. "Even to those who had their heads chopped off? How are you going to meet them and assess them?"

"Grandson, do not burden me with stupid claims. Why should I worry about those who are not able to defend themselves? In his madness, my eldest son went so far as to completely abandon his strength. I trained him enough to be sure that he would have easily destroyed Count Fardi's entire detachment. Along with him. But he did not! Why? Because he went mad! Because he broke! He turned out to be so weak that he allowed his entire family to die, just so that he wouldn't use his ungodly power. A talentless fool. A fanatical madman who imagined that he must pay for the sins of his ancestors. If you need to find a traitor within the family, look among your closest relatives. I did not interfere, because the weak cannot be helped. The weak must die. I have already done a great thing for the Valevskys. I gave them you."

"Me?"

"Grandson, don't be stupid. Sometimes you make me think that you're not quite all there. Of course, you! I couldn't give you enhancements, I couldn't give you a decent education — your father was against it, and who am I to argue with a man who's given up? Nevertheless, I found the perfect mentor for you. After all your time in the great big world, did you really think that Gustav, an ordinary Wall soldier, had managed to become a spearmaster? A man not only capable of combat meditation but also able to teach it to others? It took some effort to find such a gem. But I like the results — you're sitting here in front of me, and not scattered into a million pieces of dust or being burped out by a dark beast."

"You allowed them to destroy my family!" It

was difficult to hold back my rage.

"Don't forget, young man, this was my family too. On which I spent several decades of my precious life. But they did not justify the efforts invested in them. That's why they were wiped out! And so it will be with everyone. I am not a mother hen who shelters her chicks. Everyone must be responsible for their choice! Even if it is fraught with such consequences."

"What choice did my youngest relatives had, who were less than a year old?"

"That was their parents' choice. I gave each of my offspring some kind of gift. To you, I gave a warrior. Your middle brother — a mentor in trade. The eldest — one of the best teachers in management. You all received a decent education even by the standards of the capital! Yes, each in his own field, but together you could have become something more, if the utterly mad fanatic had started thinking with his head for a second, and not his ass. No magic stones, no enhancements, no third-party magic. They didn't even give you my simple gift that I sent you for your eighteenth birthday! I specially chose the most provincial magic stone so that my son wouldn't even have questions, but no! Even this stone seemed scarier to him than viper venom. Madman. A real madman. No matter — he has already paid for his madness. Both with his own life and the lives of his entire family. That's where they all belong. There is no place for weaklings in this world."

"You know what, Grandpa, you can leave." I

got up from the throne, ending our conversation. "I will not allow the memory of my family to be tarnished, even if they did not live up to your expectations. This is my family, and I will bite the throat of anyone who tarnishes their memory. Even if it is my own grandfather. You say that you have a bunch of other children? So go to them, why are you coming to me? I don't need anything from you, I will sort everything out on my own."

"Of course you will," Valdemar Valevsky grinned, making no move to get up from his chair. "That's why I'm here, to make you figure everything out on your own. You, young man, need to calm down, listen to me, and then, based on the information you receive, make some decisions. I understand that you were taught to wave a spear and solve problems by force, but you still have to try. Sit down, I said!"

I wasn't going to obey, but then I started to bend. There was no way to resist this force. It seemed that I had turned into a spineless doll, played with by a huge invisible giant. One who had decided to sit its toys on the chairs. The muscles that I had strained, trying to resist the external force, could not withstand and they seemed to tear. A monstrous sharp pain that flared up in my body almost deprived me of consciousness. It was good that I learned to use Heal, even in a semi-conscious state. My muscles knitted together, and I found myself sitting on the throne. My grandfather, grinning unkindly, sat on his.

"Have you calmed down? Can we discuss

things further? Or do I need to demonstrate the disparity between us once again?"

Your *Analyze* level is insufficient to obtain information about this subject.

The phrase that appeared before my eyes saved me from further reckless actions. Shooting this man with vyrma would be useless. And was he even a man? I had serious doubts about that.

"Alright, Grandpa, let's talk. What do you want? Tell me and get out."

"What's with people, eh? Couldn't you have just said that before? You jumped up and started threatening me. You reminded me of your father — he rarely thought things out either. Yes, Maximilian, we will definitely talk. First of all, about what you will be doing in the next few centuries. Okay, I see you have a question. Ask."

"Why did you destroy the offworlders? I want to hear the real reason, and not this nonsense you're feeding me."

"What an excellent question. However, the answer to it is too obvious. I am too lazy to deal with such things. Let's see if you can figure it out yourself. It's not difficult. Use your head."

"To weaken the dark ones?" I frowned, remembering Seven's emotional speech.

"See, you can reason after all. That's right — without rune magic, the dark ones lose a lot of power. There will be no more Waves, no droughts, no attacks from dark creatures. Moreover, all the locations that were sealed are now free. This is a huge avalanche of terrible beasts from the past, which the dark ones blocked, unable to defeat. Let them wreak havoc for a while. They will divert resources from the light empires. Maybe they will even send their new weapon there."

"Are you talking about Karina Fardi?"

"Who else? The girl was so mad that she opened up completely to Skron. Somehow she managed the impossible — she managed to survive. For a while I even thought that she was my offspring, I even did a little research, but no. Karina is not my descendant. Too bad — we could have used such a fine specimen."

"How can she be destroyed?"

"At your current stage of development — no way. I can't even do it now. She needs to be destroyed instantly. So that not even a particle of her body remains. Otherwise, Skron will move into whatever's left, revive her and continue sowing fear and horror anew. Karina Fardi is now inseparable from the dark being to which she swore her allegiance. The girl hasn't fully figured out her powers yet, so you have some time. A year. Three. Ten. Who knows how much time she'll need? The longer, as you understand, the better. Especially since she doesn't have any sensible teachers. Elor, who wanted to kill your Alia, is no good for this purpose."

"He wanted to kill Alia? Was it he who kidnapped her?"

"What? Kidnapped? No! Your darling girl is with me."

I wanted to jump up from the throne, but the

invisible giant continued to press on me, preventing me from moving.

"No need for an emotional outburst, Grandson. Elor lured Alia out of the palace, because he could no longer cope with your warriors alone. By the way, you have assembled a good army for yourself — keep up the good work. The more loyal people you have, the easier it will be for you to rule your city."

"Where is Alia?"

"Why are you always in such a rush?" Valdemar Valevsky grimaced with displeasure. "Elor lured the girl out, attacked and, to make sure he killed her, used dark fire. *Thunderer* is useless against it. If you want decent protection for your loved ones, make it from the flesh of the godless Pharapho. Everything else is an alternative. Elor almost killed Alia, but then I intervened. After all, my blood runs through her as well. Thanks to you. Basically, I couldn't kill Elor, but I could take Alia. I had to thoroughly tinker with the dark fire in her body, but I managed. Then I let you talk, and your girl did everything right — she realized that she needed to use the map. Now the Orthodox are being driven all over Keru. The Temple of Skron is furious that someone attacked the mother of your child without their knowledge and consent. And I left a lot of leads there, rest assured. Elor has no time to train Fardi now. And he won't be able to teach her anything properly. He is, of course, more experienced, but she is already stronger. Much stronger. I'm not sure that even the Interrogator or the Inquisitor can handle her now. Chaos, although it looks menacing, is actually weak. As for Alia, she is still too weak to return home. She will be delivered to you in a few weeks, when the effects of the dark fire have completely worn off. You don't have to worry about that."

"Why keep her unconscious?"

"Because she wouldn't last long in a conscious state. It's painful, you see, when most of your organs are mangled by dark fire. When I brought her back to consciousness to talk to you, I had to pump her with oblivion crystals to keep the pain from consuming her mind. That's why she felt so incredibly weak. But now she's fine. There are no after-effects from the godforsaken drug either. Unfortunately, there was no other way I could heal her."

"You repeatedly point out that you have certain restrictions and limitations. What are you talking about? Why can't you interfere with the current course of events?"

"Because I am dependent. Longevity, my grandson, leaves certain marks. This, among other things, was the reason why I set Meram against the offworlders. It is impossible to prolong life with the help of the symbolic magic of the ancients. It was developed for other purposes. I had to use runes, and they, as you understand, are closely connected with the abominable Skron. In the end, we reached a certain consensus — the forces do not touch me, I do not influence the world. The only loophole that was left for me was the protection of my descendants. Therefore, I have been breeding and raising them my entire conscious life."

"All this is, of course, extremely interesting, but what do you need from me now? I called you to find out the reason the offworlders were destroyed. I found out. However, you are not leaving. Why?"

"Because the time has come to repay your debt, Maximilian."

"In order to repay a debt, you must first be in debt. I don't owe anyone anything. Or are you trying to claim that you've been watching me my entire conscious life and guiding me?"

"I have nothing else to do!" snorted Valdemar. "All the descendants of the first emperor received their debt the moment they were born. Some, like your father, were not morally prepared to bear this burden. Some, like you, fully meet all the criteria. Some, like a bunch of your brothers and sisters, do not even know that they owe anyone anything. But everyone owes something. Such is fate."

"What does repaying my debt entail?"

"Rebirth. That's it, no more, no less. The rebirth of this world. You have already started it — the offworlders have been driven out. There are twelve forces left that rule our world. You, your children, your children's children, and so on ad infinitum — you will all be busy cleansing the planet of these godless creatures."

"You keep mentioning a certain god. Is it the Light?"

"This is a question you will have to find the answer to on your own. It so happened that I was not only restricted in my physical intervention, but also in my informational one. I cannot tell you everything I know. If I do, Skron or the Light will have every reason to destroy you. Even though you are a descendant of the first emperor. All the information about what is really happening in our world, you, Grandson, will have to find on your own. I can only show you the direction you should go. And teach you a few things, of course. For example, opening the Author skill for you. Is that what you want? To have at your disposal the magic of the ancients? Finally pure, unblemished. Magic that is capable of resisting even Karina Fardi."

"You talk about her as if she's the main bad guy now."

"Which is an unpleasant reality," answered Valdemar. "In the current time period, there is no intelligent weapon against it. You will have to look for it yourself. But I will give you the direction where to look. You can be sure of that."

"You know what and where to look. But instead of doing it yourself, you came to me. Why?"

"Because I no longer have access to where all the answers are. Skron's seal, obtained during the life extension ritual, imposes certain restrictions. I am no longer pure."

"Just like me. I have the dark mirror of Skron, which allows me to travel through the rifts. I have the dark magic stones that opened up magic to me."

"Magic stones do not leave an imprint on a person. They can change the predisposition, for example, make their owner more or less pleasing to the Light or Skron, but at any time you can refuse them, becoming pure. Return to a null state. As for the dark mirror...it is the reason that I am here. In fact, what you use is called something else, but let's call it a dark mirror for now. The ability that transformed your distant relative into a great entity."

"Not a human?"

"Not a human," Valdemar answered after a pause. "That is also one of the reasons why I came to you myself, but more on that later. First, we need to resolve the main issues. So, sit still and don't move. I know you're incapable of doing this, but I still must warn you preemptively. What if another one of my grandfather's abilities awakens in you? I mustn't take any risks."

The world lost all light for a few moments, but when the whole space regained its color, an inscription appeared before my eyes:

You have received the *Author* skill. All other skill paths have been blocked off.

A new icon appeared on my status bar. When I opened it, I saw the familiar alphabet, but instead of the usual description, each symbol had received a new one. And I didn't really like what I saw. Because the symbols were now just symbols, without any inner power. It was impossible to use them in the form in which they were presented now.

"You'll figure out how to use all this yourself," he said. His bloodless face told me that the process of transferring the skill was not easy for him. Which was completely untrue for me. I experienced no negative side effects. It was just a new pictogram...a new. Pictogram.

"The status bar has nothing to do with the dark ones either?" I guessed. "If the Author is a pure and ancient skill, it couldn't appear as a separate icon. But it does exist."

"I guess I didn't make a mistake with you," he smiled forcefully. "All correct. The status bar is an invention of ancient people, which was taken over by the godless Skron. But all this is unimportant now. Concentrate, Grandson. This is the key. With its help, you will be able to penetrate the closed location of the ancients. You will have to find this location yourself, I cannot tell you where it is."

Valdemar pulled out some kind of sparkling object and threw it on the floor in front of him like a trinket.

"The key and purity. Two criteria for entering the location, remember that! One more thing, grandson. Before you set off on your campaign, resolve your local issues. Two of the most influential people have turned against you. Count Vyazemsky and Padishah Bayazid the Third. They have already united and will soon strike. You need to prepare for it. It is not proper for a descendant of the first emperor to leave such enemies behind. Be careful with Kimal Sarento. For some strange reason, he likes to hover around you. I do not understand this man. I do not understand his motives. He is dangerous. So, I've said my piece, given my warnings, given you this. That's it! There's no time left. I am no longer human. It is hard for me to resist the forces that are tearing me apart from within. They thirst for new victims, and not simple ones, but those carrying my blood. Now, my grandson, you must do what is gradually becoming a tradition in our family. The grandson must kill his grandfather and take his burden. It was so with me, and it will be so with you. You have a minute to kill me. That is exactly how much time I can give you. I cannot explain why you must do this, but know that if you fail in the remaining fifty-five seconds, there will be no trace left of you or Hearth. I will have to destroy everything here, no matter how much resistance I meet. It is beyond my strength. I remove the block. Fifty seconds, grandson. Then either you become a keeper, or I look for a new one. Make the right decision."

End of Book Seven

Want to be the first to know about our latest LitRPG,
sci fi and fantasy titles from your favorite authors?

Subscribe to our **New Releases** newsletter:
http://eepurl.com/b7niIL

Thank you for reading *Condemned!*
If you like what you've read, check out other sci-fi, fantasy and A LitRPG series published by Magic Dome Books:

NEW RELEASES!

Crossroads of Oblivion
a portal progression fantasy adventure series
by Dem Mikhailov

Gakko Academy
a portal progression fantasy adventure series
by Evgeny Alexeev

War Eternal
a military space adventure LitRPG series
by Yuri Vinokuroff

The Hunter's Code
a LitRPG series by Yuri Vinokuroff & Oleg Sapphire

The Order of Architects
a portal progression series
by Yuri Vinokuroff & Oleg Sapphire

I Will Be Emperor
a space adventure progression fantasy series
by Yuri Vinokuroff

An Ideal World for a Sociopath
a LitRPG series by Oleg Sapphire

The Healer's Way
a LitRPG series by Oleg Sapphire & Alexey Kovtunov

A Shelter in Spacetime
a LitRPG series by Dmitry Dornichev

The Village
a LitRPG progression fantasy series
by Dmitry Dornichev & Alexey Kovtunov

The Dark Healer
a historical progression fantasy series
by Alex Toxic & Nadya Lee

Ghost in the System
An apocalypse LitRPG series by Alexey Kovtunov

The Last Portal Jumper
a LitRPG series by Konstantin Zubov

Lord of the System
a LitRPG progression fantasy series by
Alex Toxic and Furious Miki

Kill to Live
a LitRPG progression fantasy adventure series
by George Bor and Yuri Vinokuroff

Kill or Die
a LitRPG series by Alex Toxic

The Strongest Student
a portal progression action fantasy series
by Andrei Tkachev

Living Ice
a portal progression alternative history series
by Dmitry Sheleg

Law of the Jungle
a Wuxia Progression Fantasy Adventure Series
By Vasily Mahanenko

Reality Benders
a LitRPG series by Michael Atamanov

The Dark Herbalist
a LitRPG series by Michael Atamanov

Perimeter Defense
a LitRPG series by Michael Atamanov

League of Losers
a LitRPG series by Michael Atamanov

Chaos' Game
a LitRPG series by Alexey Svadkovsky

The Way of the Shaman
a LitRPG series by Vasily Mahanenko

The Alchemist
a LitRPG series by Vasily Mahanenko

Dark Paladin
a LitRPG series by Vasily Mahanenko

Galactogon
a LitRPG series by Vasily Mahanenko

Invasion
a LitRPG series by Vasily Mahanenko

World of the Changed
a LitRPG series by Vasily Mahanenko

The Bear Clan
a LitRPG series by Vasily Mahanenko

Starting Point
a LitRPG series by Vasily Mahanenko

The Bard from Barliona
a LitRPG series
by Eugenia Dmitrieva and Vasily Mahanenko

Condemned
(Lord Valevsky: Last of The Line)
a Progression Fantasy series
by Vasily Mahanenko

Loner
a LitRPG series by Alex Kosh

A Buccaneer's Due
a LitRPG series by Igor Knox

A Student Wants to Live
a LitRPG series by Boris Romanovsky

The Goldenblood Heir
a LitRPG series by Boris Romanovsky

The One Who Changes the Future
a dystopian portal progression fantasy series
by Boris Romanovsky

Level Up
a LitRPG series by Dan Sugralinov

Level Up: The Knockout
a LitRPG series by Dan Sugralinov and Max Lagno

Adam Online
a LitRPG Series by Max Lagno

World 99
a LitRPG series by Dan Sugralinov

Disgardium
a LitRPG series by Dan Sugralinov

Nullform
a RealRPG Series by Dem Mikhailov

Clan Dominance: The Sleepless Ones
a LitRPG series by Dem Mikhailov

Heroes of the Final Frontier
a LitRPG series by Dem Mikhailov

The Crow Cycle
a LitRPG series by Dem Mikhailov

Interworld Network
a LitRPG series by Dmitry Bilik

Rogue Merchant
a LitRPG series by Roman Prokofiev

Project Stellar
a LitRPG series by Roman Prokofiev

In the System
a LitRPG series by Petr Zhgulyov

The Crow Cycle
a LitRPG series by Dem Mikhailov

Unfrozen
a LitRPG series by Anton Tekshin

The Neuro
a LitRPG series by Andrei Livadny

Phantom Server
a LitRPG series by Andrei Livadny

Respawn Trials
a LitRPG series by Andrei Livadny

The Expansion (The History of the Galaxy)
a Space Exploration Saga by A. Livadny

The Range
a LitRPG series by Yuri Ulengov

Point Apocalypse
a near-future action thriller by Alex Bobl

Moskau
a dystopian thriller by G. Zotov

El Diablo
a supernatural thriller by G.Zotov

Mirror World
a LitRPG series by Alexey Osadchuk

Underdog
a LitRPG series by Alexey Osadchuk

Last Life
a Progression Fantasy series by Alexey Osadchuk

Alpha Rome
a LitRPG series by Ros Per

An NPC's Path
a LitRPG series by Pavel Kornev

Fantasia
a LitRPG series by Simon Vale

The Sublime Electricity
a steampunk series by Pavel Kornev

In order to have new books of the series translated faster, we need your help and support! Please consider leaving a review or spread the word by recommending *Condemned* to your friends and posting the link on social media. The more people buy the book, the sooner we'll be able to make new translations available.

Thank you!

Till next time!